The detective stuc
not to think about his 1
crowbar to break one oi these muckin stones loose.

The jack handle didn't do the trick. Opening the trenching tool and using the pick end, Thacker swung it against the largest stone. It bounced off the surface. Rory suppressed a scream as pain shot from his knee down his encased leg. "Easy!"

"Sorry, boss."

"Try removing one of the outer stones. Loosen them, and maybe we'll be able to budge these. I'll hold the light, and you make room for these damn jaws to unclasp. Try finding the cornerstone." A fine layer of perspiration covered Rory's face. He felt defeated and a little nauseous. He leaned back on his elbows and looked at the sky. "Thacker," he said, "this is damn unlucky."

The rookie moved down the mound to the edge of the pile. Using the crowbar and a lot of muscle, he attacked. Finally, he was able to roll one stone out of position. Then another. He was still three feet from Rory's crevice, working his way toward the more enormous boulders and Rory's ultimate freedom, when the rock he was prying loose rolled out of place. He hesitated. "There is something funny here, boss."

"I could use a good laugh."

"Not ha-ha funny, peculiar funny."

"Tell me anyway."

"There's someone else in this rock pile."

Praise for Terry Korth Fischer and Gone Before

". . .A mystery that will appeal on many levels. You have the classic detective, but you have an eager rookie. You have the layers of small-town life, but you have a big city-type conspiracy. [And] one can't overlook the simple value of a nice old cat. . ."

N.N. Light's Book Heaven Review

~*~

". . .Suspense starts on the first page maintains its level until very final explosive conclusion. Hoping to see more of these characters somewhere down the road. . ."

Booklover Review

~*~

". . . A good mystery filled with red herrings that kept me guessing. A mystery that I really enjoyed. . ."

LAS Reviews

~*~

". . . Fischer knows how to write a police procedural and how to lace it with suspense. She slowly created characters I cared about (and a few I hated) . . . And I definitely want to know more about the rookie cop and the strong silent handyman . . ."

Jackie Houchin, Here's How it Happened Review

~*~

". . . Quality characters with an exciting whodunit held on tight to the very end. . ."

Lori Caswell, Dollycas Reviews

Gone Before

by

Terry Korth Fischer

Rory Naysmith Mysteries

Gone Before

COPYRIGHT © 2022 by Terry Korth Fischer

Cover Art by *Kim Mendoza*

The Wild Rose Press, Inc.
PO Box 708
Adams Basin, NY 14410-0708
Visit us at www.thewildrosepress.com

Publishing History
First Edition, 2022
Trade Paperback ISBN 978-1-5092-4042-5
Digital ISBN 978-1-5092-4043-2

Rory Naysmith Mysteries
Published in the United States of America

Dedication

Lovingly dedicated to my mother, Joyce Delaine Korth.

Chapter One

Voices from somewhere down below floated up and through the third-floor apartment window. As they registered in his consciousness, Rory felt a heavy weight climb onto his chest and then a warm touch on his cheek. Without opening his eyes, he said, "If we are going to continue this relationship, you need to respect my personal space."

He felt the tabby nestle into the fold at his neck. Purring followed. "Seriously, Commander. How does it look for a middle-aged detective to snuggle with a cat?"

As feline murmurs ratcheted up, Commander laid a paw on his face again and gave him a gentle pat. "All right," Rory grumbled. "I'm up."

Throwing off the sheet and dislodging the tabby, Detective Rory Naysmith rose from his bed. Dawdling on a fine Nebraska morning wasn't acceptable. It was the Fourth of July, and he had commitments. Serving as grand marshal at the town's Independence Day celebration topped the list.

The morning promised a perfect day: parade, picnic, followed by fireworks at the fairgrounds. The parade started at ten. He dressed and put on a pot of coffee. He hadn't finished his first cup when the phone rang. He plucked it up, then rubbed a hand over his balding head.

"Detective Naysmith," he said as he crossed to the

1

window and looked out over the Winterset police station's flat roof and listened. Parade floats filled the parking lot below. Workers scurried around to add last-minute touches. "I'll be there in five minutes, Sergeant."

It wasn't like the parade was waiting on him. Rory had to admit that the advantage of living in the building behind the station was the absence of commute time. The disadvantage, though, was the ever-present responsibility.

The tabby purred as it circled his ankles. He reached down and scratched behind its ears. "Today we do the country and Winterset proud, old boy."

Rory took an extra ten minutes, not that he needed them but because it was his day off and slowing down had been his long-term goal since the heart attack that landed him in Winterset with one last chance to serve the public. In December, he had been proud to accept the town's accolades, especially after solving a rash of crimes. Little had he suspected that their gratitude would lead to him presiding over public events. In his six months as the small town's new and only police detective, he had distinguished himself in the community but managed to alienate ten of the other eleven officers in the department. Undaunted, he worked at smoothing that over by joining WPD's softball team. So far, he hadn't played a single inning.

Once dressed, he rifled through the pill bottles and selected the morning pair—one for blood pressure and another for cholesterol. Shoving them into his pocket, he crossed to the table, tore the sudoku from the newspaper, and picked up his fedora. When he emerged from the apartment on the top floor of the brick, three-story Hillard Department Store building, he wore plain clothes: dress shoes, dark slacks, button-down collared shirt, and red, white, and blue striped tie. His shapeless sports jacket concealed the shoulder holster and his Smith & Wesson 351PD. He patted his breast to check the gun's position. Tucked under his shirt, somewhere close to his heart, he carried the St. Michael medal he'd worn since graduating from the police academy twenty-five years earlier.

As he descended the outdoor staircase to the street, Esther Mullins rolled into the police station parking lot on her bicycle. The sight of her brought a smile to his lips. Her younger sister, Jesse, was in charge of the hospital float. If he remembered right, Esther had promised to help. Not that Jesse needed help or even wanted it, but after losing their mother, the sisters had grown close, sharing feelings they hadn't found time for since their youth. He spotted Jesse in a crowd of hospital workers, a sea of red, white, and blue scrubs, and headed her way, arriving in time to hear the sisters' exchange.

"Morning, Jess," Esther called. Her wild brunette hair was tucked behind her ears, and she wore an old, oversized, graying sweatshirt over blue jeans. To Rory, she looked stunning.

Jesse paused to greet her older sister. "Hey, Piglet."

"Where do you want me?" asked Esther. "I have to warn you; I'm not driving a tractor."

Jesse giggled. "We'll save that for someone else."

"And I want to ride on the float," Esther added. "I plan to chuck this shirt and jeans for a 'Winterset Proud' T-shirt and walking shorts later. For now, I'm ready to work."

"Good. I've got a job for you." Jesse, slender and blonde, had her hair clipped in a ponytail that bobbed when she spoke. Her yoga pants and T-shirt added to the illusion that she was much younger and hid the fact that at fifty she was a prominent female internist at Winterset Memorial. She shoved an industrial staple gun into Esther's hands. "I'd be happy if we could just get the skirt to hide the wagon. See if you can do something with the corrugated cardboard before the grand marshal arrives."

Rory stepped forward with a smile. "Too late."

Esther's cheeks flushed. "Hey, Rory. I sure hope nothing happens this year. It's unlucky to be grand marshal—some say it's a death wish."

She looked earnest. They'd gone to dinner a couple of times and caught an occasional movie together. Nothing serious though he hoped it would grow into something more.

"You make your own luck," he said.

"Besides being charming and dedicated—" Jesse winked at him. "—in a bald, paunchy way, you're too cute to invite trouble."

He straightened his shoulders. "There are criminals behind bars who would take exception to your assessment."

"There have been incidents," Esther warned, "to support her statement."

Jesse leaned toward him. "She's right. Last year's grand marshal sustained a concussion when that ladder fell on him. And the year before, when the mayor was grand marshal, he broke a leg after stepping in a hole while judging the pig races. There's every possibility a curse accompanies the honor." Her eyes twinkled.

"Sure hope you're careful." She wiggled her fingers at the side of her head in the universal signal for spooky, witchery spells, and mysterious things that go bump in the night.

Esther playfully swatted at her with the staple gun. Jesse sidestepped the sisterly aggression with more laughter.

"You two," he said, shaking his head. "I better report for duty."

Leaving them to button up the hospital float, Rory threaded his way through the crowd. He walked around the high school marching band and dodged the skateboard club. The Boy Scout troop huddled around their leader, receiving last-minute instructions. Scouts armed with trash stickers stood at attention; others, young hooligans, engaged in fencing matches behind the leader's back. Ms. Emily's Dance Academy girls, outfitted in Uncle Sam costumes, pranced and waved American flags. Rory felt buoyed. The town had turned out in a big way. He wasn't foolish enough to think it was in his honor.

He wondered what duties he'd need to perform. When he'd asked, the council had just smiled and said nothing odious. Still, he wondered. In Winterset, nothing surprised him. He just hoped it didn't involve kissing babies—or eating fourteen bowls of chili.

Standing beside a Tesla convertible, Petey Moss, the county coroner, waved. "Hey, Rory. Over here."

Rory lifted his chin, waved back, and made his way in that direction.

The man's ample belly moved up and down as he pumped Rory's hand, sending the scent of Aqua Velva into the festive air. Petey was this year's parade organizer. Rory suspected Viola, Petey's wife, was the real power behind the effort, but he was willing to give the man his due and looked forward to sharing a ride in the parade's lead car with his friend.

"Glad you're here. We can get this show on the road." Petey draped a scarlet ribbon over Rory. From right shoulder to left hip, the banner declared him grand marshal. "You and I will blaze the way through town in the lead car. But first—you'll judge the floats."

"Judge?"

"Yup. The grand marshal awards the ribbons for best in show, most creative, and best use of theme."

"Isn't the theme Fourth of July?"

"Usually. Although, over the years, I've seen some creative recycled floats from Founder's Day."

They made the first swing through the lined-up floats without comment. On the second pass, the inhabitants atop the floats recognized the judging was underway and tried to influence the outcome.

By the third trip, outright hostility reigned. Comments such as "How hard can this be?" or "Get a life, Naysmith," and "Just pick one, for crying out loud!" rained down on their heads.

While Rory grimaced, Petey just chuckled with bonhomie.

Some honor. No wonder the mayor and police chief had turned it down. As elected officials, they couldn't afford to alienate the voters.

In the end, Rory selected three. The bank's float, which boasted the Liberty Bell and a backdrop of the American flag, won best in show. Best use of theme went to the VFW float, whose riders included active-duty service members and veterans whose service stretched all the way back to WWII.

And last but not least, the Winterset Memorial Hospital float took the most creative award because it was the only float that could influence his future. He hoped Esther recognized the gesture.

He completed his second duty when the parade finished its swing through town. Then the convertible headed toward the fairgrounds, floats following in its wake.

****

As the festivities continued, Rory joined the mayor and Petey at the picnic table reserved for dignitaries. At fifty-eight, Mayor Hershel Becker was only four years Rory's senior, but a full head of snow-white hair and weathered face made him appear much older. Hershel was popular, and Rory admitted he got things done. Pushy, opinionated, and overbearing on occasion, the mayor's heart was always with the citizens of Winterset. It was no wonder that Bryce Mansfield, police chief and Rory's immediate boss, hid behind the well-respected man.

There was a lot of commotion as people met up with friends and family to claim places at picnic tables under the pavilion. The crowd spilled out onto the grassy fairground, spreading blankets to sit on as they enjoyed their meal or unfolding lawn chairs to claim spots not only for dinner but for viewing the fireworks that would happen later.

Rory craned his neck, trying to locate the Mullins sisters in the crowd. He thought he caught sight of Jesse by the horseshoe pits, but his attention turned to Mayor Becker when the latter rose to give a quick dedication. A prayer led by Pastor Mark from the Lutheran Church followed. Then Mayor Becker called out, "Play ball!" and amid joyous whoops and hollers, everyone lined up to fill their plates. In the mad scramble for ribs and potato salad, Rory lost sight of the slender blonde who might have been Jesse. Esther, a full six feet tall, would stand out in a crowd, but he didn't see her, either.

"What are we waiting for?" Petey slapped him affectionately on the back. "Let's chow down."

An hour later, Rory found both sisters under the pavilion, sharing a table with their family friend Marilyn Beauregard, Esther's neighbor Axel Barrow, and a man in a Panama hat. The man, ruggedly handsome, wore a string tie, an old-fashioned seersucker suit, and a mustache of which Hercule Poirot would be proud. A scar under his left eye jumped as he spoke in a Southern accent.

No one noticed Rory's approach, and he decided to take advantage of this by sitting at a nearby table, close enough to listen and keep a watchful eye. His gaze fell affectionately on Esther while his thoughts went to apple pie.

The man with the scar held everyone's attention. "I was just saying this morning, wasn't I, dear cousin, that y'all just can't imagine the delightful things y'all can discover." He puffed out his chest. "I'd never known about the plantation lands that are most likely still in our family name or the opportunities that my—our— heritage has opened up for me."

When he beamed at Marilyn, her eyes sparkled. After she laid a possessive hand on his arm, he said, "I declare, it's been the unearthing of our true lineage— and yours by extension, my dear Marilyn. The knowledge is liberating. Not to mention profitable."

If Rory remembered correctly, Marilyn's maiden name was Calley. She'd only become a Beauregard through marriage. The closest relationship she and the man with the scar could possibly have would be cousin-in-law. Rory's detecting sense went on high alert.

Marilyn turned to Jesse. "Don't you remember me telling your mother how my family lost their wealth during reconstruction? Southern Missouri was a horrible place after the war, carpet baggers, scoundrels, union troops." She shuddered from head to foot, making a dozen silver bracelets jangle on her arm. "All across the South, devastation!"

"Yes, dear cousin, but I'm speaking of the Savannah Beauregards."

Marilyn's face fell momentarily, but she quickly recovered. "Do tell us about your discovery, Henry."

Jesse listened patiently. Esther leaned back, her arms folded across her chest, her face devoid of expression.

Henry cleared his throat, straightened his tie, and raised one eyebrow in a ready-to-tell-all manner.

Axel Barrow, wearing his usual tattered jeans, headband, and tie-dyed T-shirt, made an effort to mimic Henry, but failed to carry it off. His bushy unibrow instilled the old hippie with a persona only an eyepatch would improve. Esther kicked him under the table.

"It all came to light after I sent for the DNA kit from Family Lost-N-Found," Henry advised.

Everyone except Esther leaned in. Henry's expression flickered.

What was that? Rory swore he'd just witnessed a twitch at the corner of Henry's left eye. Twitch or not, Henry now wore an intense expression, one more calculating than gentlemanly.

Esther must have registered the change as well. She slammed an empty Coke can on the table, too hard, too loud, breaking the mood. "You'll need to excuse me. I promised to cut pies for the hospital volunteers. Coming, Axel?"

Following her lead, Axel extracted his lanky frame from the picnic table. "I'm better at eatin' pies than cutting 'em, ma'am."

"It was nice to meet you, Mr. Beauregard. Perhaps we'll have a chance to chat again before you leave." Esther's voice was pleasant, but Rory didn't buy it.

Henry started to rise, but she waved him down. "No need to stand. We're informal here, and it's too hot for grand Southern manners." Esther moved away from the group quickly, taking Axel with her, before anyone, especially Henry, could object.

Rory liked the way Esther looked as she strode away, healthy and hardy. He got up and followed her and Axel. It looked like they were headed for the bake sale area behind the grandstand. Rory fell in line with them. "Enjoying the festivities?"

Startled, Esther lost her stride. "Heavens, Rory. I didn't see you coming."

"Hey, Constable," Axel said. "Are you judging the pies, too?" He took a Marlboro from the pack he had rolled in his sleeve.

Rory shook his head. "I've taken an oath and given up judging for the balance of the millennium."

Esther blushed. Good! She had noticed his judging choices.

Axel lit a cigarette, and Rory and Esther moved ahead, two steps beyond the second-hand smoke and out of harm's way. "Who was that with Marilyn Beauregard?" Rory asked.

"Henry. He claims to be a long-lost relative. Cousin, he says. I think he has Marilyn bamboozled."

"Big word, bamboozle."

"You know what I mean. Huckster. Flimflam man. Con artist."

"He comes off a little slick. Is he asking for money?"

"Not yet, but he didn't hesitate to move in. He's already staying at Marilyn's townhouse. I don't like it."

Rory wasn't sure he liked the sound of that, either. "Maybe I'll run a background check on him when I get to the office."

"Oh, he's probably harmless, and he'll be gone in a day or two. It's just that I never dreamed Marilyn could be so gullible. It bothers me that she took him in."

Rory had to agree. Strong-willed and independent, Marilyn was no one's fool. "Perhaps the family tie pulled her in. Everyone has an Achilles heel."

"I don't see any family resemblance. Henry Beauregard, long-lost cousin, my foot,"

"I'll run the background check."

"Does he think she has a ten-million-dollar slush fund?" Her eyes narrowed. "Good grief, he could be targeting her!"

Rory doubted anyone was out to get Marilyn Beauregard. She knew too many people and taking advantage of her would draw attention. Henry Beauregard was most likely who he said he was. Still…it wouldn't hurt to investigate.

They walked along in silence, with Axel trailing behind. When they reached the grandstands, Rory decided to check the firework arrangements instead of eating homemade pie. "Are you staying for the fireworks tonight?"

"Geez," said Axel. "I'm not missing the Fourth of July fireworks."

Her dark mood evaporating, Esther laughed. "Yes."

"I'll find you there, but for now, I better make sure everything looks safe at the pyrotechnic station."

When they parted, he felt tired. Too many people, too many ceremonial tasks. He looked forward to enjoying the July evening, topped with fireworks—and Esther's company.

He was halfway to the fireman's booth when Petey Moss flagged him down. "There you are, Mr. Grand Marshal. They're looking for you at the hay-bale hunt."

Officiating again?

He'd be glad when this day was over, and he could get back to being a detective.

Chapter Two

Relieved from his duties as grand marshal, Rory dropped the honoree sash in the nearest trash bin and looked over the crowd now settled along the Missouri riverbank. Mothers shushed young ones, and more than one baby slept soundly on a blanket while "Stars and Stripes Forever" played through the grandstand speakers. The pyrotechnic crew floated on the platform off the bank. Tethered and lined with rocket launchers, the volunteer fire department's pontoon boat drifted ten yards out. With sun-kissed cheeks, everyone waited for dusk, relaxing and anticipating the celebration's fireworks finale.

Rory was content to stand back and let them enjoy the twilight. He looked over the crowd, searching for Esther. Petey Moss caught his eye and waved him over. Rory raised a hand in thanks but went on looking.

He spotted a group of off-duty police officers at the water's edge. Should he take the opportunity to join them? He didn't think so. They were warming up to him, but there was a measurable distance between tolerance and acceptance.

Marilyn Beauregard sat on the lowered tailgate of Axel's pickup between Cousin Henry and the overgrown hippie himself. The hospital crew surrounded Jesse. But Esther wasn't in sight. What good was down time if you couldn't spend it with someone special? She had to be somewhere in the crowd. As he was about to take a swing through the blanket covered field, a tall brunette standing by the refreshment stand caught his attention. He made a beeline in her direction.

Sipping a pale drink from a clear plastic cup, Esther leaned against the shack. As he approached, she lowered the beverage. "Thank God the curse hasn't turned you into a porcupine or something remotely resembling a mole."

"I take it you missed me?"

"Hmmm."

He followed her gaze across the field to Axel's truck. "Do I still need to worry about a curse?"

"According to Jesse, yes. It seems anyone unfortunate enough to accept the position as grand marshal invites trouble. In past years, the GM has sustained broken bones, concussions, and all manner of debilitating injuries. But don't worry. As curses go, this one is more inclined to inflict inconvenience than death."

"Nice to know." Rory watched Marilyn and Cousin Henry move off the tailgate and unfold a pair of webbed lawn chairs. Once opened, they lifted the chairs back into the truck bed, then climbed on board. He didn't see Axel and assumed he had moved on.

Esther turned her head and looked down into his eyes. "You carry a radio and a gun. You won't suffer for long."

Rory didn't have the radio. It was his day off, so he'd left it at home while he performed his patriotic duties. "You were worried that the curse would turn me into a prickly creature?"

"And I'd miss you in the crowd." Esther lifted one foot and rotated her ankle. The size-ten walking shoe swung in a circle. "Or worse, that I'd step on you."

His lips twisted into a sly smile. She had missed him. "That's hitting below the belt."

"I've lost sight of Axel," she said. "I wonder what nonsense Cousin Henry is telling Marilyn."

Rory's cell phone vibrated. He removed it from his belt, glanced at the screen, and then sighed. "I'm going to take this."

Esther tilted her head. "I'll go check on Marilyn. Should I hunt you down later?"

"I'd be disappointed if you didn't." He put the phone to his ear. "Naysmith."

The call was from Sunny Gomez, the department's civilian dispatcher. "While you've been loafing around out there, have you seen anyone from the sheriff's department?"

"I haven't noticed."

"Even though I got to do all the work at the station, our boys deserve a day off, and a complaint just came in for a suspicious male smoking weed behind the horse trailers. Now, don't give me no grief. I know the fairground is outta the town limits, but I thought, you being the detective and all…" She let her voice trail off, but he knew what she wanted.

"Gee, Sunny. It's my day off, too." He rubbed his temple and grimaced. "All right, I'll take a look. No need to pester the boys."

The horse trailers sat at the edge of the fairgrounds behind the 4-H building. By the time Rory made it there, the sun had begun to set, and he heard the first skyrocket explode. He circled the area but didn't see a soul. Nevertheless, he checked around the trailers, cautiously sidestepped some droppings, and peeked in each empty box. And then, just for good measure, he decided to explore the poplar grove separating the parking lot from the river's bank.

It was darker beneath the trees, where the branches blocked the fading light, and the ground was moist. He listened for human sounds. Fireworks exploded overhead, but under the canopy, Rory couldn't see the bursts as they lit the sky.

Stepping out of the grove, he looked out toward the river. Solidly packed stone and dirt stretched the ten feet from where he stood to the water's edge. In the distance, the railroad bridge stretched from Nebraska over the Missouri River and touched the Iowa shore. Someone had mounded boulders farther down. Perhaps they'd been removed from the grounds and left there for a retaining wall. More likely, they were hidden from view, too heavy to move elsewhere. They were an eyesore, starting at the tree line, topping three feet, and spreading down to the water's edge. As he scrambled up the stack, intent on gaining the elevated advantage, the moss-covered boulders felt slippery under the smooth leather soles of his shoes.

When he reached the top, he caught a whiff of cigarette smoke—or was it marijuana?

He pivoted quickly and lost purchase. To break the fall, he instinctively put out his hands, and his foot slid into a crevice between two large stones. His forearms smashed against the hard surface. The force of his body slam moved the boulders which then interlocked around his foot.

From behind, he heard someone run off through the

trees. He cursed, pushed up, ignored the complaints from his knees, and hand-walked his upper body back to his feet. With one foot captive, and kneeling over the other, he awkwardly righted himself. Then gave a tug. The vise-grip held tight. His palms felt razor-scraped. He reached for the phone, but it wasn't there.

It took a moment to spot his lifeline, five feet away and out of reach. Rory looked around wearily. Withdrawing his gun, he aimed it at the sky. Fireworks exploded, lit the heavens, and echoed across the fairground. He paused. No one was likely to hear his call for help. He put the weapon away. Sooner or later, the riders would return to load their horses into the trailers. Eventually the flares and firecrackers would die down.

He stood there in a lopsided stance, one foot buried beneath rocks, one leg awkwardly bent at the knee to compensate, and realized his vulnerability. Before moving to Winterset, he'd enjoyed a special kind of notoriety in Omaha. It was said he was a dedicated detective who labored non-stop, moved mountains, and leaped buildings. Maybe the city force had laid it on a little thick, but still, this blasted Missouri riverbank had singlehandedly rendered him helpless.

He'd worked too hard to prove his worth to the citizens of Winterset, where so many were skeptical of his age and leery of his talents. He thought he was past that worry. Their praise came easy enough after the events last Christmas. Hadn't he shown the doubters? Two men behind bars, a crime boss exposed, hijackings curtailed. Grand marshal be damned—he couldn't afford to stir it all up again.

He had no wish for rescue, not if it meant he'd be

found helpless and injured. Rory's concern wasn't about looking less of a man, but at representing less of a detective—adding fodder for the skeptics.

If he could only move one stone, even a little, it might be enough for him to slip his foot out. Try as he might, the boulders were wedged in place. He looked around for a tree limb to use for leverage. Branches were scattered everywhere in the grove. Out on the rocks—nothing. The only force he could hope to muster would need to come from his free foot.

If he sat, he could use his entire body weight behind an effort to shift the boulder. He forgot his foot was locked in place and unceremoniously plopped onto his behind. In the process, he wrenched his knee. Instantly regretting the hasty move, he took a moment for the pain to subside. Then he placed the sole of his free foot on the smallest of the large stones and pushed.

Was that movement? He tried again. Nothing. Push...pause...push, he teased it out like a loose tooth. With each effort, he felt a tightening around his ankle. That could only mean his ankle was swelling. He cursed again. The boulders hadn't budged, and he called out, "Hey, is anybody out there?"

How long would it take before someone missed him? Probably next Christmas. He couldn't afford to wait if he expected to get back to the fairgrounds and Esther. He needed to be proactive.

If he could get the phone, he could call for help. Someone discreet and trusted. Rory immediately thought of young officer, Clarence Thacker. A friend and colleague, they shared a struggle for recognition from the other WPD officers. Thacker wouldn't exploit his predicament. Rory eyed the cell phone, perched on the boulder beyond reach. He unbuckled his belt, pulled it free, then re-buckled it to form a loop he could slip around the phone and drag within reach.

The leather loop slapped against the hard rock and fetched nothing but air. His arm, even fully extended and aided by a lean in the appropriate direction, still fell short. For a moment, he wished he had the blasted grand marshal ribbon he'd so hastily discarded. Then he realized his necktie would serve just as well. He made short business of removing it and fastening it to his belt. Satisfied with his handiwork, he successfully extended his range by three feet.

It wasn't as easy as he had thought. He didn't even come close until he'd thrown a half-dozen times. Then, inch by inch, the detective coaxed the phone over the uneven surface and within range of his outstretched fingers. It took close to twenty minutes, but he finally scooped it up.

Four missed calls. Crap! He found "Rookie" in the contacts, punched it, and impatiently waited while it rang.

As soon as Thacker's deep, commanding voice answered, Rory cut him off. "Thacker, Naysmith here. I'm at the fairgrounds. Do you know where the Missouri River bends in behind the 4-H building, about a half-mile from the railway bridge?" Then, "Yes, there's a poplar grove on that side. I could use your assistance."

He scowled when Thacker explained he was assigned to direct fairground traffic at ten. "This is more important. And Thacker—" Rory swallowed hard. "—bring a crowbar and a shovel."

****

Rory heard Thacker coming before he saw him. Spit and polish, dressed in his police blues, with a broad face that would give him the perpetual look of youth, he stepped out of the tree line and said, "The band's still playing at the pavilion, but it won't be long before the mass exodus to town." He carried an army trenching tool in one hand and the tire-jack handle from the police cruiser in the other. He raised them in a show-and-tell manner for Rory to see. "I'm scheduled to report in at ten. Until I go on duty, I'm all yours." The police radio crackled at his shoulder.

"This shouldn't take that long." Rory had managed to shift his weight and, with his free leg extended over the rocks, achieve a semi-natural reclining position, as if he were relaxing while perched on the large boulders and taking in the view of the river. His predicament couldn't have been evident to the young officer.

Moving closer, Thacker asked, "What's up?"

"I got my damn foot caught between these rocks."

Thacker frowned. He placed the tools on a nearby boulder and took an oversized flashlight from his belt. He pointed the light beam down the crevice. Rory leaned out of the way, giving him as wide a berth as possible.

"I can't see a thing," the rookie said. "Pull your pant leg out of the way."

"I think my guardian angel is off for the Fourth." The detective studied the cloudless sky and tried not to think about his foot. It didn't work. "Just use the crowbar to break one of these frickin' stones loose."

The jack handle didn't do the trick. Opening the trenching tool and using the pick end, Thacker swung it against the largest stone. It bounced off the surface.

Rory suppressed a scream as pain shot from his knee down his encased leg. "Easy!"

"Sorry, boss."

"Try removing one of the outer stones. Loosen them, and maybe we'll be able to budge these. I'll hold the light, and you make room for these damn jaws to unclasp. Try finding the cornerstone."

A fine layer of perspiration covered Rory's face. He felt defeated and a little nauseous. He leaned back on his elbows and looked at the sky. "Thacker," he said, "this is damn unlucky."

The rookie moved down the mound to the edge of the pile. Using the crowbar and a lot of muscle, he attacked. Finally, he was able to roll one stone out of position. Then another. He was still three feet from Rory's crevice, working his way toward the more enormous boulders and Rory's ultimate freedom, when the rock he was prying loose rolled out of place. He hesitated. "There is something funny here, boss."

"I could use a good laugh."

"Not ha-ha funny, peculiar funny."

"Tell me anyway."

"There's someone else in this rock pile."

"What?" Rory sat up too quickly and swallowed the pain. "What did you say?"

Thacker whipped another flashlight out and pointed the beam into the pit where the boulder had been. He slowly moved his head from side to side. His face, unnaturally lit, glowed like a Halloween jack-o-lantern. "There's a human foot down here."

Rory rolled his eyes up as the statement registered. "Hilarious, Thacker. I don't need—"

"It appears to be female. She has on a torn sandal.

Dried blood and—"

"Don't touch anything." Rory couldn't believe they had unearthed a body on the bank of the Missouri. He shifted into a position that relieved the pressure on his knee. "Come around from the other side and dig me out. Now!"

"I better call this in."

The detective grimaced. "Get me out first. You know WPD is better at moving violations than major crimes. We should take a look around before the hordes arrive and trample the area. We'll lose any chance to collect evidence."

Thacker immediately moved to the opposite side and began to dig in earnest. With his proven technique and the right tools, he soon removed the keystone holding Rory captive.

"Yeewow…" moaned Rory, pulling his foot free.

As soon as it was released, his stocking ballooned over the sides of his leather shoe. The whole appendage began to throb. Thacker helped him stand, but Rory couldn't balance on his own—his leg was too damaged. And his foot proved too tender to support his weight. His only recourse was to hop over to the exposed body on one foot—while ignoring the wrenched knee and aided by a young and sturdy right shoulder.

Thacker pointed the flashlight beam into the hole.

Rory closed his eyes. Who was he kidding? They needed to bring in portable floodlights or wait until sunup if they expected to see anything. It was a woman's foot, all right. Only the foot. If there was more, it was under river rock. He was a detective, not an archaeologist. They were going to need assistance.

Rory called it in.

Sunny's peppery voice came over the connection. "Did you catch 'em? I figured ya just blew me off, holiday and all. Where you been? If it wasn't Fourth of July—"

"Sunny, I found a body. Technically a body part. It's buried behind the 4-H building."

She gasped. "Part? How'd ya end up with part of a body?"

He heard wheels rolling over linoleum and then a flurry of keyboard clicks. "It's a long story. Who's on duty?"

"The boys are all out watching the fireworks."

"Perfect! I'm at the fairgrounds. I need a crew to tape off twenty feet of riverbank and secure a possible crime scene."

"Riverbank ain't fairgrounds."

"Listen, Sunny, log it in. Dispatch the whole crew." He was through fooling around. "I'll notify Officer Thacker." He chanced a glance at the young officer and found Thacker's expression was blank. "We'll secure the area until the crew arrives."

After disconnecting, the two of them hobbled off the boulders and onto the gravel and then crossed the short distance to the tree line.

"You can wait here. Keep an eye on things, and I'll get the first-aid kit," Thacker said. He left Rory leaning against the first tree they found that was strong enough to support his weight.

Thacker was an Eagle Scout. Rory had no doubt he'd come back with the appropriate splint, bandage, and antiseptic. A heavy dose of Tylenol with Codeine would do the trick. He just hoped the rookie would return before he had to explain why he'd been climbing around on the rocks doing the county sheriff's job and how he'd ended up in his present condition.

It didn't take long for Sunny to rally the boys to action. Where there is one police cruiser, men of arms gather. It seemed like every WPD police officer was either assigned to duty at the fairgrounds or celebrating the Fourth of July with family there. Before Thacker could get Rory attended to, they heard the whoops announcing the arrival of the cavalry.

"Just wrap the ankle," Rory told Thacker.

"I better look at your whole leg."

There was no way Rory was going to be figuratively, or literally, caught with his pants down. "It'll wait. The important thing is to tape off the area and get the boys working right away."

When Rory removed his shoe and pulled up his pant leg, Thacker let out a low whistle. It looked nasty, but no bones were sticking out. The rookie did a hasty job of binding an Ace bandage around the swollen ankle—and he tut-tutted as he pulled it tight. Rory was testing out the handiwork when the first responders arrived.

Officer Lloyd, a thin, angular man, and his partner, Jim Zielinski, who, at thirty-five, had a full head of prematurely gray hair, stomped out of the trees in full riot gear.

"What kind of call did Sunny put out?" Rory sniped. "You guys look like you're going to war."

"Don't start, Nay-boy. Jim and me just closed down the SWAT booth. Citizens like to know they're safe, and full gear gets them going."

"Now that we're here," Jim said, "we'll take over."

Rory gingerly put weight on the wrapped ankle and

flinched. As first on the scene, Thacker, even though he'd just passed out of his rookie probation period, would act as lead officer on the case. Rory wasn't about to let Lloyd muscle the younger man out of the position. "Officer Thacker discovered a suspicious burial site. I want this whole area cordoned off."

"Unless we can get floodlights out here now," Lloyd said, reaching for his phone, "we'll have to wait for daylight to see what we got."

"Thacker will make the call," Rory said. "Just string the tape."

Thacker's cherubic face flickered in surprise. Apparently, he hadn't considered the possibility of being the lead officer. His face quickly morphed into a more appropriate expression. In his commanding voice, he barked, "Start here. Work to the river and then twenty feet in either direction down the shoreline. I'll request floodlights and the county's forensic team."

"Ain't ya being a little premature, calling for forensics?" Lloyd said.

"I'll make the call. You secure the perimeter of the crime scene."

Thacker glanced in Rory's direction, then squared his body. "Detective Naysmith will remain here, ready to take command once we've marked the area."

The seasoned officers frowned.

Rory wondered if this meant Thacker and he had swapped roles. He was becoming substantially less than a mentor. What he knew with certainty was that he wasn't stepping in.

He wasn't stepping anywhere.

****

Celebrating the holiday meant resources were

short, and the body extraction was planned for first light.

Rory considered it fortunate that a crowd hadn't gathered. A few curious riders wandered over when they discovered the cruisers parked by the horse trailers. The officers quickly sent them on their way. The bulk of the festival-goers parked behind the grandstand and left unaware that the police force was busy at the river.

Rory waited until the last line of tape was strung and a guard was posted. Then, after limping through the grove, he accepted a ride home from Thacker. He was beyond weary. His ankle throbbed, and his knee, somewhere between weak and feeble, ached. It was time for a good soak in the tub and a shot of whiskey.

Thacker dropped him off at the private staircase that Rory typically used to reach his apartment on the top floor. Hillard's estate rented the apartment above the closed department store to him at a discount, with the condition that he keep an eye on the building. It was cheaper than demolition and eliminated the need for a watchman. Twice a day, Rory walked the first and second floors, looking for vagrants or damage. Occasionally he found something worth his time, but not often. Today he was too tired to bother.

He waited until the young officer drove away. Then he rounded the building and, using a rusty key, unlocked the alley door to the abandoned store. Aided by the flashlight on his cell phone, he crossed the cavernous room to the elevator in the back corner and stepped in.

During the store's heyday, the third floor held executive offices. Now his apartment took up much of the area. He pulled the metal gate closed and reached for the hand-crank.

It was a slow ascent, but he was in no hurry.

Tomorrow would come soon enough.

Chapter Three

The Golden Leaf on Main Street was a Winterset institution. Esther remembered when the diner's cherry phosphates were the center of her teen-age existence. The soda fountain and the counter were long gone, but the padded booths, bottomless cups of coffee, and all-day breakfasts still drew a crowd. Comfort food and friendly chatter—the Leaf was a community hub where people lingered in long conversations with neighbors, even if just idle banter or bemoaning the weather.

She slid into a booth to join Jesse for a sisterly breakfast. Between the parade, picnic, and the doings yesterday, they'd hardly spent a moment together. So, when Jesse called, voicing concern over Marilyn's newfound cousin-in-law, Esther suggested the pow-wow. Before she had time to settle onto the seat, a steaming cup of coffee was in front of her.

Jesse glanced at the menu, then set it down. "I suspect that Cousin Henry isn't truly related to Garrison Beauregard. How long has it been since Marilyn heard from the Georgia side of her family? I can't figure out what Henry is after."

Esther blew on the steaming brew and then gingerly took a sip. "Maybe he's just happy to discover he has a cousin, or second cousin once removed, or whatever nonsense." She flapped a hand trying to wave away her own concern.

"Are you kidding?" Jesse cocked her head in disbelief. "You know I love Marilyn, but I don't think finding yourself related to her is a great discovery."

Esther drew her lips into a tight line. She had to admit, Marilyn could be trying. But the striking woman had been their mother's best friend and therefore part of their family for as long as she could remember. Life would be less—she searched for the right word— colorful, chaotic, frantic? Marilyn was just Marilyn, and she always reacted from the heart. Esther thought about the conversations at the picnic, hunting for something Henry had said that had sounded fishy. He'd made her uncomfortable, yet she didn't know why.

"Did he say anything to suggest he was after something more than kinship?"

"I don't think so, but something is off."

"That scar makes him look menacing," Esther offered. "Otherwise, he's quite handsome. The picture of a Southern gentleman."

Jesse frowned into her coffee cup. "His drawl seemed a little put on." Raising the cup to the waitress for a refill, she added, "I guess I'm overprotective. Ever since Mother…well, you know…" She let the sentence fade and then busied herself with smoothing the napkin on her lap.

Esther let her sister's comment go without offering a response. They would always miss their mother, Jesse doubly so now that her husband Neil was incarcerated and the two of them were working through a divorce. The sisters needed Marilyn, and each other, now more than ever.

Jesse nibbled on a cranberry muffin. "I wonder if Abby Sue Bellman remembers a Beauregard named

Henry or Hank? What kind of nickname would a Southerner have had fifty years ago? Skeeter? Beau? Boomer?"

"I like Skeeter."

"As I recall, Marilyn's first husband was her childhood sweetheart, therefore a fellow Missourian. Hubby two was a jazz singer from the Windy City, and hubs number three a Southerner from Georgia. As a matter of fact, both Abby Sue and Garrison Beauregard grew up in Georgia. She tells a cute story about their shared hometown that involves a cabbage patch, corn liquor, and a wild cat. Let me think. It was Savannah or some small place of commerce outside the city. At least the Georgia part holds up against known Beauregard folklore."

Jesse pushed her plate away. "Enough speculating about Henry—Hank—Skeeter. Let's talk about something more pleasant, like" —she raised both eyebrows—"manly, eligible detectives, for instance. I lost sight of you and Rory last night."

"Hmmm," said Esther. "Same for me."

Jesse leaned forward. "You weren't with him? I thought you'd made plans to meet for the fireworks."

"We agreed to meet, but along the way, he must have gotten waylaid by a call to duty."

It was no big deal, she reminded herself, for the umpteenth time. She and Rory were merely friends. If he'd found someone or something more interesting than watching fireworks with her, that was his prerogative. Besides, after downing a couple of fruity concession-stand drinks, she'd felt tired and left before the last rocket had launched. At least she'd beat the traffic congestion that always formed after big fairground events and was home in her cozy bed before ten.

Jesse interrupted her thoughts. "Do you think he participated in the police action?"

Stunned, Esther jerked back. "What are you talking about? What *police action?*"

"I don't know if you'd classify it as an action, really, but something was going on at the fairground, over by the 4-H building. All the police cruisers were there with racks flashing in that annoying strobe pattern. I understand their sirens were silent, so, my guess is the situation was ugly but not perilous."

Esther wondered. Maybe he'd been tied up with police work and it wasn't a case of finding something better. She was relieved to know it could have been something urgent—and professional—as opposed to… Never mind.

"I didn't see or hear anything," she said. "It was probably nothing. You know, teens, beer, moonlight."

They chatted for a while, lingering over second cups of coffee. The waitress cleared away their dishes and offered to top off their cups.

"What time do you go on duty?" Esther said.

"I don't have an appointment until eleven. We don't need to hurry."

"Actually, Marilyn invited me to a party this afternoon. I was hoping to buy a new blouse and run a few errands before then." Esther raised her hands to ward off any potential rebuke. "I know, I know. But I couldn't think fast enough to get out of it. She wants to show Cousin Henry off, or let Henry show off, I don't know which. I avoided them as much as possible yesterday. Call it guilt, but I promised to put in an appearance. I plan to nibble a few cocktail weenies, then hightail it home."

They giggled.

"She cornered me with an invitation as well." Jesse signed the credit slip and collected her purse. "Luckily, I have a full-time job."

"Look on the bright side. Maybe I'll run into Abby Sue and the wild cat at Marilyn's get-together."

After they left the Golden Leaf, Esther ran her errands. She planned to swing by the house, change into something suitable for the two o'clock soiree, and grab a dozen cookies from the freezer. Finally on her way to Marilyn's townhouse at two fifteen, she caught a red light cutting through town and ended up idling near the police station.

Should she pop in and see if Detective Naysmith was in his office? Probably not. They weren't at the drop-in-at-the-office stage. But she hadn't received a message from him last night and, she had to admit, she'd been disappointed. Granted, Rory had grand marshal duties and whatever police business had gone down behind the 4-H building. He didn't owe her an explanation. Still, one courteous heads-up would have been considerate.

At any rate, she didn't have time now. She was running late and had every intention of finding out more about the wayward cousin named Skeeter, Boomer, or Hank.

****

The Spreading Oaks Townhouses were in a newer development on the far-west side of town which featured shady streets that boasted the best-kept flower boxes and immaculately groomed lawns. The homes faced the curb, with walkways connected to the city sidewalk and a small private patio behind, where residents parked their cars under carports running the length of the six-dwelling buildings. Marilyn's townhouse was third from the end. One of the problems with living in a townhouse community was the inherent lack of parking. Even if Marilyn hadn't invited every soul in Winterset, Esther would have found it hard to find an empty spot. Arriving late guaranteed there wouldn't be one available.

With her fears confirmed after two passes through the complex, she parallel parked three blocks away and hoofed it to Marilyn's door. It opened just as she raised her hand to knock.

"Esther, how nice of you to come." Marilyn sidestepped to let her enter. "We're out on the patio. Just grab a drink as you pass through the kitchen. I think you'll know everyone." Marilyn craned her neck to peer around Esther as if she were looking for someone behind her. "Did you come alone?"

"It's just little old me."

"Well, never you mind."

Never mind what? That she wasn't tiny—haha. Or that it was just her. Who was Marilyn expecting?

Esther set the cookie platter on the kitchen counter and filled a glass from the punch bowl before stepping out onto the patio to join the others. To her unsophisticated eye, the guests looked decked out for a Kentucky Derby brunch. She hadn't seen so many hats since the Baptist luncheon in April.

In front of a trellis overflowing with purple clematis, Viola Moss sat on an outdoor lounger next to Sophia Becker, the mayor's wife. Off to the left, the entire bridge club and several ladies she recognized from the church choir occupied folding chairs placed strategically in a semicircle facing the patio doors. She looked around for an empty spot. There were none. Viola waved and wiggled over to make room for her to join them.

The patio doors slid open, followed by an excited gasp from the collected ladies. Cousin Henry stepped onto the patio, a Panama hat on his head. Sweeping it off, he bowed deeply. Rhett Butler had nothing on Henry. Esther scooted toward the trellis and claimed the seat in the shade next to Viola. Grateful to be out of the way, she placed her arm around her friend's shoulders and gave her an affectionate squeeze.

Henry Beauregard worked the patio, pausing at each guest to formally introduce himself and offer a small compliment. From her seat under the clematis vines, Esther saw him take each outstretched hand. There were a lot of blushes and batted eyelashes. Watching made her faintly nauseous. What a load of disgraceful flirting by a bunch of tittering hens. Had they never seen a man before?

Well, this was Winterset—enough said.

Viola smiled sweetly, tipped her head, and leaned in. In a hushed whisper, she asked, "Did you hear about the body?"

By the time Marilyn's cousin-in-law made it to their location, Esther had extracted all the information Viola had on the dead body, which didn't amount to much. Sometime during the fireworks display, Rory had gone down to the riverbank behind the 4-H building and discovered a dead woman. What he was doing there was anyone's guess. The police had to remove a pile of boulders to get to her, and practically the whole force had turned out to participate. They didn't manage to extract the body and were back at it this morning. Viola didn't know how long that would take and feared Petey would spend the balance of the day working on the autopsy. Then he'd probably come home exhausted and want to tell Viola all the gory details. He always shared the ghastliest things, she told Esther, it sounded quite gruesome.

Esther agreed. She felt terrible about the poor woman but relieved to discover Rory had a good excuse for not watching the fireworks with her—or calling. Well, he still could have called.

Henry tipped his hat and said, "I believe we met at the picnic."

"We did. Esther Mullins." She didn't hold out her hand when Henry bowed. "May I introduce Viola Moss, the county coroner's wife, and Sophia Becker, our mayor's better half."

"Charmed," said Henry.

"Tell us how you're related to our sweet Marilyn," Sophia said.

"Marilyn's dear, departed husband, Garrison, was my first cousin. His father and mine were brothers. Naturally, it's been some time since we shared a table. I left Georgia at a tender age, while Garrison pursued his fortune closer to home."

"Where is home?" Viola asked.

"A small community that you may not be familiar with called Smyrola, Georgia. My family had a plantation there before the war."

While Esther pondered which war he referred to, Sophia asked, "And what do you do?" She took a sip of punch and then dabbed at her lips with a frilly napkin.

"For a living, I mean?"

Was she really doing the eyelash thing? Esther couldn't believe Sophia would fall for someone so...

Viola had just opened her mouth to comment when the patio doors slid open and Abby Sue Bellman stepped out. With her porcelain complexion, regal carriage, and head of ginger hair with a gentle gray spreading back from her temples like angel wings, she looked spectacular for a woman in her seventies. Her penetrating blue eyes searched over the guests.

"My, my," said Henry, eyeing the latest arrival.

"I believe you know Abby Sue Bellman," Esther said. "She's *also* from a little-known community in Georgia."

"My, my. I'd never have known her." He fingered the brim of his hat. "Ladies, will you excuse me? I believe I have some catching up to do."

Esther swatted at a honeybee which at that moment chose to dive-bomb her glass of punch. When she looked up, Henry had Abby Sue by the elbow, and they were stepping back through the doors and into the house.

"I thought Henry was going to tell us about Smyrola?" Viola stuck her lower lip out in a pout. "I love tales of the Old South."

Marilyn appeared from out of nowhere and announced luncheon on the veranda, which turned out to be the side yard. The group moved to where caterers had set a lovely table of salads and finger foods. Wondering why she'd bothered to bring cookies, Esther fell in line with the others. When her plate was full, she found a seat at a card table with the choir ladies.

"That Henry Beauregard is a charmer," said Mia, a

blonde soprano in a beige hat covered with netting and hummingbirds.

"Southern gentleman," Jean, a brunette with a carnation concoction on her head so tall it threatened to topple at the first stiff breeze, remarked. "Maybe he'll sit with us?"

But Henry and Abby Sue didn't join them. They must have had a lot of catching up to do. And even Marilyn seemed surprised by their absence. Coming over to Esther, she whispered, "Have you seen Cousin Henry?"

Esther had a giant portion of potato salad halfway to her lips. She stopped and put the fork down. "I saw him go into the house with Abby Sue."

"Thanks," Marilyn said absently and disappeared through the patio doors.

"Do you know anything about Family Lost-N-Found?" asked Mia. "I understand that's how Cousin Henry found Marilyn."

"Was it Lost-N-Found? I thought it was Family Finder," Jean said. "But aren't all of those family genealogy sites the same?"

Esther looked at her skeptically. "Well, there are the free sites, and there are the not-so-free sites. Some offer DNA tests and match you to your genetic roots. I wouldn't bother. You can find out a lot just by checking the Bureau of Vital Statistics for death, birth, and marriage certificates and avoid the genealogy sites."

Jean sighed. "I started to fill out my family tree, but it got so confusing, birth records, census data, DOB, DOD, all that stuff. I finally gave up."

Mia giggled. "Wouldn't it be fun to discover you're from the royal family of some small but prosperous country no one can pronounce?"

"We all wish we were princesses," Esther said.

Truth be told, she still looked in every new purse she purchased, hoping to find money an anonymous millionaire had tucked in the pocket. They all had dreams. Princess? She'd given that one up a long time ago and found contentment in her humble, impoverished Prussian lineage.

Marilyn returned on the arm of Cousin Henry. "Ladies, I trust y'all have had a chance to meet my cousin." Her face was radiant, her attitude confident. "When you've finished your refreshments, please retake your seats on the patio. Cousin Henry will tell us how Family Lost-N-Found helped him discover his family. Including little ol' me." With a giggle, she snuggled into his side.

Henry affectionately patted the hand clutching his sleeve and beamed. Esther was surprised he didn't twirl the tip of his mustache—or wiggle his eyebrows. He reminded her of a cross between Colonel Sanders and Snidely Whiplash.

Yup, there was something odd about the Southern gentleman. Hoping to grill Abby Sue, she looked around, but the beautiful septuagenarian had mysteriously vanished.

Chapter Four

Rising at dawn, Rory found his ankle hadn't miraculously healed overnight. Even with it snugly bound, he had to fight to get his shoe on over the swelling. He'd almost given up trying when he discovered his hiking boots not only fit but gave extra support to the ankle. Although it hurt to put his weight on it, an X-ray could wait, and he decided to walk the pain out.

Staying on level ground made the most sense in his condition, so instead of taking the stairs down to ground level, he took the hand-cranked elevator again. Once down, he slipped into the station long enough to pick up a city car, then headed to the fairgrounds. It was shortly after nine when he pulled into the 4-H building parking area. The earlier arrivals had driven through the grove from the parking lot, and he followed the temporary path of flattened foliage out to the riverbank and parked in line with the others.

Three men standing in water up to their shins systematically removed the stones closest to the water's edge. Their pant legs and the lower parts of their shirts were soaked and muddy. Thacker was with them.

"We've been at it since sunup," he called to Rory. "The whole lower torso is uncovered." He said something to the men and headed in Rory's direction. "Female. Hard to determine much beyond that."

"You still in charge?"

"First on the scene." Thacker's eyes shone. "Lloyd's not happy."

"He'll get over it." Rory hoped it was true. "I don't see a body bag. How much longer before we know more?"

"They can't say. But they're expediting the effort judiciously."

Rory frowned. "Can I take a look?"

"Sure."

The unpleasant odor of decaying fish and vegetation didn't mask the stench coming from the human body decomposing in the pit where the men were excavating. Rory took two steps, reached the first layer of stones, stumbled, and stopped. The putrid smell and insistent flies discouraged him. Turning to Thacker, he said, "I don't want to hinder the recovery."

Thacker glanced over at the crew. "Your expertise will expedite the effort. Wait here. I'll get some equipment from the cruiser."

Two minutes later, he returned, rolling a pole with a photo flash reflector and umbrella secured to the top. "The guys need better lighting to achieve the best documentation." He pushed the light pole toward Rory.

"You expect me to carry this up that rock pile?"

Thacker lowered his voice. "It won't be as dignified as a cane or a crutch, but it will do the job."

"Ahhh," Rory said, latching on to the deeper meaning. "Well done."

It was awkward, but with Thacker's assistance, he managed to maneuver the portable light rack next to the excavation site. He looked down into the pit and then stood unaided with both feet planted solidly and shoulders squared. "How's it going?"

A technician glanced up. "We'd be done if this river water didn't seep in from below. Got to sift through every spoonful. Makes extraction painful. Stupid, murky crap is all over."

Thacker worked the light pole into position and fired it up. Once in place, Rory leaned against the equipment to relieve the weight from his ankle. No one was the wiser, he hoped.

The rookie was correct about the meticulous recovery process. It was a woman. Identification: doubtful. Age: unclear. Bloating made her limbs look more like muddy bags of marbles than taut skin over bone. The damage could have happened when her body was buried under the boulders—or before. He'd know after the autopsy.

As the sun moved overhead, he grew impatient. The July day had served up a helping of grueling humidity. Rory fought an impulse to ask them to yank the body out, but he knew that was probably the worst thing they could do. Thank goodness his hat offered shade for his face and protected his balding dome from blistering.

The men worked in silence, and there was no telling how much longer they'd be. He hadn't thought it possible that he'd miss doing the daily sudoku. Anything that proved a distraction would have been welcomed—at least until a piece of identification or a possible cause of death was unearthed. Without something constructive to do, he watched, and a fine layer of perspiration spread across his brow as the day moved into the afternoon.

One of the technicians tossed his pick aside and

bent over the pit. "Bingo!"

"What is it?" Rory asked.

"Looks like a tote or a gym bag," the tech called back. "We'll know in a minute. Coulda been tossed onto her body before they began dropping in the boulders. She's lying underneath it."

"Fish it out," Rory demanded.

The tech mopped his brow with the back of a muddy glove, leaving a smear across his forehead. He gave Rory a look that said, "In good time," then addressed his partner. "Better record this." The tech reseated his WPD baseball cap before stepping out of the way for the video technician. The third man lifted the bag with a pole hook. River water dripped back into the pit. He flipped the muddy object onto the boulder at the detective's feet. Mud flew everywhere.

Rory almost jumped out of the way, but he caught himself at the last moment. Frowning at his splattered pant legs, he took a pair of disposable gloves from his hip pocket and pulled them on. Using his pen, he straightened the bag and smoothed it out over the rock. The video camera rolled. He stepped out of the way for the still shots.

The bag was approximately twenty inches wide and eighteen inches long, too caked in mud and grime to reveal its color. It could have been a shopping bag, diaper bag, or oversized purse. It looked too thick to be empty. He reached out to nudge it open.

"Better let us handle this, Naysmith," the technician warned.

"Is there anything in it?" Rory asked.

The pole man answered, "It's mighty heavy, but that might just be water weight."

"We'll photograph it for the record and let the sun dry it out a bit," said the technician. "I'd rather get the body out before it gets any hotter. Then we can start logging evidence."

Rory stepped back. Yeah, that made sense. At least he had one piece of evidence to speculate on while they finished the job.

It took another three hours before the body lay on the stones. It was hard to discern the bruises from the mud, but they were there, Rory was certain. Whether they had been caused by rocks or something more sinister was yet to be determined.

He still stood with the support of the light pole when Petey Moss arrived. Carrying his medical bag, the coroner ducked under the police tape, crossed the gravelly shore, and labored up the rock pile.

"Couldn't have asked for a nicer day," he said, out of breath. Sticking out a hand to Rory, he pumped it, then smirked, "I've seen lovelier bodies."

"She's not having a good day," Rory said.

"I can see that."

Petey made quick work of the examination. "Go ahead. Get her into a bag if you can. She won't be fun." To Rory, he said, "I'll let you know what I find after the autopsy."

"Can you tell me anything now?"

His friend looked him in the eye. "Female. Death confirmed. Then I could speculate if you like." He brushed mud from his pant legs. "It doesn't seem likely that she buried herself under a pile of stone. But odder things have happened. There is ugly discoloration on her wrists and throat—too early to speculate on the cause of those. And there is too much water to hazard a guess on how long she's been down there—yet I don't think long. The means and time of death all need to be determined. Give me till tomorrow? I'll have your answers." Petey glanced down at the base of the light pole. "Is there something going on with your foot?"

"No." Rory straightened and puffed out his chest. "Long day working on the rock pile. You have no idea how tedious it is staying out of the way."

Petey looked at him for a long moment but didn't ask more.

Rory remained by the open cavity, fretting, while Thacker called for the body to be picked up and transported to the county morgue. Petey oversaw the removal, and the crew sifted through the pit in search of evidence. The recovery crew was still working when Rory swapped worry for anxiety.

He'd always loved summer—heat, humidity, long days cooled by the night breeze. He'd been younger then and in top condition. His damn foot put him in an awkward position. He wasn't tip-top, that was for sure. The endless day of inaction taunted him and wouldn't allow him to shake the doubts running through his mind. Was he in shape to conduct an investigation? How long could he hide his condition from the chief? Would Mansfield push him into administrative leave?

He knew one thing. He wasn't giving up his shield—even temporarily.

Chapter Five

The Winterset Police Department took care of law enforcement within the boundaries of the town. The county sheriff's department oversaw the entire county. Their tasks often overlapped, and since Winterset was the county seat, the two law enforcement agencies often shared resources and worked crimes together. Sharing the services of the county coroner was a given.

Petey Moss had started as a pediatrician, found he had a love for forensics and pathology, and chucked the doctor's role for the county morgue, taking on the mantle of medical examiner. Winterset insisted on calling him the coroner, but current licenses and practices said otherwise. During his short period in Winterset, Rory had come to count on Petey's expertise, counsel, and friendship.

A city block away from the police station, Petey's office was in the basement of the courthouse. Monday morning, Rory called on him, using the disability ramp to enter the main hall and then taking the elevator down. The three-story stone building, listed on the National Register of Historic Places, offered cool halls even on the hottest day. The basement was almost frigid. He hobbled down the hallway and knocked lightly on the office door. No one answered. He located Petey in the morgue, with the bodies.

"Ah, Rory. Come in. I'm about ready to put our

girl to rest."

"So, she is as young as a girl?"

"Everything is relative, my friend. Compared to you and me, she is a child. Come back to the office. We'll have coffee, and I'll show you the report."

Rory followed Petey down the hall, and he quickly took the visitor's chair before the coroner had an opportunity to round the desk. Petey picked up the file and seated himself. "Before you ask, I checked the homicide box on the form. I'd sure like to get my hands on her dental records."

"Death couldn't have been natural." Rory patted his pocket, checking for his pen. "Accident or suicide then."

"Death, no."

"No identification?"

"No, not on the body."

"Then there'll be no dental records."

"I know, but her teeth are sound. Braces, evidently, at one time. Not an indigent, certainly hadn't been living on the street. Too well nourished. She hadn't been out there for more than a few days. I'd say no more than two, baking in the July heat by day and swamped with river water at night. We were lucky you stumbled onto the site. A few more days, and she would've moved beyond giving up her secrets. I've run her prints through CODA and the usual data-collection agencies. It won't take too long to match her up. Could be a runaway, but if so, very recent. There is no trauma to the genitalia. I ran a rape kit but expect submersion washed away any potential evidence. I can say she never gave birth."

"Rape unclear. Not a mother." Rory extracted his

pocket notebook and jotted the information down.

"I sent the preliminary autopsy report to your office." Petey raised a brow in question. "I imagine Mansfield's already turned the case over to you?"

Rory winced. Anxious for Petey's report, he'd bypassed the station on his way over. Mansfield hadn't called, but being the department's only detective, Rory expected the case assignment. There was a chance it would be turned over to the sheriff's department or CID, the Nebraska State Bureau of Criminal Identification, and they could always pass it off to the FBI. Mansfield wouldn't like any of those scenarios. It would be Rory's case until he heard differently.

"Drugs?" he asked, pen poised.

"The drug screen came back negative. *Nada.* The discoloration on her wrists and neck is the same width. I suspect similar leather straps, even a belt. Here's what puzzles me…" Petey paused and thumped the paper with his pointer finger. "I found a small needle mark on her right thigh."

"I thought the toxicology screen came back clean."

"Two possibilities," Petey said, balling his fist, pointer finger extended for emphasis. "One, there's something there that isn't on the standard drug panel." He unfolded a second finger. "Or two, he wasn't putting something in; he was pulling something out."

Rory let out a low whistle and slumped in his seat.

"We've got DNA, prints, and X-rays. All we need is a match, and something is bound to pop up." Petey put the report back in the folder. "There's one more thing you should know," he said, rising to his feet.

Rory stood as well.

Petey grinned. "Officer Thacker was here when I

arrived this morning." The smile found its way to his eyes. "He mentioned something about being in charge, first at the scene, lead officer, or some such nonsense. I gave him a copy of the report."

****

Rory took the shortest route back to the station, his foot smarting with each step. The hiking boots helped in terms of support and containing the swelling but didn't numb the pain. Mind over matter—he had bigger things on his mind.

Leather straps. Why did that ring a bell?

The shortest route to his office meant going in through the public entrance off Main Street instead of using the parking lot entrance around the back. Rory passed quickly through the entry vestibule that served as a lobby, ignored the glass partition, and made a beeline for his office in the no man's land between the police and civic offices at the back of the hall.

"Detective Naysmith, I see you sneaking in." Sunny Gomez's voice found its way through the payment window and into the lobby. She had caught him despite his efforts. Crap! He detoured at the last moment, opened the door to the dispatch office, and stepped in.

Pushing his fedora to the back of his head, he glanced at Sergeant Powell behind the duty desk, then turned to the dispatcher. "Good morning, Sunny."

Her usual dark curls stood out from her head in a riot of bold. Today they were an unnatural scarlet. American flags swung from her ears, and she wore an American Legion vest over her blue WPD T-shirt.

Swiveling to face Rory, she leaned back in her chair. "Chief's been looking for you since nine. Don't

48

ya ever answer your phone?"

Double-crap. He'd turned his phone to silent mode when he'd entered the courthouse. "I've been at the courthouse this morning. What's up?"

"And you the detective." As she shook her head in mock dismay, all flags waved; the curls flopped. "Nothing but Mansfield looking for an update on the river body."

He hadn't received the official assignment yet. "Is he in his office?"

"No." Sunny turned her back to him, resuming her position in front of the dispatch desk. Over her shoulder, she said, "Breakfast with the mayor, but I'd start getting my story sorted if I was a detective. You can only count on bear claws to soften the disappointment so much. And all that sugar"—more flag waving—"is bound to make him uppity."

"Thanks for the heads-up. Seen Officer Thacker?"

She mumbled something, but by that time Rory had stepped back into the hall and didn't catch it. He flipped his phone off silent and unlocked his office.

As the door swung open, Thacker looked up. He was seated behind Rory's desk, a highlighter pen in his hand. "Hey, boss," he chirped. "I'm going over the autopsy report."

Rory swiped the fedora from his head and hung it in the usual place, covering the CCTV camera over the door. Then he took the visitor's chair and frowned at the rookie. "I heard you were at the courthouse this morning."

"I'm scheduled for patrol this afternoon. I thought I could use my off hours to review the details from the autopsy. I plan to stay on top of this crime and the department's actions. Doctor Moss thought I should review a copy of the report right away."

"And you thought my desk was the appropriate place to do that?"

Thacker paled.

"Look," Rory said, "I appreciate your help, but…" He cleared his throat. What was the best way to say this? "I believe you've been replaced." The rookie's shoulders sank. "The leading police officer on any case relinquishes responsibility as the lead officer as soon as said investigative case is labeled as homicide and is turned over to a detective." He watched Thacker deflate. "If I'm not mistaken, that happened this morning."

The young officer nodded solemnly and began to collect the papers he'd spread across the desk blotter.

Rory hated this. In the last six months, Thacker's help had proved indispensable. Sure, he hadn't welcomed the rookie when Chief Mansfield had first suggested that Thacker ghost his movements, but he'd come to appreciate the young man's clear, innovative thinking and, admittedly, impulsive actions at times. Thacker's enthusiasm reminded Rory of why he'd joined the force. It spurred him to act when his own cynical attitude was reluctant.

He stood. Thacker followed suit, and they slowly exchanged chairs.

"Ever hear of Will Rogers?" The young man shook his head. "Rogers had an interesting philosophy. 'The worst thing that happens to you may be the best thing for you if you don't let it get the best of you.' "

The rookie offered another slight head shake.

"What time do you go on patrol?" Rory asked.

Hanging his head, Thacker mumbled, "Two o'clock."

"Good, we have time. Show me what you've got."

Thacker grinned.

Chapter Six

Rory and Thacker read through the preliminary autopsy report, each marking the copy in front of him. Rory pulled the wastebasket closer to his desk and propped his foot on it. "What jumps out at you?"

Thacker eyed the raised foot. "Where shall I start?"

Rory closed his eyes to concentrate. "Give me the finer points."

"Homicide, Jane Doe, cause of death pending. Approximate age is twenty-two to twenty-five. Facial features: fine, unblemished. Blonde and blue. Hyoid bone intact."

"Therefore, we can eliminate strangulation as a possible cause of death?"

Rory peeked at Thacker from under his eyelids as the younger man continued. "Damage around the neck indicates multiple or chronic choking, in contrast to a single fatal strangulation attempt. No handprints detectable. Scarring discernible. A pattern emerges that leads to the assumption"—Thacker swallowed—"the assumption that she was restrained at the throat and wrists. Perhaps with a belt or leather collar over an extended period of time before death."

It was Rory's turn to swallow. This sounded way too familiar. He blocked the image forming in his mind and reminded himself to concentrate on Thacker's voice.

"No discernible drugs in her system. No defensive wounds. Abrasions on lower back, neck, and forearms—extensive postmortem damage to her arms, legs, and lower back."

With each sentence, Rory's chest clenched. *He'd heard all this before.*

Ten years earlier, while serving in Omaha, he'd worked a Jane Doe case: a female body found in a rock quarry and cause of death pending. At the time, he'd used the newly established national missing person database, NamUs, and matched the Jane Doe to Emily Weir, a young woman from a middle-class family who'd been abducted from a grocery store parking lot and held captive for six months before the dump into the quarry. Leather straps were used around her wrists and throat. Three weeks later, her body was discovered by a group of juveniles scaling the quarry's walls on a dare—and remained unidentified for seven additional months.

It had taken Rory two more years, but he'd finally identified Tobias Snearl as the murderer. A conviction subsequently put the vile, unrepentant Snearl behind bars, where he was currently serving a minimum of one-hundred-twenty years, courtesy of the state of Nebraska, at the maximum-security prison in Lincoln.

Thacker read on. "Clothes, standard rack issue. One sandal at the scene."

"What's it say about the needle mark on her thigh?"

"I don't... Oh, here you are, at the bottom of page eight; puncture wound present that appears to be a..." Scrunching his nose, the rookie hesitated before he read, "Vastus lateralis...intramuscular injection."

Rory patted his thigh. "Yup, makes sense. That's the most powerful muscle in the thigh, more on the side than the front."

"Says here, approximately one hand-width below the groin and two widths above the knee... Circumference of the wound indicates a twenty-four-gauge needle."

Rory quickly flipped to the appropriate page and read it for himself. He wanted the full work-up. He called the courthouse. The morgue phone rang seven times before Petey picked up. "Naysmith here. I'm going over the preliminary results. I don't like the presence of that puncture wound on her thigh. When can I expect the full report?" He listened and then asked, "No way to speed it up?"

Thacker leaned over the desk. Rory continued. "So, you're sending it to Lincoln? Let me know when they get back to you."

He disconnected and stared at the hat hanging behind and above Thacker's head, lost in thought. Had he missed a needle mark on Jane Doe/Emily Weir ten years ago? And if so, what significance would it have made in Snearl's apprehension or Emily Weir's identification? He shook his head. No, that was crazy. What was he thinking? Tobias Snearl was behind bars.

"Did Petey say it would be a four-to-six-week wait before results come back from Lincoln?" asked Thacker.

"Not a day before."

Forgetting his injured foot, Rory stood. Pain shot from ankle to hip, and his knee buckled. He slammed a palm down on the desktop, drew in a sharp breath, and steadied himself.

Thacker leaped to his feet. "You all right, boss?"

"Have we requested trace evidence? Drugs? Fingerprints? Workups from the lab?" He met the rookie's gaze straight on. "I want to know about the bag and the sandal. I better take a look at the evidence log."

Thacker pushed his copy of the autopsy report together and shoved it into a valise. "I'll get copies."

"Thanks," Rory said. "Do you think you could accompany me to the apartment?" Seeing Thacker's puzzled expression, he added, "I have some old investigation records I'd like to dig out and compare to this crime."

Getting the copies of the evidence log took longer than Rory anticipated. It was Monday morning after a long holiday weekend, and several collection bags were still sitting in the evidence lockers.

He and Thacker were forced to wait while the forms were filled out, the contents were logged, and the chain of evidence was documented. Because it was a new case, control records needed to be written. It didn't help that Sergeant Powell dragged his feet whenever he felt like it, especially if Rory was involved.

Rory hated the whole rigmarole. It wasn't like he wanted the items on the list; he only wanted the list of items. He was impatient and worried about climbing the steep, outdoor stairs to the third-floor apartment, even with Thacker's help.

"It looks like it might take another half-hour or more. I'd like to get started finding that old murder case file in the apartment. What do you say? You wait for the printout. I'll go on ahead, and you bring over two copies of the log as soon as you can."

Thacker eagerly agreed.

Rory patted his blazer pockets, tugged his fedora on, and grimaced. "Later." Then with as much finesse as he could muster, he casually walked out the back door and crossed the parking lot. He thought he might pass out from the pain before he was out of the CCTV camera's range but was determined to make sure that Powell never saw him flinch. Damn competitive sonuvabitch.

The elevator's retractable metal door moaned when Rory pulled it closed. He secured the latch and then started the lift with a screech. Arriving at the third floor, he lifted the heavy woolen tapestry hanging between the shaft and his great room and stepped into the apartment. The repurposed rug had come with him from Omaha, something familiar to mix with his new digs and aid in the transition. It had been a good choice, not only did the wall-mounted tapestry hide the ugly elevator shaft but it helped with climate control. The lower floors were extremely drafty.

Commander waited on his usual perch on top of the sofa. The cat licked his whiskers and leaped down. Rory crossed the living room to the pile of cardboard filing boxes under the window. He grabbed the top box and began to rifle through the contents. Why had he never sorted these into some order?

In his mind, Rory had a master plan that called for a series of locking file cabinets where he'd keep all the stuff he'd accumulated over his career. The files would be arranged in chronological order, with labels affixed. It was a fantasy he indulged in, where he'd use the organized papers, notes, and case files to write a how-to book or memoir or relive his glory days after retirement. He'd never gotten around to carrying out his master plan. Now he wished he had made an effort.

The first box was useless. Standing erect, nor leaning over wasn't helping his foot, so he dragged the next box over to the sofa, took a seat, and went through the contents. Not what he wanted. He pulled more boxes over. When he was finished, six of them stood in a line in front of the sofa.

On the fourth box, he struck pay dirt.

"Investigation 2006–2009 Jane Doe/Emily Weir."

Chapter Seven

Stuffed somewhere among the sea of official paperwork, Rory expected to find his ten-year-old notebooks and the file on Emily Weir. He grabbed a fresh legal pad and started a list with "requests" written across the top. He wanted his thoughts from ten years ago, when he'd worked through the case's frustrating hours along with the final autopsy report to compare with the girl unearthed two days ago at the riverbank. He eyed the box with dismay. Emily's story was in there somewhere.

Was it possible River Girl had suffered at the same monster's hands?

Since he needed to call Lincoln to verify Tobias Snearl's incarceration status, he added that to the Requests list—then went back to searching boxes. Soon, he had a pile of old notebooks on the coffee table. Picking up the first, he settled into the recliner and started to read. Commander, a warm mound of fur with a running motor, settled on his lap.

Rory was used to the moans and creaks of the old building. In the winter, the windows rattled, and the pipes whistled. In summer, the windows stayed open, and the downtown noise filtered up and in. The apartment was too warm after the hot July day, and he needed cross ventilation to cool it and longed for a breeze. He struggled to his feet and checked that all the windows were up. A breeze blew in and rustled the tapestry. Commander growled at its movement. Rory turned on the radio, found a local station that featured classical music for background noise, and kept reading. He was amazed by the number of details from the case he'd forgotten.

He was well into the notebooks when he heard Thacker's knock on the door. Crap! He'd forgotten to unlock the safety bolt.

"Coming!" he shouted, stood too quickly—and wobbled. After steadying himself, he gingerly took a step. His ankle screamed. By hopping on one foot and grabbing the table, then countertops, then walls, he made it to the open-air entrance and let in the young officer.

The rookie wore a triumphant smile. Rory chose to ignore it. "What took you so long? Don't answer that. Did you bring the evidence log?"

Thacker waved the papers.

"Good. Come on in." Rory wasn't sure how, but he managed to get back to the recliner and collapse in it.

"Boss, you need to have that foot looked at."

"Yeah, later. Let's see the log."

"Powell took forever, but everything that's come in is here. What are we looking for?" Thacker cleared his throat and continued in his deep, rumbling voice. "Sorry I won't have much time to help. I'm assigned to work patrol second shift." He hesitated and then added, "You can have my lunch hour from six to seven, and I'll come back at ten tonight."

Rory greedily perused the log. He wasn't sure what he was looking for, but he was certain he'd know it when he saw it. Preoccupied, he said, "Sure. Thanks for bringing this over."

****

By the time Thacker returned at six, Rory had examined the log, evaluated it, and started an action list. The first item was "final autopsy." He had the old Weir files scattered across the coffee table. They compared the River Girl evidence, formulated some hunches, and decided they needed more proof to come to any conclusions. It was well after seven when Thacker left to report back on patrol.

Alone in the apartment, Rory pulled out the Weir autopsy and compared it to the preliminary River Girl report. Daylight faded. He lost track of time. Noise from the streets below settled into an abandoned downtown hum. Commander slept on the pillow at the end of the sofa.

He reread the full report on Emily Weir. There had been no needle marks on her body. He checked the medical examiner's name: Dr. J. B. Barnes. He knew the doctor, and experience told him Barnes wouldn't have missed something as significant as a puncture wound. Or had he? The department had been desperate to move the case forward. There had been pressure from the press. Even the governor had paid attention to their findings. If Rory remembered correctly, Barnes had been working his final year before retirement. There'd been a lot of work for the elderly, distinguished doctor.

Now that Rory thought about it, Barnes's wife had been struggling with the last stages of cancer, and there'd been talk of calling hospice in to see to her comfort. Barnes might have been distracted. No. He wouldn't have missed it.

Rory rubbed his head. He was trying too hard to see similarities between the two cases. Then he remembered there had been an intern assisting Barnes in the final months before his retirement. He couldn't recall the name and needed to find out. He jotted it on the list, closed his eyes, and concentrated on the details of Emily Weir.

As the evening settled in, the street below quieted. A few male voices calling to one another drifted up from the police station parking lot, and an occasional car passed. Rory could hear a baseball game in the park. After the dinner hour, downtown business shut down, and it was unusual to hear any activity on the streets. Winterset citizens were home in front of their TVs or relaxing on front porch swings. The Elks Lodge on Front Street saw plenty of traffic, but it was too far away to disturb a summer evening at the top of Hillard's Department Store.

Rory reached for the next notebook.

Sometime later, he was about to give up for the night when Commander sat up suddenly. The fur on the cat's back stood at attention. He emitted a low, throaty growl.

"What is it, boy?" Commander stared at the tapestry covering the elevator door opening. "Something over there? Do you hear our mouse?" Rory reached over to pet the tabby, reassuring him that all was well. Commander growled at the wall.

"Okay, if you insist. I'll take a look."

After sitting on the sofa for hours, Rory's leg tingled. His ankle was too tender to bear his weight, so he stood before moving farther. He needed to check the lower floors anyway. In his nine months as night watchman, he'd only been called to action twice. The first time was for a broken window that had allowed a family of squirrels to enter. The second time, he found teenagers using the abandoned building for an impromptu beer party. He'd cleaned up the mess both times and hadn't been bothered since. He'd take the heavy-duty flashlight and something to use as a crutch.

Both the broom and the light were in the closet by the door leading to the outdoor stairs. If he could get that far, he could throw the deadbolt on the door before taking the elevator down. With any luck, the noise from the lift would send the intruder scurrying. He'd check the doors and windows below and call it a night.

The broom helped mobility, but it was a hindrance when it came to working the elevator crank. He put the flashlight on the floor and leaned the broom against the wall, balancing on one leg while he wrestled with the lever controlling the descent. The lift made enough noise to wake the dead, and when it slammed to a stop on the second floor, he was jolted off balance. He retracted the gate and pointed the beam into the room.

The floor was empty. In the center, a sweeping staircase led to the first floor. A waist-high wooden wall encircled the opening, with a two-foot decorative railing on top. Two-by-fours were nailed in place over the stairwell, sealing it. Without stepping out of the elevator, Rory could see the room was clear, but he'd need to check behind the staircase wall to verify that the opening was secure.

Each time he moved the broom-crutch forward, the tap echoed in the cavernous room. Step by painful step, he crossed to inspect the barricade. It took both hands on the broom handle to accomplish the crossing. He tucked the flashlight under his arm and slowly made his way, finding everything as it should be.

He took the lift to the first floor. On the way down, he tested his ankle, but the effort made his foot feel like a metal bowling ball in a smelting furnace. He gave up any pretense of using it for support. Standing on one foot, he retracted the gate and swung the flashlight from right to left, surveying the floor. The area wasn't as empty as the one above.

The single room was the size of a high school auditorium, with twenty-foot ceilings, display counters, and manikins stacked in a corner. When Rory had moved in, he'd turned one section of the room into a home gym that included a weight bench and rowing machine. He kept a weighted jump rope and a medicine ball in an empty dressing stall. He and Thacker still tossed hatchets at the targets they'd built and set side by side against the east wall. Boards covered the show windows. Where the planks met, light from the streetlamps peeked through, casting shadows that danced across the marble floor. Three dressing rooms, minus their curtains, stood in complete darkness. Dust floated freely in the stale air. The elaborate staircase to the second level towered in the center. The two-by-fours nailed across the lower steps were missing, and the bottom rungs lay on the floor. The next board up was tacked only on one side.

Rory had no choice but to walk the area. Using the process he'd used on the floor above, he tucked the flashlight under his arm and moved forward. A sudden thought struck him: had he locked the back door earlier when he'd come from the station? He'd been preoccupied with what he'd hoped to find in the old files, and he had no recollection of securing it.

He pointed the light in the direction of the door and watched as it swung open six inches and then slowly creaked closed. Crap! Tomcat? Stray dog? It'd be a miracle if he found it. How could he have been so careless?

Change of plan: lock the door and then secure the area. But he was no longer certain there was an intruder. If it was the four-legged kind, Commander could sniff out the marauding culprit—one mystery solved.

He was almost to the staircase when he heard a noise to his left. Turning to illuminate the dressing area, he looked for what might have caused the sound, but he saw nothing out of place. He listened, pointing the heavy-duty flashlight first at the discarded store counters and then the manikins. They looked ominous but made no noise, revealed no movement. Cat—he was sure. A dog would be less stealthy.

Behind him, he heard a board from the stair barricade crash to the floor. He swung back quickly, turning before the wood bounced and echoed. A black form rose from the steps, spread what appeared to be webbed arms, and leaped.

Rory threw the flashlight at his attacker. It was batted back. The light went out. He didn't have time to gather his wits before being overtaken. They wrestled. Adrenaline kicked in, but he was no match for the attacker. The broom slid out of reach, and his body screamed in torment.

The intruder grunted and then laughed at Rory's feeble attempt to protect himself from the punches thrown at his head.

Rory searched for a face, but a hood hid it. "Who are you?" he demanded and was thrown to the ground. As he landed flat on his back, the wind knocked from his lungs. His ankle roared with pain.

The sinister form loomed above him, raised a heavy-footed boot, and then savagely stomped down on the detective's outstretched ankle.

Rory gasped and rolled into a ball, pulling his limbs in as close as he could for protection. "What do you want?"

Another sadistic stomp in answer. He lost track of the blows.

The mind plays tricks to survive. He'd listened to victims who'd reported out-of-body experiences while they watched, removed from shame or torture. He'd never experienced it first hand, but now he smelled pork roasting, a meal his mother had often prepared when he was young. She'd place the meat on a bed of fennel, and the house would fill with the heady aroma as it simmered for hours. He felt a sense of calm as he floated in the bewildering distraction that wasn't reality.

Then even that was gone.

****

Rory slowly regained consciousness. Through a fog, he heard a door swing open and then slam shut in the night breeze. After the day's heat, the marble floor felt cool beneath him, reminding him he was in the department store. What time was it? Had he passed out? Was he alone? Gawd, his ankle throbbed.

Rory rolled over onto his knees. He might make it to his feet from a crouched position if he grabbed something and pulled himself up. The stairwell looked thousands of feet away. The walls—beyond his limits.

The room was filled with shadows, but there was enough light for Rory to see that the flashlight and makeshift crutch were gone.

He tucked his good foot under him, tried to stand—and felt a hundred daggers stab him from toe to groin. Just don't go to my heart, he begged. His head swam, and his breath was ragged. He had two alternatives: either slither across to the door on his belly, using only his arms, or crawl, dragging the throbbing ankle behind, and hope he didn't pass out from the agony.

He checked his pockets for the cell phone and came up empty. Did the intruder have it, or had he come down from the apartment without a lifeline? His gun and radio were in the safe; that much he knew. What time was it? Thacker got off shift at ten. Mister Eager Beaver would be by to continue what they'd started in the afternoon. Could Rory make it to the door and out to the street in time for Thacker's return? Was it after ten? Damn. He'd given up wearing a watch because his cell phone was always with him. Except now—when he needed it.

Head high, belly down, he reached his right arm out as far ahead as possible. Then, pushing with his forearms, he dragged his aching body toward the alley door. Right. Left. The pain was excruciating. He would have cried, but he didn't want to waste the energy. Using grit and determination, he pulled himself into the alley where Thacker was sure to trip over him, and then he collapsed.

One thing was clear. If it was after ten—he'd probably die.

Chapter Eight

"We'll take him in triage room two."

After the EMTs transferred Rory from wheeled stretcher to bed, a stout nurse in red scrubs pushed him into a brightly lit room. If it wasn't bad enough that he'd arrived at the emergency room in an ambulance, once they slit his pant leg and cut off his boot, his blood pressure went off the charts. The attending nurse tsk-tsked and reassured him that she'd seen worse. But he knew the signs and could feel the blood pumping through his veins. He tried to slow his heartbeat. No good. When had he last taken his pills? Then a red band appeared on one wrist and an IV went into the other arm. Electrode disks were affixed to his chest, their leads connected to a monitor behind his head.

The emergency room physician blew in and took a seat on a rolling stool. "Do you know why you're here, Mr. Naysmith? What's your date of birth?" he asked, talking around the technician drawing blood. "What meds are you taking for blood pressure and when was the last time you took it?" And to the assisting nurse, he asked, "Did we contact his cardiologist?"

The doc stood. "Let's get an MRI on his leg and a 12-Lead EKG, stat." Looking down at Rory, he said, "Do you know where you are, Mister Naysmith?"

"Detective."

"What's your date of birth?" A white band was

added to his wrist. A blood pressure cuff squeezed his left arm again. "Do you have any pain?"

Rory answered all questions. He'd been to this rodeo before. Then a sharp pain shot up his arm, and everything went black.

****

A man's voice startled Rory awake. The lights were too bright. The sounds too loud. He lifted his head, saw the same male nurse, and felt a tightness in his chest. "Winterset Memorial?"

"You're in the emergency room. You'll move to the floor as soon as there is an empty bed."

The floor. Not the ICU? He closed his eyes; he was so tired. A beep sounded to his left and continued in a steady rhythm. "What time is it?"

"A little after three in the morning. You have morphine, antibiotics, and saline drips going."

Rory tried to reposition himself yet couldn't quite manage the task. It felt like a water buffalo slept on his chest, and he peeked through his lashes to rule it out. His lower right leg lay on a foam pillow, his ankle surrounded by ice packs, and his toes, what he could see, resembled overstuffed sausages. He had the urge to wiggle them but was afraid they'd burst. Not good. A buffalo might have been a cheerier sight. But at least, it hadn't been his heart.

"So, it wasn't a heart attack?"

"Not this time. You have a nasty break, and you can expect more tests to determine the extent of damage to your ankle, followed by surgery as soon as the swelling goes down. The ER doctor will talk to you as soon as he determines the course of action."

Rory's mouth felt as dry as the Sahara. "Do I have

any say in the matter?"

"Not this time. I'll check on you in a few minutes." The nurse was gone as quickly as he had appeared.

How did one sleep with the lights, the noise, and the constant clenching of the damn cuff on his arm?

The next thing he was aware of was being jolted awake when the stretcher bounced and he heard the elevator doors whoosh shut. "Where are we?" was all he could manage.

"On the way to X-ray," was the answer. "Try to relax."

Relax, the voice said. So he did.

****

Waking slowly, this time he felt a heaviness in his leg and, more importantly, the absence of pain. He was in a hospital room. He heard muffled noises from outside in the hallway, the whir of trolley wheels passing, voices murmuring in low tones, efficient footfalls. When he went to rub his head, he discovered the oxygen saturation clip on his index finger and the blood pressure cuff.

Looking around, he found Esther seated in the visitor's chair by the window—and felt his heart leap. For one happy moment, he was reassured by her beauty and calm presence. He gave her lovely face a shaky smile. "How long have you been sitting there?" His voice cracked. He licked his lips. Man, what he'd give for one sip of water.

"Jesse called at six and said you were in a room. I came to see for myself."

"What day is it?"

"Tuesday." She closed the book on her lap and tucked it into the tote at her feet. "You came in last night a little worse for wear. They're patching you up."

The morning sun backlit her figure and hid the calming smile he knew she offered. He tried to reciprocate, then let his head fall back on the pillow, and stared at the ceiling. She was, without a doubt, the best of women. "Commander is alone in the apartment. If I'm here for more than a day…" He couldn't finish the thought.

"I'll see that he's fed."

He wanted to shift his brain into a higher gear, one adept at thinking, planning. But didn't feel capable. God, he hated for her to see him in this condition.

"You'll need a key to get in. There's one on my keyring." His eyes darted around the room. Where was his keyring? He swallowed hard. His gun? His badge? His radio?

"I'd appreciate it," she said. "Try to rest. I can worry about the everyday details, and you can concentrate on healing."

"Do you think you could locate Thacker?"

"I understand he brought you in last night. It was late, but I expect he'll turn up soon."

Thacker? The night before was a blur. He remembered the dark shape with webbed arms. He pictured the EMTs and the frantic ride to the ER. And the pain. He didn't remember the rookie playing a part in it. He was glad Esther was here.

"I'll give him a call," she said. "See where he is and when he'll be by."

"I'll wait right here."

She wasn't gone more than two minutes before Thacker showed up with a bag full of papers. He sat in the same visitor's chair and dug into the bag. "I brought the lists you made last night."

"So, this isn't a social call?"

"I can get started on the requests. That will give you a few days to get back on your feet. I have more than enough free time, and Miss Mullins is a whiz on the computer. She'll help."

Rory wanted to rub his head, but everything either hurt or felt disconnected from his body. "I might be laid up for a day or two."

"The investigating officers didn't go into the department store," the rookie said. "I locked the elevator cabinet and closed the door to the alley before they could discover where the attack took place. They think you were mugged in the alley, and I didn't correct their assessment of the situation."

Rory heard the words but wasn't sure what they meant. Wasn't sure he cared.

"The only trace evidence inside the store is your blood and some scuff marks. Officer Lloyd's upset because I was first on the scene again." There was pride in Thacker's voice. "I let them work it this time." He offered Rory a lopsided grin. "I figure you'll want to do the real inspecting when you're back on your feet."

Rory grunted.

"I'll follow up on the murder investigation. You don't need to worry."

Rory concurred, but his head swam. "Maybe we can talk about this tomorrow."

Thacker stood and started for the door. "Sure, boss. Right after your surgery."

Rory's thoughts hadn't traveled as far as the need for surgery. Now, with a moment to himself, anxiety sprouted. He had a job to perform, a dead body to identify, a murder to solve. He had responsibilities.

The chief walked in on his thoughts. Taking the chair Thacker had vacated, Mansfield folded his hands between his legs and leaned forward. "Guess who almost ran me over in the hall?"

Rory didn't want to guess. He knew it was Thacker.

"We got you here in time, buddy." The chief cleared his throat and ran a hand through his abundant gray hair. His deep hooded eyes said he'd seen it all, and his chiseled jaw clenched. "Who did this to you, Naysmith?"

"I don't remember much, Chief."

Mansfield leaned closer. "Well, was it a burglary, theft, something worse? Did someone break into Hillard's building? Why didn't you call it in?" He leaned back. "You were found in the alley behind the department store, unconscious."

Rory grunted.

A tech entered the room with a cart. Mansfield waited while Rory's IV bag was changed and his vital signs taken. When the tech left, the chief picked up where he'd left off. "I don't think you were out for a stroll. Were you doing a bit of detecting? Something the boys should handle? Or anything I ought to know about?"

"No, Chief, nothing like that." As Mansfield's face went in and out of focus, Rory tried to concentrate. Last night…there had been a noise. No—that wasn't right. Commander had sensed something was wrong, and he'd followed up on it.

What was the man after? Bryce Mansfield had been in Rory's class at the police academy. Twenty-five years ago, they'd been the best of friends, but they'd taken different paths—traveled too many miles in opposite directions. These weren't the kinds of questions a friend asked a buddy who'd just woken in a hospital bed. Mansfield had always been more politician than police officer. More concerned about image than crime. More interested in himself than others. Even in his weakened condition, Rory wondered if this marked the end of his career. Mansfield seizing an opportunity to bring in a younger man.

"It's pretty much a blur," Rory said.

"You don't suppose this attack has anything to do with the body by the river?"

"They say the rookie brought me."

"Yeah, that's what they say." Mansfield shifted uneasily and then said, "He goes on patrol at two."

Rory waited.

Mansfield got up, patted him on the arm, and said, "Let me know if there's anything I can do."

Chapter Nine

The surgery went well. By doing an internal fixation procedure, the surgeon reconnected Rory's broken ankle bones with pins, special screws, and a plate. It was aligned, stabilized, and expected to heal. The entire operation was performed while he slept under a general anesthesia. Now that the la-la-land drugs had worn off, Rory had every reason to believe he would make a full recovery. That was the good news.

The bad news included a few more days in the hospital, followed by eight to ten weeks in a cast. His job required mobility. A third-floor home presented a challenge to a one-legged man. He needed to make some changes, the first of which was getting Chief Mansfield to agree to a short leave of absence and then lend him a temporary set of legs. He picked up the bedside phone.

"Thacker, what time do you have open today? Good. Bring your planner."

Rory took a pen and his notebook from the bedside table and unfolded the To-Do list pertaining to Emily Weir. He reviewed his entries, noting which items Thacker could follow up on for him. Unable to afford any downtime, he made a separate list of questions for Petey about the River Girl. The department was too small, and if he were assigned to inactive duty, the

River Girl case would be reassigned to the county, possibly the state. He made a decision and picked up the phone, again.

"This is Detective Rory Naysmith, calling from the Winterset Police Department. May I speak with Mayor Becker, please?"

They were on the phone for nearly thirty minutes, with Rory doing most of the talking. After disconnecting, he buzzed for the nurse and requested the local newspaper. He was scouring the want ads when Thacker arrived.

"You're looking better, boss. The bruises on your face should be gone by this weekend. In the meantime, they give you a rugged, devilish look."

"Look—smook. I have more important matters to discuss. Where do you live?"

Thacker sank onto the visitor chair. He seemed embarrassed by the question. "With my p-p-p-parents," he stuttered.

"Good, good. How do you feel about night watchmen?" Thacker looked puzzled, so Rory asked, "Ever share an apartment?"

"The arrangement at my parents' home works out pretty well. I pay them a little something each month. Mom does the cooking and the laundry…"

Rory shook out the newspaper and then folded it in half lengthwise. "Well, I have a proposition. Mom can still supply meals and clean laundry if you like. I am going to need some help, and I mean help beyond police legwork and the usual investigative assistance you've contributed to this year."

Thacker looked confused but remained quiet.

"This." Rory pointed to his plaster-encased foot.

"This is going to be around for a while. Maybe not the monstrosity I have on right now, but some form of mammoth foot restraint. I'll have limited mobility. It could be months. It's my right foot, so I don't see me driving anywhere because I can't feel the accelerator pedal. And chasing after a man on foot is out of the question. Take the location of my apartment, top floor, a thirty-nine-step climb to reach the front door of my penthouse puts me in the most inconvenient, or should I say challenging, situation. That's where you come in."

"You want to live with my mother?"

Rory laughed. "No, C.E." He never called Thacker by his given name, Clarence. Even his initials sounded odd, now that Rory had said them aloud. "What I propose is that you move into Hillard's. There's plenty of room, and we can fix it up so you have your own space. Or if that doesn't sound tempting—" Rory rattled the newspaper. "—we can see what's available to rent elsewhere."

The young officer glanced at the paper. Rory felt like he could hear the gears moving in Thacker's brain. "Regardless of where either of us lives, Hillard's Department Store will need a night watchman. You'd perform that duty better than ol' peg-leg here." He began to lift his foot, then thought better of it, no sense stirring up the angry nerve endings.

The rookie gave him a half-smile. "The parents count on me to mow the lawn and keep stuff fixed around the house. Plus, I took over most chores when I was in high school. Pops used to do those jobs, but he really isn't capable. I couldn't leave them to fend for themselves."

"If you think it would be a hardship for them, I'll

look elsewhere. I just thought I'd give you the opportunity."

Thacker opened his Day-Timer, flipped a page. "I never thought about living anywhere but home."

"Well…" Rory rubbed his chin. "Food for thought. You don't need to make a decision today. But the Hillard Estate could use a man to check the building once a day. I usually do it, and it's been a couple…" Gee, he hoped things were okay and that the abandoned building hadn't gone to seed in his absence.

"Sure. I can walk the building before I report for patrol. I mean, just before or just after, depending on the day's workload. I can go over when I leave now if you like."

"That would work. I'll let them know."

"Okay."

Thacker looked thoughtful, so Rory plunged on. "I haven't seen the doctor today. My discharge date is still up in the air. They're talking rehab."

"Okay."

"Sure, it's okay. It's just another nuisance."

Thacker closed his planner. "No, I mean, okay, I'll do it. Move over to the department store. Help you out any way I can."

"Good. Then you might as well know I talked to the mayor about transferring you to the detective department. You'll report directly to me."

"WPD has a detective department? What about Chief Mansfield?"

"Mayor Becker will smooth all of that out. Now, where are we on the River Girl?"

Thacker grinned and then tried to hide it.

Rory pretended not to notice.

After Thacker left, Rory pulled out the newspaper. He was getting pretty good at the sudoku. Most days, he could complete one in under five minutes. Those were the good days, when his mind wasn't occupied with assaults and injuries. Today's puzzle was a bear, the kind Esther could knock out in two minutes flat. He'd keep trying.

"Knock-knock." Jesse Wallace poked her head into his hospital room. "Have time for a concerned citizen?"

"Always," he said, stowing the paper.

"I know you're anxious about your cardiac condition." She moved into the room and stood at the foot of his bed. "I've read your tests. Blood pressure under control, cholesterol and sugar levels reasonable. There's nothing to indicate you'll be the one-in-five who suffers a second heart attack after surviving the first. As far as your heart goes, you're in good shape. The ankle is—" she raised one brow "—another matter. But the prognosis is that you'll live."

"Yes, but I'll be shorter." She laughed and gave him an encouraging smile.

"I don't suppose you have any medical insider information?" he asked hopefully.

"I'm just a humble internist. The orthopedic surgeons are gods."

"That's what they tell me."

"I'm just leaving for the day." She stuck her hands in the pockets of her white lab coat. "Are they treating you all right? Can I bring you anything?"

There were things Rory could set in motion. And then there were the other hundred, the ones he had no control over. "I'm concerned with the time they've estimated for my full recovery. Are those textbook numbers, or am I destined to spend a year on crutches and then limp for the rest of my life?"

She hesitated, smoothed the blankets at the foot of the bed, then finally returned her gaze to meet his. "Usually, the professionals add a fudge factor to their recovery estimates. Results that happen faster than expected are always welcome and speak well for the surgeon. Don't be discouraged."

"Easy for you to say. I'm looking at an extended time as a one-legged pirate. No weight-bearing. Casts and crutches, then progressing to a walking boot if and only if I'm lucky. My head is swimming with visions of being permanently disabled. There's got to be a way to protect my foot, allow it to heal, and still let me move freely. You're one of the professionals. Can't you suggest something?"

"Hmmm. I'll see. I'm a doctor, not a miracle worker." She made as if to leave but then stopped. "Do you know who hurt you?"

He hadn't expected her question and was caught off guard. He had a suspicion, but it was too early to say. Even to him, it didn't make any sense. He wondered, was she worried about him, or did she suspect danger would bleed over to threaten her sister? He shook his head.

"I'll check on you tomorrow, then. You don't mind if I tell Esther you're doing well?"

Ah, Esther. She hadn't been by to see him since yesterday morning, when he'd been in a pain and drug induced delirium. Had he said something that discouraged her from coming back?

"Please tell her to come anytime."

They exchanged polite smiles, and she was gone.

Who had hurt him? The sixty-four-thousand-dollar question. Someone who knew enough to cripple his already injured foot. There wasn't anything worth stealing in the old department store, so burglary seemed unlikely. There were easier routes into his apartment, but once there, what would a robber expect to find? It was unlikely that Rory's old papers were the goal. There were no hidden jewels. It would have been easy for the attacker to discover that in his role of night watchman, he walked the abandoned building after dark each night, then lie in wait and strike.

Why target him? Who wanted him out of the way? And if so, out of the way for the murder investigation or something else?

Chapter Ten

Dr. Jesse Wallace usually reserved her mornings for research and paperwork. Today the time allowed her to look for answers to Rory's mobility problem. Finally satisfied, she printed a sales sheet and retrieved it from the printer. Was she getting in the middle of something she had no business stepping into? She wanted to talk to Esther about him, but there never seemed to be a good time. With twenty minutes to kill before her first patient, she picked up the phone. What were her sister's feelings for the detective? She put the phone down. It wasn't a topic to discuss over the phone. She needed to see Esther's eyes and watch her body language.

And that called for a face-to-face meeting.

Instead, Jesse buzzed her receptionist. "Bev, what do I have after the two o'clock today?"

"Let me look." After a pause, Bev came back on the line with the results of her search. "You have back-to-back appointments until five."

"Thanks."

Shoot. She couldn't squeeze Esther in. And after five, she wanted to check on Rory and give him the information she'd found on the orthopedic equipment—unless she changed her mind. But her evening was free. She made the call to Esther.

"Hey, Piglet. What are you doing for dinner? I can pick up a couple of plates of brisket and be at your place around six for sister time."

Esther hesitated before answering, "Oh, wow. Tempting. But I've been neglecting my clients lately, which isn't good for a self-employed bookkeeper. I really should catch up on some of their accounts."

"You can do that anytime. Right now, I could use a big sister."

"What's wrong?"

Jesse bit her lip. Esther wasn't anyone's fool. "Nothing, just feeling blah."

"In that case, come on over, but don't expect a clean house or to be waited on."

"It's a deal. See you around six."

****

Shortly before the appointed hour, Jesse knocked at the kitchen door and then walked in, asking, "Anyone home?"

"I'm in the bedroom. Be right out."

Jesse put the bags on the kitchen table, took two stoneware plates from the cupboard, transferred the dinners from their Styrofoam boxes onto plates, and added napkins and silverware.

Esther came in, her face flushed. "Thanks. I decided I smelled like old cash register receipts and jumped in the shower. Yum, this smells good." She pulled some bread-and-butter pickles out of the fridge and put them on a plate. "Onions?"

"Sure. Got any red wine?"

"Maybe. Check under the sink."

Finally, they were seated. Esther raised her glass. "To quiet evenings at home."

"To sisters." They clinked glasses.

Esther leaned forward. "So, what's wrong?"

"Nothing is wrong." Jesse wasn't sure how to broach the subject. "Mostly, I hate going home to a quiet house. You're used to it, but I don't have an attentive neighbor like Axel. I can feel isolated out there by the golf course. Neil wasn't a decent companion, not the last few years, anyway, but a least he was a body in the house."

She didn't add that he belonged in prison, where he couldn't cause her more heartache, or that their divorce had been long overdue.

Esther wrinkled her nose. "You're better off without him."

"I know."

They ate in silence. Finally, Jesse said, "How do you feel about Rory's accident?"

"Terrible."

"I stopped to check on him after my last patient. He's doing well, but it's probably going to be a while before he's back to walking around. I'm worried they won't let him continue with his job or that they'll put him on restrictive duty."

"That would kill him."

"So, you feel terrible about him getting hurt. How do you feel about your relationship?"

Esther blushed. "Huh? What relationship?"

"Don't try to fool me, Es. You care for him. And from what I see, he feels the same way about you."

"We're not teenagers. Nor are we going steady."

"What I meant was, what would you do for him? How much does he mean to you?"

"Well, I'm willing to make him Sunday dinner."

"No, beyond that."

"I'm not offering to do it for anyone else. His

mother made pot roast with fennel from their garden. His favorite meal. Comfort food, I guess. He remembers the heady aroma. I thought I'd try."

"I'm talking about your feelings."

"I don't understand what you want, Jesse. We're good friends. I think he respects me, and naturally, I hold him in high regard. The two of us are middle-aged and set in our ways. He's married to his job, and I'm married to no one."

Jesse pushed her fries around on the plate, speared a bread-and-butter chunk with her fork, and, using the implement for emphasis, said, "You sound like you've given up." When she pointed it at Esther, the pickle flew off the prongs and landed in the BBQ sauce.

With the tension broken, they burst into giggles.

"Don't threaten me with pickles. I'll come clean."

When their giggling was under control, Esther turned serious. "Here's the way I see our relationship. He's interested in a friendship. I haven't had anything deeper than that in over two decades. I'm okay with it. Once you turn fifty, there's no good reason to change your name. I certainly don't want to think about moving in with him. Then again, I'd like to count on an escort to the policeman's ball."

"Do you admit you like the idea people think you're an item?"

" 'Couple' would do nicely."

Not wholly convinced, Jesse eyed Esther. "Is this the same sister who was disappointed that Detective Naysmith was detained after the Fourth of July picnic? Or the sister who waited impatiently for a phone call the next morning?"

Esther took a bite of brisket and washed it down

with a sip of wine. "I don't think a woman needs a man to be complete."

"I'm not saying that. You can love someone without being subservient. Where you live has nothing to do with your commitment to each other."

"You want me to make some kind of declaration?"

"No, I want you to be honest with yourself."

Esther finished her wine. "If I fill your glass, can we talk about something else?"

Well, at least she'd broached the subject with Esther. There'd be time later to make her confess her true feelings. Esther had to have serious thoughts about the detective.

"Like what?"

Esther continued: "We should figure out how to help Marilyn. Cousin Henry is still in her spare bedroom, and she seems to have fallen under his spell. There's no telling how long he'll hang around."

Jesse agreed with her concerns. "He is nauseatingly charming."

"I can't find any trace of him on the Internet. I Googled Henry Beauregard and got over three hundred hits. Mostly obituaries and find-a-grave sites. But not an actual, living, breathing Henry Beauregard with a driver's license or a speeding ticket anywhere in the United States, let alone Georgia. He doesn't seem to exist."

"Maybe, Rory—"

Esther raised a hand. "Between the two of us, what can we do?"

Jesse frowned. "What about this ancestry service that he's touting?"

"It seems to be legitimate. At least, there are no

claims against them with the Better Business Bureau, and the reviews online are mostly favorable."

Jesse started to clear the table. "We should do this more. I enjoy your company."

"Same here. Do you really think people are interested in sending in DNA to find out where they come from? Who doesn't know? Why risk finding out you're related to the pool man?"

"Not everyone is as lucky as we are. Grandma's old Bible answers most of my questions. I'd be afraid to use the free sites, and the ones that charge a fee make me feel like they're stealing my money. You still have it, don't you, Es?"

"Yes, the Bible is in my bedroom dresser. Let's talk to Abby Sue Bellman. I'll call her tomorrow."

"I thought you were doing that at Marilyn's party. Wasn't she there?"

Esther thought for a moment. "She was. But I didn't get a chance to talk to her. She left almost immediately after arriving."

"That's funny."

"Yeah, isn't it. Cousin Henry was the guest of honor, and he disappeared after making a whirlwind dash around the patio. There was a lot of hand kissing and eyelash batting. Viola Moss and Sophia Becker said they were disappointed and particularly wanted to hear about Smyrola, Georgia, and the Beauregard plantation."

"If there was a plantation," Jesse said.

Esther drew her lips into a stern line. "Yeah, if there was a plantation."

Chapter Eleven

With Axel's help, Thacker managed to motorize the old elevator by attaching a marine battery, a steel arm, rubber straps, and a relay switch. Together they hauled in a gas generator, strung lights around the room, removed the barriers on the steps, and added battery-powered lights in the stairway.

The flimsy cabinet door that fronted the lift was replaced with a more substantial roll-up steel curtain operated from a key fob that could raise and lower the covering remotely. He even installed a red light in the third-floor apartment that flashed when the curtain opened. The way he figured it, when he took up residence, there would be more than one way to get in and out, and he didn't like dark corners.

When remodeling to the 'elevator' was finished, they started in the apartment. Hillard's had converted the third floor to function as an apartment for Rory. At that time, unused offices were walled off from the apartment by plasterboard over plywood. Axel wielded a sledgehammer to make mincemeat of the partition.

After knocking the final piece of gypsum out of the newly created doorway, Axel stood back to survey his handy work. "Not bad. Geez, I better make a run to the dump before we start the next phase."

Thacker headed for the lift. "We need to get this mess down to street level. I'll get the hand trolley."

"No need." Axel opened a window and tossed out a piece of destroyed plasterboard. A loud thud echoed when it landed.

"Wait!" Thacker hustled over and leaned out the window. The plasterboard lay in the alley behind the building, and plaster chunks sprinkled the ground. "Nope, this will work. I'll give you a hand." He pulled his head back in and pushed the window up as far as it would go. "I'll get the ax; we can chop the larger pieces into manageable slabs."

Axel pulled a headlamp from his vest and set it on his head, over the soaked-through sweatband. His stringy hair stuck out in confusing directions. "I'm going in. We need a recon of this area. Yell when you get back." He flipped the lamp on and stepped into the newly opened warren of dark offices.

Thacker retracted the gate and descended to the ground. Axel's beat-up metal toolbox sat where they'd left it in the middle of the floor. He took the hacksaw and a couple of blades and then stepped outside to check the locked storage mounted in the bed of Axel's pickup for a power saw. No luck. His dad had one, and he could run home for it if the hacksaw didn't do the trick. But knowing Axel, they'd improvise. He was headed back up in the lift when he heard a shout.

He stopped the ascent. "Is that you, Ms. Mullins?"

"Where are you? The door is wide open."

"Back corner. I'll be right there." He reversed directions and landed with a thud. Esther was at the cabinet door when he retracted the elevator gate.

"What is this thing?"

"Used to be a hand-crank elevator to the penthouse. Now it's a motorized lift behind a steel curtain." He demonstrated the retractable steel.

Esther whistled in appreciation. "I want to see the place where Rory was hurt."

"Oh, that'd be by the stairs, though everyone thinks it was in the alley. But actually, his first injury happened on the riverbank."

If he hadn't heard the "Huh?" her puzzled expression said it for her.

"It's a long story," he added.

She folded her arms across her chest. "I have plenty of time."

He filled her in on the Fourth of July escapades, explaining how Rory, being a nice guy, had covered a call for the county sheriff's department. Then, how his good deed led him to the riverbank, where he trapped a foot, Rory's call for help, and the discovery of the body.

"You know how single focused Detective Naysmith can be when there's a dead body? He hobbled around all weekend, downplayed his injury, and tried to keep it from anyone's notice. I wasn't fooled for a minute; I knew it was a lot worse than he let on."

As he told the story, they moved back to the room's center, stopping at the staircase. "This is the spot of Monday's attack. He crawled out of the building and closed the door behind him. I found him in the alley."

She looked into the middle distance. "I was right there."

Thacker gazed at her, not understanding.

"Not the alley. I'm thinking about the Fourth of July and being at the fairgrounds that night."

"Detective Naysmith is his own man. He would never call for help."

"He called you."

"That's different; I am his enabler. You know, assistant."

She wasn't buying it. "So, what happened here?"

"I had an arrangement with Detective Naysmith where we'd discuss the details of the River Girl autopsy. But he wouldn't open the door, even though he was expecting me. The truth is, I was late—really late. When he didn't answer, I went around to the alley to throw a rock up at his window. Instead, I found him bloody and hardly conscious, lying in the alley."

Staring at the dried blood on the marble floor, Esther hung her head and let him tell it all.

"I couldn't bring him completely around, but he put a key in my hand before he passed out. I called for the EMTs and then found the lock the key fit. Before the ambulance arrived, I dropped the steel bar and padlocked the department store's door, making sure it was secure. Then I called the station. Once Detective Naysmith was on the way to the hospital, I came in. The evidence tells the story."

"Okay, let's hear *that* story." She sat on the second step, with her long legs stretched out in front of her.

"When I came in, the elevator door was open, the lift was on the first floor, and the gate was pulled back. Therefore, Ror…Detective Naysmith—"

"You can call him Rory."

"Yeah, therefore, Det—Rory had either come down from the apartment and planned to go up again or hadn't had time to go up in the first place." He looked at Esther, trying to gauge how well she was following his story. He figured he was doing okay and continued. "A heavy-duty flashlight and a broom were against the far wall. The marble tiles displayed evidence of an object disturbing the dust and grit running from the stairs to their exact positions at that wall. I surmise the perpetrator kicked them there. This whole area"—he spread his arms, backed up to the bottom step, and held his hands in front of himself at waist level—"was rife with scuff marks where they struggled."

"Rife?"

"You know, full of…" He paused, trying to think of a better description, and then gave up. "I couldn't read the exact sequence of blows, but I could read Rory's footprints coming into the area. None from the perpetrator, evidence that the person behind the attack came from the stairway."

Esther turned and looked over her shoulder. Then she frowned at Thacker.

"Axel and I destroyed the trace by putting up the lights and installing the generator, et cetera. Rory said it would be a distraction to use police department resources to apprehend a cowardly villain. That's also the reason he wanted me to lock up the building, write down what I found, and keep the incident to myself."

"But…you're telling me."

"I think you should know."

"You betcha," she snapped, rising from the step in one crisp motion. She began to inspect the floor tiles, stooping down every so often to rub at the dried blood. "You didn't clean up?"

"There was no reason to do it right away and he, Rory, wants to have some input in the process. He doesn't remember the details of the fight. Perhaps there is DNA evidence."

She rubbed her hands on her thighs and nodded. "I get why Rory had the flashlight. You can't see what's going on in the dark. But the broom? What's that about?"

Thacker thought she seemed angry. Maybe he'd made a mistake by taking her into his confidence. What if Rory intended to keep the details of his injury from her as well as everyone else? His cheeks burned. He'd gone too far to turn back now. "I concluded he was using it for a cane—you know, a walking stick, a makeshift crutch. There are small circular prints the size of the broom handle."

"And do the police"—she made quote marks in the air—"have any leads on the culprit that attacked him in the alley?" Another set of air quotes.

"No." Thacker felt defensive. He knew that withholding the real story would lead to complications. He knew better than to lie, even by omission. "Rory thought it would be distracting if—"

"You don't think there's reason to believe he, she, whoever will come back and harm him further?" Raising her voice, she asked, "Why did he attack Rory?"

He didn't have an answer. Swallowing hard, he decided he'd better not tell her about the old case files Rory was hunting through upstairs.

Esther huffed. She stomped around and then seemed to cool down. Shaking her head, she said, "What was that man thinking?"

Thacker shrugged.

A jubilant whoop sounded from the alley. Axel, in sweatband, headlamp, and a crown of cobwebs, appeared in the open doorway.

"Hey, Thack. Guess what! I just slid down a fire escape. Ya—" He stopped abruptly and looked sheepishly at Esther. Flicking the cobwebs from his unibrow, he added, "Ya gotta try it."

****

They went up in the elevator. Esther was puzzled by Thacker's story, perturbed by Rory's actions, and anxious about what it all might mean. Thacker retracted the gate and held the tapestry out of the way for her to exit into the apartment, and she was followed by a jubilant Axel.

The day before, when she picked up Commander, the apartment, although it looked very much like the domicile of a middle-aged, bachelor detective, had been tidy. Today demolition debris was everywhere. Plaster dust covered the tabletops, drywall had been split and piled on the floor, and there was a gaping hole where a wall had been. She didn't even want to think about the elevator, hidden behind a rug on the wall. Commander, who had been her mother's cat until she disappeared last December, was used to a placid, orderly environment. Most times, she was grateful to Rory for adopting Commander. Today, she was thankful she'd taken her mother's cat home with her for the duration of the detective's hospital stay.

"It's down here," Axel said, flipping on the headlamp and making for the hole in the wall. "The windows are all boarded up. Watch your step."

"Wait a minute," Esther said. "What's going on?"

Thacker looked sheepish. Axel had already fled through the gaping hole.

"It looks like remodeling."

Thacker cleared his throat. "It is remodeling."

"And the purpose for home improvement is…" She was tapping her foot. She made it stop. "Does Detective Naysmith need additional room now that he is…" She couldn't think of a scenario that would call for enlarging his apartment: a live-in nurse, his mother was moving in, the children were returning?

"I'm going to perform the night watchman duties."

"And that would require extra rooms?"

"Rory thought—"

She held up her hand to warn him off. "Just give it to me straight, no he-said-she-said. Just the facts, jack."

Thacker moved a box out of the way and sat on the sofa. She took a seat in the recliner. "Go ahead, officer, spill the beans."

"I'm Rory's enabler."

"So you said."

"His foot is going to put him at a disadvantage." She nodded, so he continued. "For the last year, the chief has let me do the footwork for him. Research, smoothing the way around town, you know, police work that would have taken him longer alone. So, now that he really doesn't have both feet, I'm going to do a bit more. It only makes sense that I am accessible when the need arises."

"The room is for you?" She hadn't seen that one coming and didn't know if she resented Thacker's opportunity or was relieved that he would be able to watch out for the detective.

"The details aren't really worked out yet. Axel and I are trying to get things set up before Rory's discharged. Maybe I'll move in. Maybe I'll just spend extra time here to help out, and the additional space will be like a war room where we can lay out the cases we're working on."

"Like the River Girl and what else?" She put her feet on the coffee table and dislodged a folder, causing it to fall to the floor.

"I'll take my lead from Detective Naysmith."

"Hmmm. What does the chief think about all this?"

Thacker paled.

The phone rang, and neither of them moved to answer. After six rings, the answering machine kicked in. "*Detective Naysmith, this is Cecil Rudd, warden at the maxim-security prison in Lincoln, returning your call. I have the information you were after. Give me a call back when you can.*"

Esther picked the folder up off the floor. Across the front was stamped: "Incarcerated." Under the stamp, Rory had scrawled, "maxim-security prison, Lincoln."

She slapped the folder onto the table. "Well, Mister Enabler, what's the story about Lincoln?"

Chapter Twelve

Pushing a wheelchair, two green-clad therapists came for Rory at eight in the morning. The girls outweighed him by a hundred pounds of cheerfulness and enthusiasm. They parked the chair by his bed. The day before, he'd lost the argument about sitting in the recliner and been forced to sprawl across the imitation leather with his foot elevated. They'd left him there for hours. Two days after surgery, he'd had enough coddling and was ready to get back to his life. The wheelchair didn't play a part in that—he wasn't an invalid.

"Baby steps, Mister Naysmith."

He gave them a gruff bark. "I'm not getting into that thing."

"We're here to take you for therapy. We don't want to damage the delicate work the surgeon performed. Do we?"

He gave them a stern look.

They manhandled him into the chair and secured him with a seatbelt. "Here, put your hands on the wheels. Push down to move forward." He knew how the chair worked. He wasn't convinced he needed it. Definitely didn't want it.

He spent a humiliating hour in the hospital's physical therapy gym. When he propelled himself back to the room, accompanied by the unrelenting therapists,

Thacker was sitting in a folding chair stationed by the door, dressed in full WPD blues. The young officer leaped to attention as they approached.

Rory, wheeling past, snarled, "Inside. I thought you'd spend your off-time working on the renovations. Why aren't you sticking close to Petey Moss, applying pressure to get the final River Girl autopsy completed?"

Thacker hung his head like a scolded puppy, but Rory didn't let up. "Who's collecting the details on River Girl that are coming into the station? What are you doing here?"

Rory threw on the brakes. The room had an antiseptic aroma and a hushed atmosphere. On the second bed, which had been vacant when he'd left for his insanely unnecessary therapy, lay a man with the sheets pulled up to his chin. The man's face was hidden behind bandages. Blankets had been mounded over his body, exposing no details of his anatomy.

Therapist-gal cooed, "Oh, your roommate is here. How are we, Mister Brown?"

The man barely opened one eye and grunted. She sprang to his bedside and smoothed the blankets, tucking them smartly and enclosing him in a flannel cocoon.

Rory expertly pivoted the chair, smoothly maneuvered around Thacker, and called over his shoulder, "Outside. Now!"

Outside meant all the way outside, where there was sunshine but no prying eyes, overeager ears, or inconvenient roommates. Outside was easier said than done. First, there was the hallway, then the elevator, and then getting past the lobby receptionist, who stopped him.

"Whoa, there! Where are you charging off to?" The lobby security guard eyed Rory suspiciously as he stepped between the wheelchair and the door. "Not exactly ready for an unsupervised outing. Patients do not take themselves outdoors."

Prepared to run the man down if necessary, Rory bristled. "I'm not an invalid. I'll go out if I want."

Thacker quickly took command. "Detective Naysmith needs a little fresh air."

"You're with this patient?"

Thacker puffed out his chest and grabbed the handles of Rory's chair. "I'll keep him on the hospital grounds. Shut up in a hospital room isn't the best therapy."

"Detective Naysmith? You're the one what solved those cases last Christmas. My sister works out at the Old Orchard Restaurant, and I heard firsthand how you waylaid that dude with nothing but your wits and an ax." The guard stepped back with an admiring grin. Then he turned to Thacker. "I'll need to sign him out in your custody."

Rory harrumphed. The rookie nodded and said, "Officer Thacker, WPD."

Recognition and a full police uniform did the trick because they were allowed to roll through the door, down the handicapped ramp, and into the parking lot. They headed for the new senior center footpath between the two buildings.

The lawns were tastefully landscaped and sprinkled with benches. They stopped at the first one they came to. Rory remained in the chair; Thacker took a seat on the bench. Rory didn't miss the younger man's despairing gaze. Visible from their position was the area where they'd found the body of Homer Coot last November. "That's all behind us, son. You did a helluva job."

Thacker brightened. "I do my best, sir."

"You do. That's why I'm amazed you would waste time here at the hospital. Are you guarding my door?"

"Private duty, sir."

"Who put you up to that? Don't tell me." He waved his hand dismissively. "If it's the mayor, I'm impressed because I confided in him. If it's my mother, she's blinded by love, and I'll want to know who bothered her with the details. Outside of those two individuals, no one has a reason to be concerned for my safety."

Thacker's cheeks pinked. "It was Ms. Mullins, sir."

Rory glared at him. The young officer cleared his throat. "I had to tell her, sir."

At least he had the decency to be embarrassed. Backed into a corner, Thacker would always blurt out the truth—once a Boy Scout, always a Boy Scout. Rory was still trying to help him learn to think on his feet. "I suppose that means Doctor Wallace and Mrs. Beauregard know as well?"

"Oh, no, sir. Not Mrs. Beauregard."

"What's done is done. I guess we'll have to trust the Mullins sisters. However, having a roommate is a problem. It means we can't work from the hospital. I'll have to move up my timetable. How are you coming with the living arrangements?"

"The apartment is almost converted. One more day, and I'll be able to take up residence." At Rory's nod of approval, he continued. "By the way, Axel found two exits in the closed-off area, a fire escape that hasn't been used for over fifty years and a back stairway leading to the second floor."

"That's two more than we need."

"That's what I thought. In any event, the fire department wants to inspect the fire escape slide."

"A second stairway, you say? It might be nice to have another way down to the lower levels, but I think you better figure out a way to secure it. We don't want anyone coming up the backstairs and catching us flat-footed."

They talked for another few minutes. Rory outlined Thacker's priorities on the River Girl case. The tote/gym/duffel bag found at the scene contained no trace evidence and was the generic kind offered at most hardware and grocery stores. The second sandal had been located and revealed nothing new. When his foot began to ache, he knew it was time for another hit of pain medication, and he let the rookie push him back to the room. Brown wasn't in his bed. With Thacker's assistance, Rory moved to the recliner. They'd make him sit there anyway.

Thacker took his Day-Timer out. "Except for this special duty—"

Rory slapped the arm of the chair. "Consider that assignment canceled. No one's going to bother me here." He realized he was a little too loud and lowered his voice. "I'll talk to Esther."

"Tomorrow starts my weekend off," Thacker said. "Axel and I can finish up at the apartment. He'll help me move a few things over from my parents' home with his pickup."

"While you're in the apartment, watch for a call from the maximum-security prison in Lincoln. It's important. I may want to run down there for a meeting."

Thacker straightened. "A man called yesterday."

Rory opened his mouth to ask how he knew. Then he noticed a new piece of equipment in the far corner and stopped. At the foot of Brown's bed sat a mobile camera on a pole. He had enough experience with this particular model to recognize it anywhere. A sign hung under the camera, "Patient Monitoring in Progress," and a red light flashed behind the lens. If he wasn't mistaken, it was pointed in his direction. What was the deal with the surveillance unit?

"Just let me know if the guy calls again." He scratched his forehead. "He is an old pal from the academy. He's collecting phone numbers for the guys in our class. Reunion roster of some sort."

Thacker looked confused. "Sure."

Rory hoped whoever was watching through the camera was just as puzzled.

"For now, go on and finish getting things set up. I'll be out of here soon."

After Thacker left, Rory tried Esther's cell. It went to voicemail, and he decided not to leave a message. He didn't know if the monitor transmitted sound as well as video. Besides, she'd be by sooner or later. Plenty of time to sort out the personal bodyguard business.

The orderlies brought Brown back to the room around seven. Rory put his notes away and took out the sudoku. He noticed his roommate was able to get into bed without assistance.

Once they were alone in the room, Rory rose to pull shut the curtain separating their shared accommodations. Brown's body was tucked under his coverings. Gauze wrap hid most of his facial features, yet the detective noted a scar that shaped one eyebrow into an unnatural arch. Balancing on one foot, he said, "Rory Naysmith, pinned ankle. I'll be out of here in a day or two."

Brown turned intense black eyes in his direction. They appeared glossy and unfocused.

"I hope the light doesn't bother you."

Brown closed his eyelids.

Wondering why a detective didn't warrant a private room, Rory hobbled back to bed. His discharge couldn't come too soon.

Chapter Thirteen

Old Orchard was as close as it got to fine dining in Winterset. Contemporary in an old farm community setting, the restaurant was light and airy by way of large plate-glass windows overlooking plush gardens, peacocks that wandered the lawns, and a view of a working apple orchard. Esther and Marilyn arrived in mid-conversation and found Jesse waiting in the gazebo by the garden door.

"I tell you, it's the real thing!" Marilyn exclaimed to Esther. Then, to Jesse, she said, "Sorry we're late. Esther wouldn't get a move on." She pecked the younger woman on the cheek and turned back to the conversation. "Cousin Henry assures me that all you do is mail in the simple DNA test, and it gets analyzed and sent back with oodles of information."

Esther gave Jesse a sisterly hug. "I looked Family Lost-N-Found up on the Internet. There is a website. And they charge money. Why would anyone pay to have their DNA analyzed and added to the databanks where millions have access?"

"It's not like you're a criminal, Esther. It's so you can learn about your ancestors."

"I think I already know enough."

"Oh, pshaw." Marilyn turned to Jesse. "Convince your sister."

"Oh, no." Jesse laughed. "You're not getting me in

the middle of this."

"But Cousin Henry—"

Esther shook her head, opened the door, and let them enter the restaurant ahead of her. Every second Tuesday, they dined together in honor of Lydia, their mother, who had also been Marilyn's best friend. The hostess seated them by the window, where they could enjoy the view. They accepted menus and ordered drinks: iced tea for the sisters, white wine for their family friend.

When Marilyn's wine came, she lifted her glass and offered the toast. "To Lydia, devoted mother and beloved friend, rest in peace." They clicked glasses. Esther had had a hard time in the early days of this ritual, choking up when Marilyn reverently whispered the words. But as time passed, she'd found them comforting and enjoyed dedicating the moment to her mother. As usual, they picked up menus, spent whatever time they needed to compose themselves, and selected their entrees.

After a moment, determined to have the last word, Marilyn turned to her and said, "Well, if you aren't interested in doing it for yourself, why don't you do it for Rory?"

Esther almost choked on her tea. "Rory? Why?"

Jesse jumped in. "You haven't heard. Our charming detective is in the hospital."

"Bless his heart. Whatever for?"

Jesse paused, but Esther wasn't about to pick up the tale. When she didn't, Jesse continued. "He was attacked, and his ankle got smashed. He underwent surgery to repair the damage which included placing a pin in the bone. It's too early to tell if his mobility will be impaired. As it is, he'll spend weeks in a cast, and who knows how long in physical therapy."

"Goodness. The dear man. So, it wasn't an accident."

"No," Esther said. "It was deliberate."

"Oh, my stars! First, a dead body is found, and now a mugging. What is happening to Winterset?"

"This was more vicious than a mugging."

Esther paused. How much did she know about the attack on Rory? And how much should Marilyn hear from her? Marilyn was sweet, but she didn't know anything about discretion, and everything shared with her would soon become general knowledge. Gossip moved fast in Winterset. Esther didn't need to toss speculation into the wind.

Thankfully, Jesse changed the subject. "Enough about death and destruction. I want to talk about the hospital silent auction."

"Oh, goodness." Marilyn took a sip of her wine. "Did you volunteer to chair the hospital charity event?"

Nodding, Jesse said, "I'm counting on you and your contacts."

Marilyn blushed. "Yes, I imagine you do need my help. There is the card group, the ladies at St. Matthews, the choir, of course, and..."

Esther stopped listening; Marilyn would go on for another fifteen minutes. Over her tea glass, she gave her sister a grateful smile. She wasn't foolish enough to think Marilyn wouldn't ferret out the details of Rory's mishap within the hour, but Jesse had successfully diverted the inquisition—for now.

"I can get Axel to put up posters around town." Marilyn started ticking off locations on her fingers.

"There's the lodge and the VFW hall…"

Their entrees arrived, and they dug in.

"Where is Cousin Henry today?" Jesse asked when the waitress served their desserts: a small bowl of mixed berries for each sister, a generous slice of rhubarb pie for Marilyn.

"He's with Abby Sue Bellman. They've been seeing a lot of each other since the soiree last weekend."

Esther stopped with a spoonful of berries halfway to her lips. "So, Abby Sue does remember him from her Georgia childhood?"

"I didn't say that."

"What would you say?" Jesse prompted.

"They have quite a few common memories that involve the area around Smyrola. There's a great story about a cotillion at one of the plantations; it was the harvest moon, and—"

"Garrison and his cousin were at this plantation dance?" said Esther.

Marilyn waved a dismissive hand, which set the bangles on her wrist jangling. "I didn't say that."

"Then who did supply this information? Henry or Abby Sue?"

Ignoring Esther's question, the older woman dug into her pie. "Delicious."

Esther eyed her suspiciously. "So, it's fair to say Abby Sue, your late husband, and Henry didn't share a childhood? Are they even cousins?"

The older woman laid her fork down, patted her lips with the napkin, and successfully avoided Esther's glare. "You know, in those days, dear, immediate family included uncles, aunts, cousins, and cousins once, even twice removed. Cousin was a term of endearment. A neighbor might be called cousin when there was no blood relation whatsoever. First and second cousins married all the time. Relationships were intertwined; gentility bound them with a common thread. Garrison and Henry might have attended the same military school and not been blood-related at all, but rather called each other cousin as a symbol of their mutual respect for one another."

Esther narrowed her eyes. "There was no real Cousin Henry?"

"Oh, yes, there was, is," Marilyn corrected. "The people at Family Lost-N-Found say there's genetic proof."

Esther put down her spoon. "What kind of proof?"

She still couldn't figure out what that man was after. Or why Marilyn was so willing to believe him.

Chapter Fourteen

The Elks' barroom was dark and smoky. Behind the mahogany horseshoe-shaped bar, an equally smoky mirror displayed a handful of men watching the afternoon baseball game on TV. The regulars sat on imitation red leather bar stools, cheering for the underdogs, the Chicago Cubs. Ed, Freddy, and Sarge, cousins on their mothers' sides, mowed for the county in the summer and plowed in the winter. They were inseparable and always appreciative of any newcomer who enabled them to retell old stories.

A slim but muscular man, Jerry Ames said he was from Fargo. He had a shaved head and spoke softly, explaining that he was passing through and needed a decent hotel for the night. Omaha was close, but their town looked friendly. He pulled out a membership card with an early-bird sticker and declared twenty years of Elks' membership. The Kaulburg cousins welcomed him with open arms, especially when he offered to buy the next round.

"Passing through, you say?" Freddy leaned back on the barstool. "Where you on your way to?"

"I started up in North Dakota, and I'm working my way down to Joplin. Going to connect up with the old Route 66."

Ed asked, "You in a car or on a bike?"

"Parked my Tahoe outside, and I'm pulling a '62

Corvette on a trailer. I have a friend down in Missouri. The plan is to leave the truck in his garage and drive on in the 'Vette."

Sarge gave Ames a disapproving squint. "Ain't the sports car of choice in these parts. What year was that red beauty you had, Ed?"

"You mean the one we had down to the state fair? You remember those girls from West Point?" Ed tossed back a shot, signaled for a refill, and picked up his beer.

Sarge followed suit, shaking his head. "Talk about wild women."

"You fellows have a recommendation on a place to stay?" Ames asked. "There needs to be room to park a trailer."

The cousins considered the problem for a moment.

"Can't say I've ever stayed at any of the local motels hereabouts," Sarge said. "Max, what would you say is a decent place?"

The bartender stopped rinsing glasses at the sink and came over. "We don't have any four-star hotels in Winterset." He took Ames' measure while wiping his hands on a towel. "If you're not too particular"—he said it like he thought Ames might be—"you could try Beaver's Best Western. It's out by the interstate, and I've heard they have a breakfast buffet."

"Sure," Sarge said. "That'd be the place."

"So, what do you do for excitement in this town?" Ames asked, drawing a square on the cardboard coaster with his beer glass.

Ed stopped with his beer halfway to his lips, shook his head, and then took a swig.

"They roll the sidewalks up every evening at seven," Freddy said. "We got the lodge here and the

VFW down the way. Every once in a while, there's a church festival, and everyone stays out till nine. You shoulda been here last week. We did the Fourth of July up in a pretty big way."

"There's a lot of weddings," said Sarge.

"We had us a police detective get mugged a couple of days ago." Freddy looked at Ames. "You ready for another drink?"

"Not quite. Tell me about the mugging; that must have been something. Don't those guys wear their guns all the time?"

Freddy said, "I don't know much about the mugging, just that it was good for a laugh."

The Cubs loaded the bases and then ended the inning without scoring. The cousins wanted a grand slam, and the conversation turned into a discussion about the league's lousy umpires. Then it progressed to the batting coach.

It took more rounds before the cousins got back to talking about the police department. But they finally came around.

Freddy paid for a round and said, "They hired a new detective last fall. He came out of Omaha, some sort of hotshot with a big reputation. Winterset isn't a hotbed of crime, you know. He was kind of uppity, but once we broke him in, he turned out an all-right guy."

"North Dakota is like that," Ames said. "Most towns don't have a police department with a budget large enough to keep a paid detective."

"We pay Detective Naysmith?" Sarge asked. They all laughed.

"Probably all the corn he can carry home on payday."

"It can't be much; he lives in an abandoned building." More laughter.

Jerry Ames smiled. Now he was getting somewhere. "You fellows interested in taking a spin in the 'Vette?"

****

Esther was balancing books when her phone rang. She glanced at the clock and was surprised to see it was already after nine. "Hello?"

"It's me, Jess."

Should she tell Jesse what she'd learned about the attack on Rory? "Hey, I was going to call you."

"I have a concern," Jesse said. "It has to do with your friend, the detective."

"Our friend. What has Rory done now? There isn't a problem at the hospital. He didn't—"

"It's nothing like that. He's been moved off the floor and into rehab. I stopped to see him after my shift, you know, wondering if he needed anything or I could do something for him. He said the funniest thing."

As Jesse paused to take a deep breath, Esther wondered, ha-ha funny or strange funny. "He can be a card."

"No, Es, this was strange. He wanted me to see about mobility aids, as in bionics or stimulators, or anything that would speed up the healing process. You know I'm just an internist. I don't know what kind of new technology is out there. I don't have the slightest idea if there is something that can help his healing. I don't have the training. He needs to listen to his doctor—"

"Calm down. He's probably frustrated with the physical therapy routine. The man isn't the most patient human being on the planet."

"I think he means to check himself out AMA."

"He wouldn't do that. He isn't a fool. That ankle hasn't even begun to heal."

"They say the surgeon does the best he can, the patient and the doctor take every precaution to keep the break stable, and everyone hopes the mend will be successful," Jesse said. "Moving around too soon can play all kinds of havoc with fragile bones. I don't think he realizes this is what they call the *hope stage*. He has to finish therapy, and if he doesn't, he could end up crippled for life."

Esther hadn't considered the surgery might leave Rory disabled. She thought it over, trying to decide how much of the attack and the events that had led up to it she should share with her sister. Rory was strong enough to get through the pain and healing. He had the experience to flush out the villain and apprehend the demons—he'd already proved his crime-solving prowess. He might be "his own man," but she needed someone to help her navigate her emotions and filter out the nonsense. Jesse, she thought, would be perfect for that.

"Are you still there, Esther?"

"I was just thinking that you're right. Rory is in real danger."

"Of course he's in real danger if he intends to shortcut the healing process."

Esther pictured Jesse standing at the kitchen island with a glass of wine. After she heard a glass clink on the countertop, she was sure that's where her sister was. "Are you drinking wine?"

"Uh-huh. Want to join me?"

"I wish I could. Pour yourself a big glass; I need to tell you a story."

It took thirty minutes to cover Fourth of July night, Rory's attack in the department store, and the cover-up that followed. Jesse had many questions. Esther did her best to answer them all.

When she was through, Jesse said, "It seems that Rory has decided to make Thacker his bodyguard as well as his roommate. I wonder. Do you think the rookie is experienced enough to handle the task?"

"When you say it like that, it makes me worried. You should have seen Axel and Thacker at the apartment today. They acted like kids packing for a trip to a Florida theme park."

"We have to do something to keep him from hurting himself." Jesse's voice sounded urgent.

Esther glanced around. Then her gaze settled on the darkness outside the window. "Agreed. But what?" Her stomach felt hollow, and she fingered the top button of her blouse. "Do you have something in mind?"

"I do."

Chapter Fifteen

Jerry Ames helped himself to a waffle. The breakfast buffet offered overripe fruit, prepackaged pastries, and runny eggs. The sight of greasy bacon made selecting the do-it-yourself waffle station a no-brainer. Beaver's Best Western had seen better times, but his room was comfortable, and the coffee was hot. Taking a seat by the window, he looked out over the parking lot, where his truck and trailer took up eight full spots. The night clerk agreed that leaving it there for one night wouldn't do any harm. Most of the rooms were empty, and people traveling cross-country tended to stay closer to the city. But, he said, Ames shouldn't expect to park it for an extended period.

Yesterday's foray into the doings in and around Winterset had been a success. He was especially pleased to have run into the Kaulburg cousins, who had been a font of information. Through them, he'd learned about the three-day classic car show at the Strategic Air Command & Aerospace Museum in Ashland, thirty miles to the southwest. The perfect cover. Any real car guy would understand that a man setting out to travel the old Route 66 in his classic wouldn't miss a chance to attend the show. Maybe even participate. He had three days before he needed to produce a better excuse for being in Winterset.

After breakfast, he stopped at the check-in counter.

Instead of the night clerk, he found a dumpy, middle-aged woman in a cotton shift. "We'd be delighted to let you have the room for a couple more days, Mr. Ames."

"I have one problem," he said, looking around the empty lobby to see if anyone was listening. "I'm pulling a trailer. The night clerk said parking it in the motel's lot would create difficulty for the other guests. Perhaps I could speak with the proprietors?"

The woman straightened, plastered an artificial smile on her face, and said, "You've come to the right person; I own this motel. How long is your trailer?"

"I'm towing a car. Twenty feet would probably cover it."

"Guests like to park close to their rooms; no one likes the spots away from the doors. You can park it around the back by the dumpster if you don't block the waste management truck's access to it." She eyed him as if sizing up her opportunity. "We own an RV and boat storage lot. For a nominal fee, my husband would be glad to store your trailer while you're here. It's fenced in, and he turns a pair of German Shepherds loose at night. Might be safer for the car and your peace of mind." She winked.

"Let me think about it this morning. I'll pull the rig around back and unhitch it for now. If that'd be okay."

"Sure, hon. I'll tell Ralph you're interested in short-term storage. Stop in after lunch. He's always here then 'cuz he comes home to take his noonday meal."

"Great. What time can I expect to have the room cleaned?" She gave him a suspicious look, so he quickly added, "I have paperwork to do. I don't want to be in the way."

She laughed politely. "You can have it to yourself after lunch. The girls are gone by then."

"Thank you, ma'am. Is it Mrs. Beaver?"

"Beavers were the previous owners, and I never bothered to change the motel's name. Why don't you call me Sheila."

"Well, then, thank you, Sheila."

Jerry Ames pulled the trailer behind the motel and unhitched it. As he checked the bungee cords that held the tarp over the corvette, he decided the storage lot would be a better location. For all he knew, the local police checked the motel lot regularly. There might not be a problem, but he didn't want to arouse suspicion. It was best to stay off the local law enforcement's radar.

At nine o'clock, he parked in front of the police station and went into the lobby. Sheila had said a fishing license could be purchased there or at the hardware store on Main Street. He wanted to check the station's layout. Afterward, he entered the public library, asked for the reference section, and spent the rest of the morning reading through old issues of the local newspaper. He started six months back, looking for articles on the town's detective. December turned up the most references and some pretty bold editorials. Then he read six months' worth of "Police Blotter," noting the level of local crime. By noon, he was satisfied he'd learned all he could and walked over to the county building.

The Winterset courthouse held the offices for the county clerk, assessor, and treasurer. Ames knew any record filed was accessible to the public. Enduring the lines and miles of irritating red tape, he came out two hours later, satisfied.

It was too late to catch Ralph having lunch at the motel. He checked the address he'd taken from his record search, found Steel's Boat & RV, and fired up the Tahoe. At the end of a short drive, he found an eight-foot chain-link fence surrounding a storage lot and a four-by-eight-foot hand-painted signboard that confirmed he was in the right place. He drove through the open gates and parked at the mobile trailer with an office placard hanging over the door.

Stepping into the metal building, he asked, "Is Ralph Steel around?" A window unit air-conditioner clunked a steady rhythm and moved warm air around the cluttered room.

A chubby man in overalls and a ball cap and with a three-day beard stood up from behind a wooden desk. "You found him," he said. "What can I do you for?"

"I'm interested in storing a car and trailer for a couple days."

Ralph's head bobbed. "We can accommodate you."

"I'm staying out at the Best Western, and your wife suggested your storage lot was a secure alternative to parking out there at the motel."

Ralph stretched to look around Ames and check the space in front of the door. "Don't have it with ya?"

"No, but I can bring it over right away."

"We charge by the square foot. Covered storage is more than exposed storage. You got a tarp over the car? The car worth anything?"

Jerry laughed. "I'm afraid it has more sentimental value than monetary value. I'm looking to move it somewhere for a few days where it isn't a public nuisance, and I won't have to worry about it day and night. Any old cubbyhole will do."

"Want I should put the charges on your room? Wait. That won't work. Two different businesses." Ralph grinned sheepishly. "I'm always getting into trouble over my taxes. The wife insists I take credit cards or cash. We'll figure out what you owe when you bring it in. Three days, you think?"

"That should do it." Ames and Ralph shook hands, and then Ames asked, "Say, there isn't any reason to let anyone know the car is here, is there?"

Ralph hesitated, giving Ames a beady-eyed inspection. "Don't know why anyone would notice or ask. It isn't stolen, is it?"

Jerry moved close enough for an old-buddy-around-the-shoulders hug. "That's a good one. I'll bring it over within the hour."

Ralph stood at the trailer door, watching as Ames cranked up the truck. He was still there when Ames cleared the lot.

****

Back in his room after a bland dinner in the motel dining room, Jerry Ames reviewed his progress. There was more reconnaissance to do, but it was too early. Booting up his laptop, he connected to the Internet, opened the search bar, and entered the name for the surveillance site. He typed in the password and waited. The connection was slow. The monitor screen showed dancing static, unfocused, and then, pixel by pixel, the image materialized: Rory Naysmith on his hospital bed at Winterset Memorial and his roommate, Brown, on another.

It made him laugh at how easily he'd slipped into the hospital wearing beige scrubs that matched every other orderly on duty. The nurses were too busy, and the doctors too aloof, to notice one lowly staff member pushing a patient surveillance monitor. Heck, the hardest part had been locating an unassigned camera in the equipment closet. That and waiting until both men were out of their room.

But it had paid off. He could see the detective working a newspaper puzzle on the tray table, with the bedside lamp switched to low. On the other bed, Brown wasn't moving at all. The image refreshed ten times a second, and the low internet speed made the transition slower. A fast-moving object would have jerked worse than a silent movie, but stationary objects, like Naysmith and Brown, didn't pose a visual challenge.

A blonde in a doctor's jacket came and went. He wondered if it was Dr. Jesse Wallace. He set the laptop on the bedside table, where he could keep an eye out for any movement. Then, prepared for a long evening of not much happening, he plumped the pillows and stretched out on the bed to wait for the sun to go down.

Chapter Sixteen

The red light in the monitor blinked on and off all night. Tossing and turning, Rory wondered who was watching. His roommate, Brown, snored, and when he wasn't snoring, he moaned. Between the distractions, details swam around in Rory's head, and he couldn't settle down enough to sleep. Instead, he stewed over the list of things to do, like talk to the surgeon at the first opportunity and, if a walking cast were doable, have it put on. Thacker would see to the apartment, so Rory could put that worry out of his mind. He should look over the old Weir case, return the phone call to the warden, and plan the trip over to Lincoln. The pain? He had endured suffering before. It was only a matter of putting it out of his mind.

At two in the morning, he used a pair of crutches to hobble over to the door and looked into the hallway, half expecting to find the rookie standing guard. The brightly lit hallway was empty. His mind circled to Esther. He should have called her. He'd had every intention of doing so. It wasn't that she didn't matter to him; there hadn't been an opportunity. He would do it first thing in the morning—from the physical therapy gym so Brown couldn't listen in.

He must have dozed off, because he was jolted awake by the image of the webbed creature swooping down on him. A fine sheen of perspiration covered his body. The sheets had twisted around his injured leg and made his ankle ache. The room was overly hot, and he wished he could pull the curtain to block Brown from his sight.

Not sure what time it was, Rory's internal clock told him it was well into the night. He heard voices in the hall but dismissed them as nurses and orderlies checking on the other patients. He was tired of the persistent blood pressure readings and the dispensing of medication one pill at a time throughout the entire day, until it was impossible to remember if you'd had one or needed another.

The parade of nurses, assistants, and doctors was never-ending. It was no wonder patients went home feeling like zombies and pincushions. It had been like that after he'd had his heart attack and subsequent surgery. He had forgotten the feeling of helplessness, hopelessness, of having your fate in someone else's hands, wanting to live but so endlessly tired of the pain. Until now.

The IV bags hung from a pole on the frame of Stryker frame bed behind him. They were essential to his recovery and traveled with him everywhere, although he didn't know their contents. Intentionally keeping them out of view was part of the conspiracy. What was dripping now? Fentanyl? Electrolytes? At least, after the heart surgery, he'd had control of the morphine pump.

This time around, his hospital stay felt like a covertly executed torture. Nurses came in on cushioned soles and traded out the bags—too many times, too many faceless caretakers. He hurt and felt cowardly about it. He needed to regain control of his life. When the nurse came at dawn, he took a pill for the pain.

He awoke in the hospital room, and the sun was fully up.

Mr. Brown's bed was empty, and the mobile camera was gone.

Chapter Seventeen

Esther knocked on the door to the third-floor apartment. She had a key, but now that Thacker was in residence, she didn't want to barge in without an invitation. The Tupperware container of stew under her arm was a housewarming gift, along with the pecan cookies and garden salad in her tote. After the second knock, she began to worry that he wasn't home and pulled out her phone.

He answered on the first ring. "Hey, Ms. Mullins."

"Hi, Thacker. I'm at the door. Are you at home?"

Seconds later, the deadbolt was pulled back, and the door swung open.

"Gosh, my first official visitor."

"I don't know about an official, but I brought you some homemade fare." She put the gift on the kitchen table and looked around. "You'd never guess what a mess this place was two days ago. You've done wonders."

He opened the container and sniffed the contents. "Wow, I love beef stew. Mom makes one, but only in the winter. Did you bring enough for two?"

"Comfort food is good in any season. There's enough for two, but I brought it for you. Show me what you've done."

Thacker proudly walked her through the apartment expansion, pointing out the room he was using for a bedroom and the stairs to the second floor, where they'd added a roll-up curtain like the one installed to secure the elevator cabinet on the first floor. It operated from a locking switch mounted on the wall. "We can open the curtain and use the stairs from up here," he said. "It doesn't open from below."

"That seems smart."

He grinned proudly. "When the curtain goes up, lights come on in the stairwell."

"Where's the fire escape Axel is so enamored of?"

"The fire department condemned it. They plan to remove it, so we just boarded up the access."

"I see, and this door over here?" She indicated a closed door directly across from Thacker's room.

"That is the war room."

From a retractable chain attached to his belt loop, he withdrew a key and unlocked the door. "Axel put an automatic lock on the door. Unless you have the key, you're not going in. It's sort of a safe room, without the safe part." As the door swung open, lights flooded the room. "I was in here when you knocked."

Esther stepped in. The boys had built desks along two walls, using filing cabinets overlaid with full sheets of thick plywood. Computer equipment sprawled over one, and stacks of paper covered the other. Cardboard boxes stood in the center of the room. She presumed the two Office Depot cartons contained matching desk chairs.

"No windows in your safe room?"

"Wouldn't be safe. Did I tell you the door closes automatically?"

Esther turned. Sure enough, the door had closed behind them. A sudden sense of claustrophobia sent a shiver down her spine. She wrapped her arms across her chest. "There isn't enough space in here to breathe, let alone maneuver a wheelchair."

"Rory doesn't expect to need one."

She silently thanked Jesse for the plan to intervene in Rory's healing. If Thacker knew Rory intended to walk out of the hospital, throwing caution into a box, they couldn't move too fast. But were they moving fast enough?

She picked up a notebook from one of the boxes. "What are these? Rory's case notes?"

"Closed cases from his Omaha days. Ancient history, before he joined the WPD."

Esther flipped the notebook open. Reading down the page, she tried to make out his scrawl and realized he employed a form of shorthand, most of which was indecipherable.

"Besides delivering your housewarming gift, I wanted to find out if you're ready to have Commander back. I mean, before Rory returns home. I'm willing to keep him if that works out better for you."

Through the closed door, she heard the shrill ring of the telephone in the living room. "Better add an outlet for a phone extension and a doorbell you can hear from in here."

"They're on the list." Thacker pushed the door open, and she preceded him out. The answering machine picked up the call before they reached the handset. They listened as the caller left a message. *"Naysmith, it's Cecil Rudd again. I'll be available tomorrow. Give me a call."*

"Why is this Cecil Rudd person calling Rory?"

Thacker shrugged. He had an impish expression on

125

his face. Esther suspected he knew perfectly well what Mr. Rudd wanted. Then again, maybe she didn't want to know.

"I don't have any plans for tomorrow," she said. "I can bring Commander by any time and help you set up the computer equipment."

"Axel is putting in extra outlets in the morning, and I'll be on patrol. The afternoon would work best."

"I thought—"

"Chief Mansfield hasn't signed off on the arrangement Rory proposed to the mayor. It's a political stand-off. Rory says the mayor will win, but until it's official and the town council has approved the detective department, I'm still on patrol. I work the early-morning shift."

When she left, it was dark. Too late to swing by the hospital and visit the detective to explain the extra precautions she and her sister had planned. She had confidence Jesse would monitor the situation.

Chapter Eighteen

Not only did the streets of Winterset roll up at seven in the evening, but they also didn't unroll until nine the following day. A half-dozen farmers met at the Golden Leaf Diner for coffee and heated discussions about local politics as soon as it opened at six each morning. Except for their battered farm trucks in front, the streets were deserted when Thacker came down the outdoor stairs in his blues and crossed to the police station.

He had a million things on his mind, but patrol came first. Then, he wanted to see Rory at the hospital. If Axel was rewiring the war room this morning, an extra ringer for the doorbell should go inside there. He wondered if Axel had all the right cables because Esther would be by to help set up the computer equipment after two. Thinking of Esther reminded him that Commander was coming home. Should he make extra space for the cat? Probably not.

Rory would ask about progress on the River Girl, so Thacker should see Petey Moss before the end of his shift. If it was a slow morning, maybe he could slip in a stop at the courthouse and then run by the hospital, even if he was on duty. It wouldn't hurt to buzz by his parents' place just to check in. And he needed to tell Rory about Cecil Rudd's call.

Planning his day, he stepped off the curb and

almost into the path of a Tahoe as it rounded the corner. Geez, as Axel would say, he needed to pay more attention to his surroundings.

No sooner had he picked up the cruiser and left the department's lot than Sunny dispatched him to a possible break-in on the west side of town.

He punched the address into the dashboard computer and discovered it was Marilyn Beauregard's townhouse. He flipped on the flashers, made a U-turn, and headed in her direction.

Marilyn, in a silky, multi-colored robe, green mule slippers, and turban, waited under the carport in the back. A man sporting a red smoking jacket over baggy lounge pants stood beside her.

"About time you got here," Marilyn said, giving Thacker the evil eye.

"Now, Cousin Marilyn, we only just called it in," smoking jacket guy said.

"What's going on, ma'am?" asked Thacker.

"Well, Cousin Henry was telling me about the plantation, and I was having a hard time picturing the map of Georgia in my mind, so he said... What was it you said, Cousin Henry?"

"I have an atlas in the car, and I'll show you, or something to that effect." With a glance at Thacker, he said, "You see, I do a lot of traveling, and one can never depend on a GPS for directions. I always get the route laid out beforehand by the American Automobile Association. I carry their map and a complete United States atlas. I came out here and discovered someone had tried to pry the doors open."

"We've never had any trouble on this side of town." Marilyn swung her arms for emphasis. Her silver bracelets jangled. Thacker wondered if she slept in the durn things.

"Do you keep valuables in your vehicle?" He walked over to the passenger door of the sedan to check for signs of attempted theft.

Taking both hands from his pockets, "Cousin" Henry reached for the door. "Look at what they did to my car."

"Fingerprints," Thacker warned.

"Right." Henry snatched them back. "You might get evidence or something."

There were scratches from a tool used to jimmy the lock. In Thacker's opinion, a professional would have completed the job in seconds and left no marks. "The car alarm didn't go off?"

"Cousin Henry hit the clicker because we thought it was squirrels. They are fearless creatures that run shamelessly throughout this neighborhood."

Thacker took out his notepad. "How much time elapsed between when you turned off the car alarm and when you went to retrieve the maps?"

"Let's see. We were having our first cup of coffee around five thirty. That's when the noise started. Naturally, we stopped the alarm as quickly as we could. This neighborhood is mostly retired, early risers but not particularly fond of predawn noise." Marilyn checked her watch, setting off another round of jingles. "I'd say thirty or forty-five minutes later."

"Maybe less than that," said Cousin Henry. "Remember, I got the brochures out of the trunk. There wasn't any damage on the door then, unless I didn't happen to notice."

"The brochures were retrieved between five thirty

and…" Thacker consulted his watch. "Let's say fifteen minutes later, five forty-five, six?"

"Oh, for heaven's sake, who cares what time he went for the brochures? It's the theft we're reporting."

"Just trying to establish the timeline, ma'am."

"Oh, pshaw."

Cousin Henry said, "We wouldn't have noticed then except the same car kept driving past. We were seated in the kitchen nook, and I was facing the window. There isn't traffic back here because it's only residential parking. It's not an alley and certainly not a through street. I noticed it the first time because of the tinted windows."

Thacker perked up. "You didn't see the driver?"

"No, but I wasn't trying to see who was driving. I just noted the windows and thought to myself, that looks like a government vehicle, FBI or Drug Enforcement."

"And it came back?"

"Sneaky as a polecat." He twirled one tip of his mustache between finger and thumb. "I said as much to Cousin Marilyn, but she assures me there's no crime in this neighborhood."

"And you didn't see it stop?"

Cousin Henry agreed he hadn't.

"You didn't get the model of the vehicle or the license tag number?"

Again, Cousin Henry agreed he had not.

"But you did come out and subsequently discovered the damage?"

"Yes." Henry's eyes gleamed. "But actually, I came out because I wondered which townhouse y'all had under surveillance."

Thacker shook his head. Watching TV sure gave people some crazy ideas. "You can go back inside and finish your coffee if you like." He tucked the notepad into his pocket. "I'll take prints, fill out the report, and bring it in for your signature."

"What?" Marilyn said, raising her voice. "You're not going to investigate?"

"I will log a complaint, ma'am. We will look for similar incidents. Sometimes that leads to charges. Sometimes it only helps to recover the cost of repairs from your insurance carrier."

"Well, that's ridiculous. Cousin Henry didn't drive all the way to Nebraska from Georgia to have his car vandalized. I'll be in to talk to Chief Mansfield."

"There, there, Cousin Marilyn." Henry put an arm around her shoulders and steered her toward the door. "No real harm has been done. Officer Thacker is only doing his duty."

Thacker watched them go. Then, using his phone, he took a few pictures of the door handle and the scratches before climbing in the cruiser to start the paperwork. He wasn't too far into the report when his cell phone rang. He glanced at the display: Rory. Shoot. His heart skipped a beat. He hadn't had time to get any information from the coroner.

Chapter Nineteen

"Of course, I can wait," Rory said into the phone. "But get here as soon as you can. I'm at the bench in the senior center park." Out of view from the hospital and camouflaged by a half-dozen seniors walking around the landscaped track, he disconnected and settled in.

It had been surprisingly easy to commandeer a wheelchair after his physical therapy session. Getting dressed and staying out of the watchful view of the nurses had been a bit harder. The staff was preoccupied with dispensing morning care to those patients already admitted and running down the new arrivals' paperwork.

First, Rory had to get rid of the monitors. Returning from the rehab gym, he was wearing the transistor-radio-sized portable unit. It wasn't reliable, a fact he'd learned while exercising. The routines constantly caused the leads to detach, which set off the alarm. He'd watched as the therapists called the monitoring attendant to say they were with him and would call again once everything was reconnected. Rory made a call and told the attendant that he was in the restroom and had noticed the dang leads were loose again. He'd call in a few minutes when he was back in his bed. Close monitoring diverted.

Next task, a change of clothes. With Brown still

out of the room they shared, there was no witness when he changed out of the backless hospital gown and bathrobe. His trousers were completely unwearable since the right leg had a slit from cuff to waistband. Brown's closet, however, had a pair of baggy sweatpants. Perhaps not generous on his roommate, Rory found plenty of space in them for his cast and the protective boot that fit over it. Elastic in the cuff allowed him to tuck the pant leg back up inside, shortening the length considerably and keeping it out of the way of his step-hop-step manner of getting around.

His shoes had disappeared, so he settled for a yellow gripper sock to cover his left foot. Dirt and dried blood clung to the shirt on the hanger. He opted for a clean hospital gown instead of the conspicuous mess. He grabbed a blanket, then climbed into the wheeled chair. Propelling around the room, he collected items and smoothed the cover over his injured foot and as much of the loot as possible before rolling into the hall.

The breakfast trolley blocked the sight of those at the nursing station. He did a slow turn in the opposite direction and stopped at the elevator. He held his breath as the door opened. Unoccupied. Slowly letting the air out of his lungs, he rolled in, pushed the button for the first floor, and descended.

The doors whooshed open to the expanse of the main lobby. A guard sat at the information desk. Recalling their confrontation the day before, Rory hung back, watching. The funny thing was, no one paid the slightest attention to him. He moved closer to the doorway, glancing often at the guard, hoping it looked like he was waiting for a ride. After five minutes, the guard stood, stretched, and headed to the drinking fountain. Seizing the opportunity, Rory wheeled on through the doors.

He had walked out the front doors of Winterset Memorial countless times, yet on this morning, he was disoriented. He couldn't remember the location of the disability ramp and feared he'd have to stand to find it, which wasn't a possibility with his lap full of stuff, including his fedora. Luckily, a woman using a walker saw his dilemma and pointed out the ramp.

Relieved to be out of the building without mishap, he followed the signs leading to the park between the hospital and the center. He felt like a fugitive—which he was. It didn't make him feel better. Unexplained incidents were piling up: an unexpected attack, room surveillance, prolonged disability. He needed to get a grip if he expected to keep his physical condition from playing a major part in his future. He was itching to get started when Thacker arrived thirty minutes later.

Eyeballing the bulging blanket on Rory's lap, he said, "Good morning, boss."

Rory took out the fedora and put it on. Gritting his teeth, he said, "Get me out of here, now."

There was one problem with Rory's plan. The wheelchair fit fine in the cruiser's trunk, but he didn't fit into the front seat. With all the electronic equipment required in a modern police cruiser, he couldn't get his foot in with all its protective covering. After trying various methods, he agreed to lie on the backseat if Thacker drove quickly through town, used only back streets, and pulled up at the alley door to Hillard's— where they could finally get back to business.

****

Rory was amazed at the work that had been

accomplished in such a short time. Under his praise, the young officer beamed as he took Rory through the first and the second floors, pointing out the improved security features he and Axel had installed. They finally reached the apartment.

"I'm still on patrol," Thacker said, dropping the tapestry back into place after pushing Rory's chair clear of the elevator. "I hate to snatch and grab, but if I don't report, Sunny will send the hounds after me."

"Call in a ten-forty-one. I can find my way around up here alone."

"There are still a few things to do. The war room isn't complete. Axel put extra electrical outlets in this morning, and I'm setting up the computers this afternoon."

"Good. I'll go through my files and organize until you return."

"You'll need a key." Thacker filled him in on the self-locking door and handed him one. "Also, I discovered that it's almost soundproof in there, though we didn't intend it to be. We'll need a way to hear if someone comes to the stair door. And the red light for the elevator is still in the living room."

"Right. We can work all that out." Provided they didn't come to haul Rory back to the hospital. He wondered if his escape had been discovered yet. Feeling smug about outsmarting the staff, he indulged in a lopsided grin.

"Expect me back after two. And Esther Mullins might stop by."

Esther. Crap! Rory swallowed the smile. She needed a heads-up call.

****

As soon as Thacker was gone, Rory struggled into a fresh set of clothes. A shower would have been nice, but he wasn't sure how he would manage. He hopped over to the phone, pulled out his notebook, and dialed the number to the prison. He had to clear two secretaries before warden Cecil Rudd came on the line.

"You understood correctly, Mr. Rudd. I've run across a similar MO." Rory scratched his head. "Tobias Snearl has plenty of years left to serve, but there are just too many similarities. I can't shake the notion he's involved. Him or someone close to him, even a copycat. I'd like to question him face to face if you could arrange it without going through the governor."

After a lengthy conversation, the warden finally agreed to help eliminate some red tape and set up a visitation. "I can't guarantee he'll talk to you."

"You're welcome to sit in on the interview."

Cecil laughed. "Then I can guarantee you'll get no cooperation out of Snearl."

With that one item out of the way, Rory thanked the warden and disconnected. He should pull out his notebooks and have another look, but instead, he punched in the number for the courthouse. On connecting to the morgue, he learned Petey Moss had left for the state lab in Lincoln. He thought that could mean anything, but he didn't know if it was good or bad. Without identifying a foreign substance introduced to River Girl's body, extraction hadn't been eliminated. But damned if either of them could speculate on what that meant or what purpose it served. He left a message for a return call.

The old case files and notebooks weren't in front of the sofa where he'd left them. Deciding Thacker must have moved them into the new office, he used his key to open the war room and entered. The door closed solidly behind him.

Even with a mess of boxes and equipment to unpack and assemble, the room looked great. His notebooks were placed exactly where he thought they'd be. He transferred to a chair, stretched out his throbbing leg, and started to read.

****

Esther arrived at two o'clock, letting herself in through the third-story door. Commander leaped from her arms and started an inspection of the new digs as soon as she was inside. It took four trips to bring up the things she thought the men needed. She piled them all on the kitchen table.

The food items, a plate of fried chicken and a bowl of potato salad, she put away in the fridge, along with fresh milk, a pound of butter, and the dozen eggs she'd picked up at the farmer's market. Her special granola, strawberry jam, and homemade bread went into the pantry.

Axel had taken off early that morning. She'd watched her neighbor's old pickup leave around six. If she was lucky, he'd finished the electrical work. She didn't have a key to the war room and would have to wait for Thacker to begin the computer assembly. No matter what, she wanted to check with Jesse and get an update from the hospital. She called her sister.

Jesse's answer came as no surprise. "Just as we expected, Rory is gone."

"I'm at the apartment. He hasn't shown up here, unless he's hiding in a back room." Esther glanced around and spotted Commander, who had finished his inspection and was curled up just outside the war room door. "Did you get it?"

"Yup. I had to pull a few strings. It's still in a box and so heavy I can't even lift it. I'll get one of the guys to put it in my trunk. Should I bring it to the apartment, or do you want to see it first?"

"I trust you, sis. It's a great idea."

"By the way, his latest X-ray shows perfect alignment. We can still worry, but he's on the way to healing unless something catastrophic happens. I have one more patient to see before I'm headed in your direction."

"If it's that heavy, we'll never get it up the outside stairs. Ask Axel to swing by the hospital and bring it over. Thacker should be here any minute, and together they can use the lift to bring it up."

"Done. Changing the subject, did you get a chance to talk to Abby Sue about Garrison Beauregard?"

"She was at Marilyn's luncheon-cum-soiree, but she disappeared with Cousin Henry soon after she arrived. Why?"

"We had a planning meeting for the hospital's silent auction this morning. She didn't show up. It's so unlike her to miss a meeting."

Hmmm. Abby Sue Bellman, the only Winterset citizen who was more Southern than Marilyn. Jesse was right; Abby Sue wouldn't miss a meeting. It didn't match her conviction that a Southern lady had a duty to society, which, in her case, meant participating in every charity event.

"She must have had a conflict. She's on every citizen's committee in town."

"True. I was counting on using her notes from last

year. I'll just give her a call."

They disconnected. Wondering where the men were, Esther checked her watch. It was only two thirty. Too early to start worrying.

Chapter Twenty

Across town, Jesse looked up when her receptionist poked her head in with news the three o'clock appointment had called to cancel. Good news. Jesse could squeeze in a quick workout at the gym after arranging for help to deliver Rory's package.

She called Axel. It took five rings before he picked up. They exchanged greetings, and she said, "I have a surprise for Detective Naysmith."

"Does Miss Esther know?"

She laughed. "Yes. We're cohorts. The problem is I'm at the hospital, and the box is too heavy for me to manage. I wonder if you have time to deliver it to the downtown apartment?"

He hesitated. "I'm down at the lodge." She could hear a broadcast of a ball game in the background. "I was hoping to take the afternoon off. Geez, I worked all morning."

His answer amused her. She often speculated on Axel's aversion to steady employment. He was young enough, and fit enough, to work for one of the local companies, but instead, he preferred to function as a local handyman. Odd jobs were his specialty, and he was always available for friends. Plus, he was devoted to her sister. Esther might complain that he smothered her, but Jesse was grateful he lived next door.

"Geez, the Cubs are playin' lousy," Axel said. "It's

painful to watch. But, hey, I got all the new wiring in place and ready for Miss Esther to connect the computers. So, sure, anything for the constable. What I got to do?"

She explained where to meet her and where to deliver the box and then headed to the employee parking lot.

She snicked the trunk of her vehicle open. Sizing up the area, she decided that there wouldn't have been room for Rory's box even with everything removed, including the spare tire. She pulled out the red gym bag and closed the lid. Opening the back door, she gave the bag a toss, then paused and wondered if they were doing the right thing for the detective. Rory needed to be in the hospital and receiving daily physical therapy. Should they interfere?

Lost in thought, she started to close the door when a shape moved at the edge of her vision. Whomp! She was hit from behind and lost balance. She grabbed the door frame, dazed, then crumpled to her knees.

She felt the shoulder bag go as it was wrenched from her shoulder and found herself on the ground. Time slowed, sounds muted, and flutters kicked in her stomach. She fingered the back of her head and found blood on her fingertips. The asphalt beneath her felt gooey and smelled of pothole patch and tar. This wasn't right. Not in broad daylight. Not in the hospital employee parking lot.

Jesse sat up slowly and assessed the injuries. She was more alarmed than harmed and decided to remain close to the ground until her breathing was under control.

Axel arrived in a plume of burning oil. He revved

the engine, skidded to a stop behind her car, and jumped out, leaving the engine running. "Dr. Jesse, are you all right?"

She struggled to her feet. "Not really. Someone hit me and took my bag."

He looked around. "Your gym bag is on the back seat."

"No, I mean my purse. He took it. Look around. It's tan leather and about the size of a laptop computer."

Axel circled the car and then bent down to look under the frame. "Got it. Right here by the front tire."

She grabbed it and inspected the contents. "This doesn't make sense. Everything is still in here, wallet, change purse, hospital ID. Everything."

Axel opened the driver's door. "Sit down in here." He took out his phone. "I'll summon the police. Don't move a muscle."

"No. I don't think we need the police."

"All right, I'll notify security."

Jesse put a hand on his arm. "No, Axel. I'll go back inside to let someone dress my wounds. You go on over to Rory's and make the delivery."

"I better see that you get inside."

Now that she was standing, she felt much better. "I know Esther is in the apartment setting up computer equipment, even if no one else is there. We want Rory to have the gift right away."

Axel's beady eyes drilled into hers. "Ain't he in the hospital?"

Chapter Twenty-One

Esther opened the door and found Axel wrestling a heavy box onto the landing. "Doctor Sister says to bring this right away. She's at the hospital getting a bandage on her head."

"Why? What happened?"

"Oh, sorry, Miss Esther. Can I put this down?"

"Of course." Impatient for news about her sister, she stepped out of the way. Axel grunted as he hefted the container into the middle of the room.

"She was bashed on the head, then thrown into the car but didn't think it could be a concussion and you are not to worry." Axel recited it all in one breath, then drew in a lungful of air, placing his fists on his nonexistent hips. "I said call the cops. But she said the constable is out of the hospital and waiting for this surprise package. I woulda called the cops, only she said—"

"Jesse's not hurt?"

He shook his head. She uttered a deep sigh, picked up the container of cookies, and held it out to him.

"Wow, pecan sandies! It happened in the employee parking lot at the hospital. She was putting something in her car, and someone came up from behind, whacked her on the head, and grabbed her purse."

"A purse snatcher? Isn't there security in the lot? I thought—"

"Her purse was still there. She looked inside and said nothing was missing. Did you bring any chocolate chip?"

Esther took out her phone. "I think I better give her a call."

"Miss Jesse said she'd be here as soon as she gets her noggin patched up and not to ruin the surprise."

"Thanks, Axel. I think I'll still give her a call."

The call went straight to voicemail. Typical.

The red light above the tapestry started to flash, and she heard the lift start up. Stepping around the cardboard container, the two neighbors waited for the elevator's arrival. Commander leaped onto the sofa back, joining their vigil and concentrating on the wall.

Anxious that Jesse wasn't truly hurt and grateful that the young officer was there to help, Esther wasn't prepared for the voice that came out of nowhere.

"What's going on out here?"

She jumped.

"Geez!" Axel exclaimed.

Commander ran over and twined around Rory's boot, purring loudly. "I heard the elevator coming up and thought the rookie was home. I didn't expect to find a crowd." Balancing on one foot, he leaned his weight against the hallway door jamb. "What's up? Or should I ask, who's throwing the party?"

Recovering from her shock at his sudden appearance and realizing he'd been closeted in the war room all this time, Esther asked, "How long have you been here?"

He smiled at her appreciatively. "Thanks for bringing the cat back."

"Looks like he missed you. I always suspected he

was a man's man—cat."

They heard the metal gate retract. Thacker stepped out from behind the tapestry.

"Looks like the gang's all here," Rory said. Pushing off and hopping forward, he turned his gaze to the box. "Hey, is that my scooter?"

"I thought it was a surprise," Axel said, narrowing his eyes.

She guessed not—Rory was a detective, after all.

Axel and Thacker made quick work of unboxing the steerable knee scooter. Unfortunately, it required assembly. Thacker took the instructions, sat, and began to read. Axel retrieved his toolbox from the war room, laid out the parts, and began to put it together. She was content to sit side by side with Rory on the sofa.

"Where's your sister? I want to thank her for arranging this."

"Axel says she was hit in the parking lot at the hospital, an attempted purse snatching. The man got away. Let me call her and see if she's on the way." The call went to voicemail. "Well, she's either still inside the hospital, her phone is off, or she's talking on it. Axel, are you sure that goes that way?"

"Yup." Axel attached the wheels and tightened them with a wrench.

Thacker lowered the instruction sheet and asked, "How tall are you, boss? There's a height adjustment for the seat and the handlebars."

Axel answered, "That comes later, Thack." He had the wheels on the scooter frame. After turning it right-side up, he began to string the brake cables. Thacker went back to reading.

Rory fidgeted, obviously enjoying the sight of the

scooter coming together. Two wide front wheels, a sleek bicycle-like frame attached to a single rear wheel. Handlebars on a shaft running up from the bar between the front tires and tall enough to allow him to stand up straight while traveling or using the handbrake.

"Okay, I get it." Thacker folded the instructions. "You begin by…" He looked up to find the scooter mainly assembled.

Axel attached the padded seat. "Done."

The rookie slumped on his chair, letting the instructions drop to his lap.

Rory smiled. "Great job, boys. Let me see if this thing fits me." He winced when he tried to stand from the cushy sofa. The booted cast might hold his ankle steady, but it weighed a ton and did nothing to alleviate his pain. Esther wondered when he'd get used to it or if he would remove it before he did.

Thacker adjusted the height of the seat and the handlebars while Axel went for another cookie. "That looks like fun," he said around a mouthful. "Too bad we boarded up the fire escape." Esther gave him a don't-even-think-about-it look.

Rory chuckled. She hoped he understood how fortunate he was to have such devoted friends. She had no doubt the roommate arrangement would be great for both the detective and his young protege.

"I'm getting worried about Jesse," she said. "Shouldn't she be here by now? Maybe they found some real damage."

"Let's call the hospital," Rory suggested. He picked up the phone. Before he could dial, the back door opened, and Jesse peeked in.

"Anybody at home?" She had a gauze bandage

wrapped around her head. "Don't worry. It looks worse than it is." She set pizza boxes down on the kitchen table. "I thought everyone would be hungry, so I brought sustenance."

They clustered around the table, ate pizza, and listened to her tell how she had come to wear the lovely headgear. "But actually, it's not a deep cut. Head wounds are like that; they bleed a lot. The wound has been cleaned, and of course, I had an MRI just to be safe. It wasn't bad enough to require stitches. I'll keep this on until the morning, then I'm good as new."

"So, you were attacked, not hurt, and nothing was stolen," Rory said. "Thacker, has anything similar been reported?"

"Not that I know of, but I can check tomorrow. Wait a minute. This morning…" He paused as if retracing his earlier movements. "No, that wouldn't be the same. Never mind."

"Go ahead," Rory prompted. "What are you thinking?"

"Marilyn Beauregard reported an incident this morning. An attempted car theft. But when I got there, there hadn't been a theft. The car door had been jimmied open, but nothing was missing. The only damage was a few scratches around the lock. I filled out a report and filed it."

"Marilyn loves that old Cadillac," Jesse said.

"It was the vehicle registered to a Henry Beauregard," Thacker corrected.

Esther exchanged a look with Jesse. Cousin Henry again.

"I think you're right. These events aren't related, at least not on the surface. Jesse's incident was bodily harm; Beauregard's involved personal property." Rory stood. "It's just a coincidence that something happened to two parties that you know personally. Anyone up for taking the scooter down to the first floor and giving it a whirl?"

Axel was already across the floor when Thacker answered, "I'd like to see it in action, but we still haven't set up the computers."

"You boys go on downstairs." Esther began to gather the empty pizza boxes. "Jesse and I will clean up and start on the electronics, if someone will give us a key to the war room."

Once the men had gone down in the elevator, Jesse turned to Esther and said, "If we're talking about the Beauregards, I have another strange coincidence to add to the list of odd things happening to our friends."

"Oh, who else?"

"You know how I told you Abby Sue didn't show up for the silent auction committee meeting?"

Esther raised one brow.

"Well, her absence started to bother me, and I called around." Jesse's grip tightened on the empty pizza box in her hands. Blinking rapidly, she added, "Abby Sue hasn't been seen since Marilyn's party."

Chapter Twenty-Two

Long after everyone departed, Rory sat listening to Thacker's snores escaping from the spare room. Sitting in the living room recliner with his lousy foot up and Commander curled in his lap, he reviewed the day's events and worried over the attack on Jesse. It seemed random and unprovoked. But so did his attack.

In both incidents, the villain must have stalked them and sprung at a time when they were most vulnerable. Jesse was preoccupied after work, in a familiar place, and not paying attention to her surroundings. In his case, once his physical condition was compromised, he was inside an abandoned building where it was unlikely anyone would come to his aide.

His injuries had been worse than Jesse's, and there was a lot of anger there. But at what? An old grudge? Revenge? To keep him off the River Girl case? He suspected his inquiries into Tobias Snearl were the cause. He still thought River Girl was somehow connected to Emily Weir. If not the women themselves, then the modus operandi linked them to a single doer. Someone wanted him out of the way. He sighed.

Jesse didn't have a connection to Tobias Snearl. There wouldn't be a reason to harm her unless it was her link to Rory. She'd helped him by arranging for the knee scooter. They'd been seen together at the hospital. That was a stretch. Maybe it was as simple as wanting to get him out of the way. Then a thought struck him. What if it was a warning? What if this degenerate intended to send a message by showing he could get to anyone close to him? Were his friends in danger? You couldn't get any closer than working side by side. Then there was Petey Moss. Was he back from Lincoln, and what had he found?

Thacker could take care of himself. But Esther... kind, trusting Esther... If he'd had both his legs, he'd drive over to her place right that minute and verify she was safe.

The Beauregard incident was something else. He'd come to understand the crazy woman—to be close to the Mullins sisters, he had to accept Marilyn would always be part of their lives. And a thorn in his side. He harrumphed. She reminded him of his mother, determined, opinionated, and a little off balance. If he was looking for a connection between Jesse's attempted purse snatching and the would-be car theft, what would it be? He couldn't see one. Two different cars, two different women, too many points of separation. The only thing even the slightest bit similar was that both women were close to Esther.

Nah. He was spinning his wheels, connecting dots where there were none to connect.

When he awoke in the chair the following morning, Thacker was in the kitchen, frying bacon. It smelled delicious. Living without bacon was one of the things Rory hated about a heart-healthy diet. If he was lucky, maybe crispy fried eggs were also on the menu and Thacker had made enough for two. "Sure smells good."

"You're awake. I didn't want to disturb you."

"Live-in-chef isn't an imposition."

Thacker smiled, moved the meat from the pan onto a paper towel, and cracked an egg. "One or two?"

"Two." Rory made an effort to stand, failed, tried again. He reached for the knee-scooter, pulled it within range, and then, using it for leverage, finally managed to get up. After making his way to the kitchen counter, he poured a cup of coffee. Filling the cup didn't present a problem. Getting the full cup to the table was. Before he could ask, Thacker picked it up and put it on the placemat, where he'd already dispensed Rory's morning meds. Rory eyed the setup.

"Sorry, boss. I thought you'd find a few tasks difficult. It takes two hands to maneuver the scooter. I took the liberty of setting a place for you. Your pills are there. I hope I did right. If I'm out of line, just let me know." He added the eggs to a plate and delivered them to the table.

"No. This is fine." Rory discovered he was on the wrong side of the kitchen chair, so he backed up and moved around to the other side. Still, he had to hop-step on his tender foot, grasping the edge of the table for balance. Even the most straightforward actions were brutal. It was like learning to walk again.

"Mom is researching our heritage through that company Marilyn Beauregard's cousin used, Family Lost-N-Found. I thought she knew our family background, but she's keen to see if we're linked to a famous personage. Even the neighbors have signed up. The Kaulburg cousins are convinced they're descendants of the kaiser. There's a sort of competition going: who will make the first astonishing discovery? Mom's hoping it's us. Dad thinks it'd be something if the Thackers of Winterset were related to the Earl of

Sandwich, or someone equally famous."

Rory was amazed at the number of citizens who had taken an interest in their ancestors. It was harmless, but a waste of money, in his opinion. "The Thackers are jumping on the bandwagon with the others, then?"

"I guess you'd say that. But only the introductory package has arrived. Mom hasn't sent in the DNA swab."

"How's it work? Do you send DNA for your mother as well as your dad?"

The rookie hesitated and then said, "It could be done that way."

"Don't tell me. They are having your DNA researched?"

Thacker made a strange sound in his throat and turned his back to the detective. After filling Commander's bowl, he said, "Once we eat, I'm going down to the station. There might be something new on the River Girl. While I'm gone, you can practice getting around." Standing straight and with his shoulders back, he added, "I think Chief Mansfield wants to see us."

"I plan to run Petey Moss down first." Rory speared a bite of egg. "He went to Lincoln yesterday, and I haven't heard the results. We're on for the trip to the prison on Monday. Mansfield better have our reassignments set before we go."

Rory ate his breakfast. It was perfect—bacon crisp, eggs crisper. He wondered if Thacker knew how to bake biscuits.

Chapter Twenty-Three

The complimentary breakfast area at Beaver's Best Western was busy. The night before, Jerry Ames had watched as a bus full of teenagers offloaded. Each had a duffel and a baseball glove. Traveling through for a tournament in Denver is what he'd surmised from the snatches of conversation overheard in the lobby. Moving on this morning, they were six deep at the waffle station. The steam table had been scraped clean, and a woman in a hairnet, with a similar build and facial features to Sheila, was madly filling the bread, muffin, and pastry bins.

Ames could count on hot coffee and not much more. It didn't matter. He planned to go by the Golden Leaf and see what he could pick up from the locals. Plus, the diner was within sight of the police station. He hoped to catch Naysmith when he reported for duty.

He added three packets of sugar to his cup and opened the newspaper.

Sheila materialized at his elbow with a fresh pot of coffee. "Can I fill that up for you?"

"Thanks. Full house last night?"

"You better believe it. Between the ballplayers and Miller's relatives, we didn't have an empty room. Good thing you took your trailer to the boat lot. They parked the school bus in the back."

"The boat storage is working out fine."

"Are you taking the 'Vette down to Ashland tomorrow?"

Jerry looked at her sharply. Nonchalantly, she looked back. "I heard you were putting it in the car show this weekend."

It was a small town. What did he expect? "It's an opportunity."

"Don't suppose you'll be giving up your room? I only ask because Beau Miller wants to know if we got space. Relatives from Minnesota decided to drive down to attend the wedding. Otherwise, he's stuck with them at his place, and they're already wall to wall."

"Ashland isn't all that far. I thought I'd commute."

He didn't count on the Steels being interested in his movements. Now he'd need to move the trailer. He could find something on this side of Omaha and not lose too much of the day.

"In that case, I'll tell Miller no," Sheila said. "Maybe Mr. Brown's plans have changed."

Jerry Ames shifted his eyes to the doorway, where a middle-aged, middle-sized, nondescript man had appeared.

As Sheila moved to the next table, she called over her shoulder, "Let me know if you're planning to stay past Monday."

****

Ralph Steel hadn't slept well, either. He wanted to talk to Sheila about Jerry Ames and the big man's car. He'd tried to tell her, but he'd been afraid she'd find something wrong with how he'd gone about making the discovery. He always did something, and she'd find a reason to make it his fault, and until he figured out what was going on, he'd keep mum. He was more convinced than ever that something wasn't right.

Okay, it wasn't a stolen car. But when he'd jimmied the window and popped the trunk, he hadn't been prepared for what he'd found: two trombone-sized cases, one containing a long gun and the other an assortment of weapons. He'd seen those shows on TV, where the hitman assembled a rifle out of parts in a briefcase, added a silencer and a sight, took a position on the third floor of a building, and then took a sniper shot at his intended victim. Hollywood stunts. He'd never believed they were true. Wait! Winterset didn't have any three-story buildings…well, except for the courthouse.

He pulled on his overalls, took the loose change and nail clippers from the top of the dresser, and shoved them into his pocket. There was the grain elevator that was as high as a three-story building. Only, it was at the end of Front Street, and there wasn't likely to be anyone snipe-able in the vicinity. He was pulling on his steel-toed boots when Sheila came in.

"Ralph, you gotta fix the commode in room six before you go off and hide at the storage lot all day. I can't run this place and be a plumber, too."

"Yes, dear."

"And don't you go slipping off with those Kaulburg cousins. They can do what they want, but you've got responsibilities."

"Yes, dear." He had planned to squeeze in a bit of fishing after the cousins showed up. So much for that idea.

"I asked Jerry Ames if he planned to check out. It doesn't sound like he's leaving before Monday. Miller will be disappointed. Oh, and you better check on room twelve. Mr. Brown just got out of the hospital, and I don't want him dying in one of our rooms. He should be home, where family can look after him. We're not running a rest home."

"Yes, dear." Maybe there was a clue in Ames' room, something that would tell him what the man was doing with artillery in his trunk. Ralph knew he could use the master key, but he didn't want to run into Ames. "Was Ames in the dining room?"

"Certainly was. Reading the paper and drinking coffee. I think he's headed out. What do you suppose he does all day?"

"He checks in at the boat storage. Other than that, I don't know."

"It must be nice to live a life of leisure."

Ralph figured that by the time he had plumbed Room 6, Ames would be gone. If Ames' car wasn't in the parking lot, he'd slip in and check the plumbing in his room as well. After all, he was the proprietor and had every right to inspect the property. And anything in or on it.

Jerry Ames' Tahoe wasn't in the lot when Ralph slipped the key into the lock and entered his unit. The room was as neat as a pin. Probably Sheila's doing. The bed was made up, and fresh towels hung in the bath. The closet contained slacks, shoes, and polo shirts. A search of the pockets came up empty. The leather roller bag stowed in the corner contained only its silken lining. The vanity and medicine cabinet held those items Ralph expected to find: toothpaste, toothbrush, and shaving supplies. He didn't expect to find anything in the bed or under the sheets—too easy for housekeeping to discover. He checked between the mattress and the boxed springs just in case, leaving under the bed for last.

Leaning down, he lifted the spread and opened up a whole new territory. A laptop computer and two heavy, old-fashioned sample cases were hidden there. He pulled them out, which proved no easy feat. The significant cases were wedged in tightly. He worked up a sweat, invented a few new words, and finally managed to get them out from under the bed and into the room.

The cases had a pair of built-in locks and an extra strap with an official-looking padlock. Given the right tool, he could get the padlocks off. The built-in locks were recessed, and a bolt cutter wasn't going to do the trick. He'd need the keys or a set of lockpicks. He only knew one person who had a pair.

He whipped out his phone. When the man answered, Ralph felt giddy. "Hey, Axel. Doing anything special?"

Chapter Twenty-Four

Esther parked in the hardware store's bicycle rack. The owner, Tom Hutchinson, had learned long ago that if he didn't provide parking for the two-wheelers, their bikes littered his front walk. Outdoor displays, especially in summer, brought in business. Keeping the space orderly helped to promote his family-owned business. The bell over the door jingled when she entered.

"Morning, Esther," Tom called from behind the gun display. "Your order came in this morning. I'll be right with you."

She looked around, not sure what she'd find. Hutchinson's Hardware had a diverse assortment of items that made browsing an adventure. He even had a display of handcrafted items from local artisans. Computer parts, however, were not among his eclectic offerings, but Tom was always willing to order an article he didn't keep in stock. He tried to accommodate the community's needs and ward off the big box store competition. Heaven knew Winterset didn't need another business to entice customers away from the local businesses.

"Take your time," she called. "I'll just look around."

An impulse rack had been added by the cash register since her last visit. Beemans, Clove, and Black

Jack gum were among the treats displayed. The licorice and clove flavors, popular when she was a girl, didn't tempt her. Wandering into the gardening section, she spotted a bench with end-of-season, marked-down plants. As she reached for a pot of bedraggled petunias, she caught movement in her peripheral vision. It turned out to be a man rifling through a display of seed packets.

"It's pretty late in the season for those," she said, waving a hand at the droopy flowers. "Just look at these."

He turned the packet of peas over and read, "Sow in full sun in early spring or late summer. Will tolerate some frost and very sensitive to heat. I suppose you're right. No danger of freezing, but pretty late in the season. If it wasn't July, what would you recommend?"

In tan dress slacks and beige golf shirt, and with sunglasses resting on top of his buzzed-cut head, the man didn't look like a gardener. He had the air of a casual businessman, retired military, or an out-of-work golf pro. She didn't recognize him. Not that she knew everyone, but having lived in the town all her life, she knew most people. "You're asking the wrong person. Whatever I pick will surely die. Even if it managed to break through the soil, it wouldn't stand a chance. The horticultural gene bypassed me. No one who knows me would accuse me of being a gardener."

"I have the same problem." Swapping the pea seeds for summer squash, he read the back. "What about these?"

"Radishes and lettuce come up quickly. But I'm afraid it's already too hot to grow anything that won't taste bitter." Curious, she asked, "Are you thinking of putting in a fall garden?"

He laughed. "No, just speculating."

She noticed one brow grew in a pleasing arch, giving his expression an eager look, as if her answer would be appreciated.

"Are you new to town? I don't—"

Tom came around the corner, cutting off her question. "Truck dropped this off this morning, and I hope it's the right one." He dropped the box on the indoor plant table and stepped over to the drooping petunias. "Good, I see you've found the walking wounded."

"I was just asking Mr..." Realizing she hadn't caught the man's name, Esther turned to ask, but he was no longer standing at the seed stand. "Strange," she mumbled.

"What's that?"

"I was talking to a gentleman about gardening, and now he seems to have disappeared."

Tom narrowed one eye and, using his nose for a sight, studied her. "I didn't see anyone."

"Well, he was right here, same as you."

He glanced toward the nearest gondola. "Maybe he stepped into one of the aisles."

"Don't bother, Tom. I only wanted to introduce you. He had some gardening questions. You know me and my talents with soil."

Tom didn't head down the aisle, but she could see he didn't want to let a potential customer get away. "What did he look like?" His voice sounded eager.

"All kinds of beige. Pretty average. Nicely dressed. Clean."

"That's the kind of description I'd expect from a

bookkeeper. Average. Clean. Polite. You're leaving out respectful and trustworthy. You sound like Pastor Mark."

"Sorry. I didn't really look at him. You know how that is. He seemed pleasant and had some questions."

Tom shoved the box into Esther's hands. "I missed him, so let's see if this is the right connector. Did you bring the printer?"

No. Why would she bring the printer? She'd supplied the manufacturer's part number. The bell tinkled, announcing activity at the front door. They exchanged a look. Did somebody new enter the store?

"Sorry, I need to go up front; I'm the only one here this morning."

"Of course. I'll wait."

After Tom disappeared to the front of the store, Esther resumed perusing the marked-down plants. Finally deciding against taking one home, she wandered to the checkout counter with the printer cable.

Tom was by the handcrafted goods, talking to a woman holding a brightly colored bag with yarn and knitting needles poking out from the opening. Esther stepped up in time to hear him say, "I'm still waiting for the results to come in. I sent off my DNA last week and was hoping to have the information by now."

"I expect it takes time," the woman said.

"Good news for you, Natalie. Two of your quilts sold over the weekend."

She beamed and then noticed Esther. "Good morning. It's my lucky day. It appears I finally sold some of my handiwork. I was ready to give up since I hadn't tickled anyone's fancy. Clancy wants me to set up an online store. That's so not me. I think Tom's hardware store here is the perfect outlet. Don't you think?"

Clancy? Then it clicked. It always amused her to hear Thacker called by anything other than his last name. Then again, his mother wouldn't be inclined to call him by it. She didn't know what Natalie's arrangement was with Tom, other than it was none of her business.

She smiled with what she hoped was encouragement. "I can see why, if the ones sold were anything like these—they are beautiful." She fingered the edge of a baby quilt, admiring its design.

"You can only make so many infant blankets before they start piling up. I have so many that I've taken up knitting."

"My mother and grandmother were both knitters. I never learned how." Another skill that had bypassed Esther's generation. "Wouldn't know what to do with them if I did knit."

Natalie made a sour face. "I was hoping to have a grandchild before now. But Clancy doesn't even have a girlfriend. I'm afraid I got hopeful and started too early. There are no little ones, and I don't expect we'll see any." She had a dreamy look on her face when she added, "Any time soon, that is." Her lips parted, and her gaze darted to Esther expectantly, asking if she knew anything that Natalie didn't.

Ha! Like the rookie would confide in her. "Your son is a nice young man, Natalie. You and Bill should be proud."

"Oh, we are." Natalie smoothed the quilt and gave it a little pat. "I know Detective Naysmith is pleased with his work." Her eyes glazed over.

Tom cleared his throat. "Why don't I get your money, Natalie." He hurried into his office as if he couldn't get away fast enough.

"I hope you aren't worried that Thac…er, Clarence is sharing an apartment with Detective Naysmith."

"Oh, no. We knew the day would come when we'd lose him. And Mr. Naysmith is such a nice man and so helpful to Clancy . It's just that"—she swallowed hard —"we've always been close. He's such a blessing. It's, well, it's an adjustment for us."

Natalie was Jesse's age, three years younger than herself, and they had never run in the same social groups. Esther didn't have firsthand experience in raising children, but she had always heard that when a child left home, it could cause grief. Thacker had moved out of the family nest, and they were feeling lonely and at loose ends. It was a significant change for Bill and Natalie.

Esther could, however, put a positive spin on the situation. "Maybe he has left home, but he hasn't left town. That should be a comfort."

"Yes." Natalie ran a hand over her handiwork. "We have dinner together every Wednesday. And there isn't anything he wouldn't do for his dad. The problem is…" She hesitated and then said, "We have the strangest and most unsettling conversations. Clancy gets so involved and excited, always has, you see, and he can't help but share his enthusiasm with us."

"That sounds delightful."

"It is. But we find it hard to listen to talk of blood splatter, and crime scenes, and debilitating injury. Oh, listen to me." Not meeting Esther's eye, she wiped a hand along her cheekbone as if smoothing away her embarrassment. "I'm going on like Clancy doesn't enjoy every moment of what he's doing. We want him to be happy…"

Esther put a hand on Natalie's arm. "I understand. Truly, I do." She had the same dilemma in her relationship with Rory. Sure, she wanted to know everything that went on, but not the sordid details. It took a special person to enforce the law. Most days, she was proud Rory felt the calling. Other days, she feared for his safety and prayed and remained silent. At the same time, he investigated horrors beyond her understanding—nothing simple about being a detective, or a police officer, for that matter.

Natalie shrugged off the thought. "We're thankful Detective Naysmith will be with Clancy when he interviews that horrible Snearl person."

Tobias Snearl was an unpleasant threat to Esther's peace of mind. From the minute she'd heard Rory planned to visit him in prison, she'd started to fret. He was a vicious and evil man, convicted of murder. Maybe he was locked up, but she knew all too well that crimes outside the prison walls could be contracted, even controlled, from within those walls.

"They're going?" she croaked. "I didn't know they'd made plans."

"Monday." Natalie's eyes widened, and her lips drooped, as if she realized she'd said something out of line. Esther's expression involuntarily followed suit.

Returning with an envelope, Tom handed it to Natalie. Looking from her to Esther and back, he asked, "What did I miss now? You two look like you've seen a ghost."

Esther smiled and said, "We were saying things

never stay the same."

Tom picked up a pack of Black Jack gum. "Here's a blast from the past."

"Ugh, licorice gum? I don't think so." Esther recoiled from the offering. "I'll just take my cable."

Chapter Twenty-Five

Rory practiced using the scooter in the apartment. It didn't take long to decide the mobility aid was much more effective in a large area. His plan for the day included an inspection of Hillard's first floor.

The trip down in the lift went without difficulty, but once on the ground floor, he found himself facing into the elevator cage rather than ready to exit. To resolve the problem, he needed to back out of the elevator, pick up the scooter, and turn it around to face the right direction. Performing the maneuver ticked up his impatience level. Maybe he didn't need the scooter. He had on the walking cast with the protective boot over it. One step without the scooter reminded him that his logic was faulty. The orthopedic specialist had insisted the pain would gradually decline as his ankle healed and he regained strength. He could tolerate the pain. It was the inconvenience that grated on him.

He wheeled over to the staircase, parked the little bugger, and walk-limped as he inspected the area of his assault. True to his word, Thacker had left the trace alone. The spot showed where he'd wrestled with his assailant, including disturbed dust and blood spatter. Rory wanted to collect a blood sample, but that would require getting down to the tile level to gather it. One-legged squat? Not in his lifetime. He'd need Thacker to collect the trace—supervising, he could handle.

After making a full circle of the area and not discovering anything new, he sat on the scooter's knee rest to check his phone. One missed call from Viola Moss. Strange. He returned it.

After a hurried greeting, she said, "I haven't heard from Petey. Is he with you?"

"No. I just got out of the hospital and haven't had a chance to catch up with everyone."

"I know it's not your problem, but I'm worried. Petey went to Lincoln yesterday to check in with the state forensic lab. He called me about dinnertime and said things had gone well and he had something for you. He planned to drive home but wanted to eat a meal before he headed out. Take the boys out for a thank-you meal is what Petey said. When it got dark, and he wasn't here yet, I went to bed without him. When I woke this morning, he still wasn't home. It's a drive, but it isn't the other side of the state. I don't know what's going on. I hate to bother you, but he doesn't answer his phone."

"It's all right, Viola. No bother. I'll see what I can find out. He has a phone, and the drive is interstate most of the way."

"I know it's silly, but it just isn't like him to let me worry." Her voice was husky.

"Sit tight. I'll call you back." Rory called the state lab and talked to the duty chief, who confirmed that Petey had been there the day before and had gone to dinner with some of the guys. The man hadn't gone himself, but the crew had all made it in that morning.

Rory asked to talk to one of the guys and was passed off to Kent, who told him the group had parted ways around nine after eating and polishing off a little wine. Kent insisted no one was drunk. Petey had been in great spirits and anxious to get back to Winterset after saying his trip had been fruitful. Petey expected to wrap up the autopsy on his desk now that he had the missing link.

No. Kent didn't know what link.

What had the boys in Lincoln discovered? And where was Petey? Maybe he was in his office at the morgue. Rory hated to call Viola back with news of no news. He'd better contact Thacker and ask for the use of his legs again. He hated this!

Thacker agreed to run over to the courthouse and call back. Patience wasn't Rory's superpower. He used the scooter to cross the room, and then he unlocked the back door. The alley looked innocent, with no large rocks, no potholes. He wheeled out. Coming around the building, he managed okay, but then he had to cross the street. Winterset hadn't put in wheelchair ramps, and the curbs looked intimidating. He mentally counted how many times he'd need to take the scooter up or down if he was going to make it to Petey's office on his own. He felt helpless. He sat on the knee pad and waited for Thacker's call.

When his phone rang, it wasn't the rookie. "Rory, thank God!"

"Petey?"

"I need to get word to Viola. She'll be frantic. The house line has been busy for twenty minutes, and she isn't picking up her cell."

"She already called me. Where are you? Are you all right?"

"Yes, it's a long story. I'm calling from a garage in Prairie. Please don't ask me where that is. They tell me it's an hour's drive from Winterset. Can you send someone to the house and let Viola know I'm among the living? The car is in one piece, and I'll be home in time for dinner. Shoot, I'm on a payphone. You can even tell her to call me at this number."

"You got it." Rory disconnected, called Thacker, and sent him to carry the message to Petey's wife. Then he returned to the alley. Sitting side-saddle on the scooter, he stretched out his legs, tipped his hat to shade his face, and leaned back to await the coroner's return.

****

Petey pulled his car into the alley and climbed out. Before he could start, Rory said, "First things first, what were you doing in Prairie?"

The coroner laughed and took a relaxed position leaning against the car door and facing the detective.

"I feel like I was in *The Twilight Zone*," Petey said. "I went to dinner with the boys from the lab. We had a great meal, said our thank-yous and goodbyes, and I drove out of the lot. It was a little restaurant that one of the boys recommended, and it was west of Lincoln but not too far off the interstate. On the way over, we followed a feeder road that ran parallel to the highway and then made a series of switchbacks, and since it was getting dark, I didn't see all the landmarks as we made the turns. Heck, I was just following along, not paying much attention.

"When I left after the meal, I must have gotten turned around because I didn't hit the interstate where I thought I ought to. I have a pretty good sense of direction in full daylight, but last night, I ended up in Timbuktu. Or the road leading to it. I must have been going west when I thought I was going east. And then, the next thing I knew, I was on a dirt county road. I recognized it as one that would eventually bring me back, not to the interstate, but back to Winterset by way of the old state highway that comes down from the north. I was feeling pretty satisfied, had the windows down and the radio cranked up on the oldies station."

"I remember night runs like that," Rory said, flexing his injured leg.

"I was really enjoying the drive, and then I ran into the detour. Out there in the country, a thing like that can run you back and around for twenty miles just because a bridge is out or something."

"Didn't think to turn around and go back the way you came?"

"By that time, I'd gone too far to double back. You have to understand, I was still feeling good, but I knew I was lost. I pulled over and fired up the GPS, only I couldn't make a connection. That's also when I discovered the lack of cell phone reception. There wasn't much for me to do, so I decided to trust the county boys and their signs. It seemed like I drove for an hour without seeing another detour sign leading me back to the northern route and home."

"Never hit another town?"

"I can tell you've never been up that way. There was a crossroad with an old train depot, a gas station, and three houses. The station hasn't seen a train in forty years. The pumps were locked, and the lights were out in the houses. When I drove through, I wasn't feeling desperate, just a little agitated. I could have stopped and knocked on one of the doors. But I didn't."

Rory nodded. Petey stood. "I've got some pop in the car. You want one?"

"No, I'm good." Rory knew the storytelling would progress at Petey's speed, so he steepled his fingers and waited.

"I'm looking for detour signs," Petey said, returning and taking a position where he could lean against the bricks. "I'm running low on gas. The GPS and the cell are useless. And then it gets worse."

The detective knew there would be a zinger, and he lifted one side of his lips in a wry smile.

"Out of nowhere comes a car. It must have been going eighty, ninety miles an hour. One minute, the road's clear, and the next, here's this yay-hoo on my bumper. I tried pulling over to let him pass. Flashed my high beams. He wasn't buying it. Taps my rear bumper. Finally, he nudges me into the runoff ditch and hightails it up the road. Left me sitting at a fifty-degree angle, with the front bumper kissing dry earth and the back end without an inch of traction."

Rory whistled, shaking his head at Petey's dilemma.

"It's a long way from one farm to the next out there. I wasn't sure where I was. There wasn't a light on in any direction. I couldn't even think about walking to the nearest town. I wasn't sure there'd even be a next town."

Petey stopped talking and took a long drink. "I decided to wait until morning light and then try to get the car out if it looked like I could. Or walk out if I found no better way. It was a long night, and the whole time, I was hoping someone would come along and rescue me."

"And…"

"Damnedest thing. This morning, right at daybreak,

a wrecker drove up the gravel road. He said a fellow had paid him to come tow me out and into town if necessary. Now, I ask you, doesn't that sound like an episode from *The Twilight Zone*?"

"No aliens? No physical harm to you? No damage to the car?"

"You're right; there wasn't any car damage. I could have bent an axle or something. I was lucky. The front tire was flat, so I let them tow me in."

Rory scratched his head. Petey's tale was crazy. "Do you think someone was following you when you left the restaurant?"

"I don't see how. I would have seen him. I was on the road for a long way. Another set of headlights would have been visible. I don't even remember passing a car going the other way once I turned off and onto the detour."

"Think about your time in the restaurant. Anything fishy happen there?"

Petey paused like he was replaying the scene, looking for something strange. "Nope. Good food and a couple of swell guys to enjoy it with."

"What about when you were in Prairie?"

"No. But I spend most of my time on the payphone, convincing Viola I was all right. Have you ever been to Prairie? Grain elevator, gas station, IGA grocery, not the most scenic community. Didn't make any new friends."

Many strange things were happening: Jesse's attempted purse snatching, Marilyn's attempted car theft, and now Petey. What would you call this incident? A hit and run? He wondered if he should share the other accidents with his friend. None of them made sense. Petey seemed preoccupied with his own misfortune.

"You're right. It's the damnedest thing," Petey said.

"What did the boys at the state lab find?"

"Oh, yeah. Wait till you hear." Petey straightened to his full height, pushed up his sleeves like he was getting down to business, and said, "I owe you an apology. There's no excuse, but with all the talk of 'find your ancestor' and just finishing an online course about matching up and harvesting organs, you see, I had these crazy notions in my head."

He looked sincere, maybe a little rattled. "I led you down a rabbit hole. Once I came to my senses, I realized it was more likely that the puncture meant something administered before death. That something wasn't on the tox panel, and it wasn't a known date-rape drug. I was out of my league."

"No chance it was the other way around?" Rory didn't know if he was disappointed. Heck, he would be happy to just have an answer.

"Nope." Tipping the pop can, Petey took a long draft before continuing. "Those boys in Lincoln have a great setup. They knew right away what direction to go in. I gave them the samples, and it was no time until they had an answer."

"Which was?"

"Chloral hydrate."

The drug sounded familiar but not particularly exotic. Rory couldn't place it. "And that wasn't on the standard toxicology panel?"

"The FDA hasn't approved drugs that contain chloral hydrate since 2012."

"What's it used for?"

"Sedative. Doctors and hospitals used to sedate patients before surgery or invasive tests. It fell in the sedative-hypnotic category and was used for over a hundred years. However, because it was an oral liquid administered through IV, it resulted in countless dosing errors. Oversedation and multiple deaths. Finally removed from the market."

"But only for the past couple of years."

"True, but it was never an over-the-counter drug, and there wouldn't be any in the back of someone's medicine cabinet. A major alarm went out from the FDA. There was a broad reaction to the deaths, and most healthcare personnel have a healthy respect for malpractice lawsuits. After two years, you wouldn't find any chloral hydrate in a clinical environment."

"What about other places? Military, for example. Aren't they notorious for stockpiling?"

"It was probably part of the supplies carried by EMTs."

"What would be the shelf life of chlora-whatever."

"That, I don't know. What I do know is that our River Girl had it in her system."

Rory rubbed his head. "I'm headed to the prison in Lincoln on Monday. There are similarities between the Emily Weir murder case I worked in 2006 and our River Girl. Do you remember hearing about that case? Ugly business. Vicious murder by a heartless man, if you'd even call him a man. This drug gives me something I didn't look for back then, maybe something I missed during the original autopsy. I plan to find out."

"I remember the case. Abduction, torture, a sad

story. But if this murderer is locked up, there's not much chance—"

"Tobias Snearl is a psychopath, as charismatic as Manson and as handsome as Bundy. I doubt he murdered our River Girl, but he knows something that I need to know."

Petey's demeanor changed from jovial to serious. "Do you suspect a copycat or strings pulled from behind bars?"

"I don't know. I don't mind telling you it's a drive I'm not looking forward to taking." Rory raised his booted foot and moaned at the effort.

The coroner's playfulness returned. "You can look forward to a less eventful trip than mine."

Rory laughed. "I hope to go straight there and back, despite having a damn bowling ball attached to my leg."

"If Tom Whittaker could climb Mount Everest with one foot, you can get to Lincoln and back." Petey crushed the empty pop can and tossed it into a nearby trash can, preparing to leave. "Waylon Jennings had his left foot amputated in 2001 and kept on singing."

Rory waved him to silence. "Enough. I know it's not the end of the world."

"I better head to the house and report to Viola."

Rory watched as Petey got into his car and pulled out of the alley. Then he locked up and took the lift up. This time, he pushed the scooter in and carried it out.

Using the walking cast and his determination, he left the scooter parked in the living room and headed straight for the war room. In one of his boxes, he felt he would find information showing Emily Weir had had chloral hydrate in her system.

Chapter Twenty-Six

Esther was delighted when Jesse invited her to join the other ladies for the silent auction planning meeting. Most times, Esther hesitated to volunteer. Many town ladies made a career of working the charity functions, and she didn't want to compete. She was content to lend a hand when they called in the worker bees. However, this one was different. Her only sister was chairperson.

Jesse pulled up and tooted the car's horn. "Climb in, Es. I'm running late, and I want to talk to Marilyn before we get started."

Esther buckled up. "I think you mean Marilyn and Cousin Henry."

Jesse laughed. "I thought the same thing when she called this morning. But no, Cousin Henry is off in the Cadillac today. His car is at the body shop, getting the scratches smoothed out."

"There were only a few, tiny, little…nothings."

"I guess the nothings bothered Cousin Henry. Besides, I want to see Marilyn without him around."

"It does seem like he's always underfoot or lurking in the background."

"I'll say. Do you know he went with her to the lady's card game this week? Oozing charm and twirling his mustache at the ladies. He's got everyone stirred up about finding out their heritage. It's uncanny. Do you suppose he gets a commission?"

"I wouldn't know."

"Are you interested in finding out?"

"Not really. Rory checked him out and didn't find anything on him or the company. I'm only concerned that he doesn't take advantage of Marilyn."

They rode the rest of the way to Marilyn's townhouse in silence. Esther, for one, felt content to enjoy the lovely lawns and flower beds they passed. She wished she had her grandmother's green thumb. For years, she'd struggled to maintain the beds planted around the house she'd inherited. Esther's talents lay elsewhere. Occasionally she purchased a pot of geraniums to add color. Curb appeal, Jesse called it, but they always died.

Marilyn was standing on the curb when they turned the corner. She had a large portfolio under her arm and was wearing a new hat. She pointed out the fashion accessory and left the sisters to wonder why she had the portfolio.

Arriving before the rest of the committee, the three used the time to straighten the hospital's small conference room. Esther put on the coffee. Marilyn claimed the chair at the head of the table. Jesse ran down to the cafeteria to buy a dozen donuts, and she came back with two dozen assorted.

"I wish I'd asked Viola to bake a coffee cake."

"Why didn't you say something? I have plenty of goodies in my freezer." Esther poured a cup of coffee and added some creamer. "Do you want some?"

Marilyn said, "She won't be here." She cut a sprinkled donut into two pieces and took the larger half. "I talked to Viola earlier. It seems Petey joined the ranks of the missing."

Esther gasped. Abby Sue Bellman and now Petey Moss!

Jesse sat down, and Marilyn continued. "Sorry, dears. He joined the ranks and immediately turned in his membership card."

Esther wiped the coffee spill she'd created by thumping the cup down too hard. "What are you talking about?"

"Petey went to Lincoln yesterday. Viola didn't expect him back until late and fell asleep waiting for his return. Naturally, when he wasn't there this morning, she was worried. I just happened to call to remind her of the committee meeting, and she told me the whole story."

"You better fill us in." Esther scooted her chair under the table, folded her hands, and placed them on top. Rory was going to the prison on Monday. Ranks of the missing weren't something she took lightly. Both she and her sister had spent agonizing days waiting while the whole town had searched for their mother. Marilyn knew better than to make light of the situation.

The older woman recounted the events from the preceding night, including Petey's expected return before dinner today, and employed more hand-waving and bracelet-clinking than Esther thought possible for a woman her age—or any age.

"Poor, Viola," Jesse said.

Poor indeed. Esther wondered how a grown man had gotten himself into such a predicament, and she was relieved it had nothing to do with Tobias Snearl or the prison.

"Viola said to assign her any tasks we thought her

capable of performing. And she promises to make next week's meeting." Marilyn nibbled on the half-donut.

The other committee members shuffled in, helping themselves to sweets, half-donuts, and coffee. Marilyn had at least four half-pieces. It was a good twenty minutes before Jesse got them started on the committee business.

"Ladies, we have two major decisions on today's agenda. A poster to draw in community participation and support." She flapped a hand in Marilyn's direction. "And the items to offer at auction."

Marilyn jutted her chin at the portfolio propped against the wall in the corner. "Madam Chairman, I brought a mock-up poster. Could I get an easel to display it so we can all see?"

"Oh. Ah, sure." Jesse glanced around. "The hospital should have one somewhere."

Her panic-filled gaze landed on Esther, who took over. "Why don't we make a list of possible auction items while we wait?"

Relieved but flustered, Jesse called the hospital's staff-training supervisor and asked if there was an easel.

Esther recorded the auction items on the whiteboard as members made suggestions: a night at a local B&B, a gift certificate from the nursery, dinner at Old Orchard, a lecture series at the community college.

The list grew. Unfortunately, each item set off a debate on its merits. Soon the discussion grew loud and out of hand. To regain control, Jesse finally suggested they write ideas on paper and turn them in for consideration. The whole time, Marilyn fussed with the contents in her folder, waiting for the poster stand to arrive.

A knock at the conference room door drew their attention. A middle-aged, slightly stooped, but otherwise undistinguished technician entered. The bill of a baseball cap concealed his face, and ginger-colored hair stuck out around the edges. His complexion, what Esther could see, which was mostly chin, matched his beige hospital-issued jumpsuit.

As she watched him set the easel up in the corner, she felt a spark of recognition. Had she seen him around town? Should she know his name? Without uttering a word, he left after placing the easel where Marilyn indicated and before Esther could identify him.

Jesse leaned in and whispered in Esther's ear, "Was that Sheila Steel's brother?"

Esther shrugged. She didn't recall that the motel proprietor had a brother. But he was someone's father, son, or brother.

Marilyn produced a sheet of poster board. Careful to keep her body between the display and those assembled, she placed it on the easel. Then, stepping out of the way, she said, "I thought I'd save some time by having this mock-up made. Any suggestions for modification are welcome." She glanced around with a bright smile, rubbing her hands together and setting her bangles jangling.

The room went deadly silent.

Across the top were the words "WINTERSET MEMORIAL WINGDING — SUPPORT YOUR HOME TOWN HOSPITAL" in bold letters.

Prominently centered on a background showcasing the senior center park was Mayor Becker's image. His expression, usually the conveyor for trustworthiness, held a hint of mischief by way of a nefarious grin.

Although the Winterset High School colors were gold and purple, the eggplant bow tie at his throat turned his complexion sallow and clashed with the neon lemon of his dress shirt.

Everyone found their voice at the same time. An animated thirty-minute discussion followed. Marilyn shot down all changes while encouraging more comments. Finally, they caved. The poster was accepted as proposed, with one primary revision: Albert Winterset would replace the image of Mayor Becker. Albert Winterset, for whom the town and hospital had been named, had been a pioneer settler and currently resided at Winterset's Boot Hill Cemetery. A committee was appointed to find an appropriate photograph of him.

Esther used the time to worry about Rory and his upcoming trip. Then her thoughts turned to his recent hospital stay. She half-expected a hospital administrator to barge into the meeting, demanding to know why she had allowed Rory Naysmith to walk out of the hospital under his own power and without signing the appropriate medical and financial release documents. Jesse wasn't Rory's primary physician, and red tape was red tape. Maybe they'd be after her, too.

Then there was the procurement of the scooter to help facilitate his return to detective duties. And the guilt. She knew he had discharged himself way too early in the healing process, and if anything happened to him, she deserved to bear the guilt for not coming forward to stop him. She didn't feel well.

****

Ralph watched Axel pull in at Beaver's Best Western fifteen minutes after he'd made the plea for help. Sheila had gone to their private quarters just off the main lobby for a rest, but he didn't want to run into her and risk having to explain himself. It was uncanny. She always saw through him. It wouldn't do any good to lie, and he was in no mood to listen to one of her lectures. Behind the dumpster in the back parking lot seemed a safe bet. He was in position when the pickup pulled in.

"Psssst, Axel. Over here." Ralph stepped out and windmilled his arm to signal him over.

"Compadre, what are you doing back there?" Axel took a Marlboro from the pack he kept rolled in his shirt sleeve, lit the end, and then tucked the lighter into his cut-off blue jean's pocket.

"Shhhh, I don't want Sheila to see me."

"I got the pick set like you asked. What's up?"

Ralph filled him in while Axel smoked. Crushing the butt under his Roman sandal, Axel said, "Let's get with the program."

The drapes were drawn in Jerry Ames' room. The computer case and two sample cases sat in the center of the room, by the bed's maple footboard. Axel nudged the computer with his toe. "We ought to let Miss Esther look at this."

"I'm not interested in the computer. I want to know what's so secret that it needs a lock and a padlocking belt."

"See your point," said Axel, and he squatted down to examine the locks. "Interesting hardware."

Ralph flipped the "Do Not Disturb" lock on the door and joined him. "Can you get them open?"

"Is a duck bow-legged?"

Ralph frowned. Axel took out a leather package,

untied a leather thong, and unfolded the tri-fold pouch. From the variety of picks, he took one. Sized it up with the padlock mechanism. Swapped it for another. With one tool inserted, he employed another to swing the lock open.

"Piece of rhubarb," he said. The belt fell away.

The recessed hinge-locks were more challenging, but not much.

"You're not going to scratch them, are ya? I don't want him to know we've been in here."

Axel raised his eyebrow. "Not in this lifetime." He had all four locks sprung before Ralph blinked.

"Good. Open 'er up."

"Holy cow!" Ralph reached into the first case and lifted out a curly wig. "What do you imagine this is for?"

Axel took it from him.

Ralph pulled out another. This one was longer, fuzzy, and shoulder length. "There's four or five of these in here. He wouldn't be one of them female impersonators, do ya think?"

He pulled out a black cape and a deep purple boa and tossed them on the carpet. Next came a bag of cosmetics, which he dumped onto the bed. A cigar-sized box contained rubber noses—or covers or something. Ralph didn't know what to think.

Axel thought a minute, tapping a finger at the end of his mustache. "You mean like a drag queen? Not unless there are female things in this other case."

They opened it. The case contained filing folders, and each folder had a handful of newspaper clippings.

"I don't get it," Ralph said. "What's these girlie things got to do with old newspaper clippings?"

"Is there a label on those file folders?" Axel took a cigarette from his sleeve and hung it on his lip.

"This here is a no-smoking room. Sheila will kill me if you light that thing."

Someone rattled the doorknob. They froze.

Ralph's heart jumped, and he forgot to breathe. Axel stuffed the cigarette in the pocket of his cut-offs and started loading the cosmetics back into the bag. Ralph could feel his heart hammering in his chest. Jerry Ames was linebacker bulky, strong, and could be one of those special forces guys, probably able to take them both on—at the same time!

A light tap sounded at the door. "Housekeeping."

Ralph gave a little nervous laugh and slapped a hand over his mouth. After a moment, he heard the housekeeping cart move down the hall. "Let's get this stuff put away."

They'd just put the computer under the bed and were discussing how the cases didn't look like they were in the right spots when a heavy hand knocked on the door. "Ralph, are you in there? I know you're in there."

Sheila! Shoot.

"Open this door! You're not running an illegal poker game, are you? You know what happened last time."

"No, dear." He looked askance at Axel. "Just a moment, honey."

The door rattled. "Don't sweet-talk me. Open this door."

Ralph timidly turned the lock and admitted his wife. He talked fast. Arms crossed and nose flaring, Sheila tapped her foot the whole time while Ralph explained the setup. Axel nodded in solemn agreement while Sheila gave him the evil eye.

"Well, let's see this booty."

Ralph checked the bedside clock. When could they expect Ames back? "Wouldn't it be okay for ya to believe us, and we leave before Ames shows up?"

"I don't trust the two of you to describe the contents of those sample cases. I want to see for myself."

Axel did the magic with the picklocks again.

Sheila pulled each wig out one by one, turning them over and feeling the texture. Tsk-tsked. Then she spread the make-up out, opened each case, and sniffed the contents. Shook her head. "This here is theatrical quality. Let's see the folders."

Axel repacked the first case while Sheila examined the second.

"These are about murder," she said. "News accounts from Tulsa." She tossed the folder on the bed. "Lubbock." Toss. It landed on top of the other. "Wichita Falls. Grand Island." She fanned out the rest like she had a fistful of cards. "Ralph, there are at least eight accounts of murder. Did you read them?"

Biting his lower lip, he eyed the door. "No."

"Let me get my phone out." Sheila reached beneath her blouse and extracted the cell phone from what she liked to call her "left bank."

"Spread the clippings out, Ralph. I'll take a picture. Eight files, eight pictures, eight seconds. Stop being so nervous."

Axel took the Marlboro from his pocket. The cigarette was crumpled, and the paper had a hole. He put it between his lips. "If you don't mind, ma'am, I'll

185

be outside standing lookout while you finish the photoshoot."

"Good idea, Axel. I don't know what we got here. But it ain't good."

Chapter Twenty-Seven

The war room was extremely quiet, almost eerily silent except for the hum of the computers. Rory liked the feeling the closed door provided—shutting out the world. Here among his records, with the tools technology made possible, he could touch archived files, search databases, and record new theories. Several websites were open, and he was working in a two-fingered style on a cross-reference file when the new doorbell announced someone at the door to the apartment. He clicked on the camera icon.

Esther Mullins waited on the platform outside. He clicked the audio button. "Hello, Esther. I'll be right there." He watched her confusion turn to pleasure.

"Hi, Rory. I'll wait."

He was still working on leg strength, so he used the scooter to help him reach the door. He let her in, parked the scooter at the kitchen table, and hobble-limped to the living room, with Esther following. "I shouldn't have accepted my key back." He sat on the recliner and elevated his foot.

"There was no reason for me to keep it," she said, sitting on the sofa, her face flushed.

He winced. "I like what you and the boys did to the office. Real handy."

"I hope it postpones your return to the office in the police station."

"Here is more convenient." He looked at his booted foot. "Chief Mansfield isn't a fan of the work-from-home philosophy. I have to report to the station in the morning."

She nodded as he spoke and allowed Commander to climb onto her lap. "Then it's official. Thacker will become a detective?"

"Technically, Thacker is assigned to the temporary detective department Mayor Becker has authorized. The town council has the final say, but I think we can count on them doing what the mayor considers prudent. They won't give Thacker a detective shield because he'd still need to take the test and qualify. But instead of being put in the patrol rotation, he will report to me."

Esther gave him an encouraging smile. "That will make his mother feel better. She's worried about his choice of profession."

"He'll work on investigations as needed, but never alone. And always without authority. The mayor made that clear. It's not exactly a win-win, but it works for now, and the boy is willing."

"I'd say he's ecstatic."

Rory grinned. "It helps that he's enthusiastic."

"And Chief Mansfield?" she asked.

"Will do what the mayor says."

"Where is your bodyguard-roomy this evening?"

"He's having dinner with his parents. It's meatloaf night. Mom makes a mean meatloaf."

She stroked the cat. He was sure she'd come for more than a social visit, although that would be nice. "Would you like to get yourself something to drink?"

"No, I'm fine." She concentrated on Commander, tickled his chin, and then looked up suddenly. "I'm sorry. How about you? Can I get you something?"

He laughed. "No. And I'm not an invalid. I've been figuring out this mobility thing. You know when the scooter is helpful and when it's in the way. Mostly it's the latter. Thanks for helping Jesse find it for me."

She put up her hands. "Innocent. It was all her doing."

"I'll tell her it's appreciated. Or you can tell her for me if you see her first. And about not calling..." He didn't know where to begin. Surely, she knew how he felt.

Esther waved the subject away. "I have a couple of things to run by you. If you have time?"

What was this? Had he made another faux pas? He didn't know why she made him nervous, worried he'd say the wrong thing, and naturally, only after he'd spewed out something without weighing its impact. Crap.

"Always. What's on your mind."

"First are the coincidence incidents." She chuckled and added, "Wow, that sounds weird."

He smiled indulgently. "Tell me."

"I'm worried. Marilyn, Jesse, and Petey have all been involved in incidents. And there is your attack. I can't for the life of me figure out how suddenly everyone I know is experiencing a near brush with the criminal element. The criminal element. Listen to me. I sound like Thacker." She pulled her lips into a tight line. "For all I know, there have been more accidents—incidents."

"True."

He wanted to say he was afraid she was on a hit list, albeit more of a nuisance hit list than a fatality hit list. Even thinking it puzzled him. "Coincidence incidents?"

"It seems like the targets all have a connection to me. Well, of course, or I wouldn't even know about them. My point is that in each case, the person involved is a close friend. And then it dawned on me. You were the first, and the others are all close to you as well." She fidgeted, adjusting Commander's collar and then smoothing his fur. "I know this sounds crazy, but do you think these incidents are messages?"

She laid one hand on Commander's head. He squirmed out from under and shot across the room. They watched him go. She brought Rory's attention back to her by adding, "A message for you personally, Mister Senior Detective."

He watched her closely. "What's the message?"

"I don't know. I can get to them, so I can get to you again." Esther fingered the collar of her blouse absently as she looked into middle space. "I'm out here, so I'm right in your backyard." He frowned, and she went on, "I can hurt them, but they are not my real target?"

She sat for a moment as if trying to decide to say more. Then she turned to him, her eyes glassy, her voice husky. "Rory, I'm afraid. I think someone is out to get you. The first incident didn't do the job, and there will be another."

He swallowed and then cleared his throat. "No real damage was done in the subsequent incidents. No one was hurt. Jesse got a scare and a little cut. Marilyn was inconvenienced, and Petey had an overnight adventure. They are all home safe, no worse for the wear."

"Someone is out there. Watching. It can't be good for any of us. You, especially, must be careful."

"I'm always careful." He looked at the cast resting on the extended footrest. When he looked up, Esther was looking at it, too.

She stood. "Do you have any wine? I could use a glass. There's another situation that I want to tell you about concerning Abby Sue Bellman."

"Who's Abby Sue Bellman?"

Esther rummaged through the cupboards until she found a bottle of Merlot, the corkscrew, and two glasses. She poured the wine and brought it back to the living room area. "Abby Sue is one of Winterset's prominent citizens. She was born and raised in Georgia and moved here with her husband after he retired. You might or might not have met her, but I can guarantee she knows who you are. She's one of your biggest supporters. Behind the scenes, as it were, at the Lady's Aid Society, Chamber of Commerce, Friends of the Public Library. She's active in all the local charities and civic clubs."

"I had no idea."

"You mean a lot to Winterset, Rory. Justice, integrity, we count on you to be impartial. The citizens expect you to not only uphold the law but to always do it with their well-being foremost in your mind."

If she hadn't been so sincere, he would have been embarrassed. These were the things he wanted the citizens to count on from him. It pleased him that she'd voiced them. He hoped he didn't look smug because he felt honored.

"What coincidence has happened to Abby Sue?"

"She's gone."

He had a sinking feeling, déjà vu all over again. "Gone? As in no longer with us—dead type gone?"

"Hopefully not dead," she said, "but something is mighty smelly."

She relayed Abby Sue's connection to Marilyn's cousin-in-law Henry Beauregard and the fact that she'd last been seen in his company. "No one's seen her since Marilyn's party last Saturday. Cousin Henry claims to spend time with her, but no one has seen them together, including Marilyn. We only have Marilyn's word, and she only has his word that Abby Sue is carrying on her life as usual. She missed the silent auction committee meeting this morning, unheard of for a professional society matron."

She searched his face. "I've called around, but nothing. It's as if Abby Sue vanished."

Esther seemed to swallow the end of her sentence. Wow, talk about stirring up emotions from the past. The situation called for his calm, reassuring voice, the one he reserved for frightened children. "What seems like a coincidence is nothing more than a question as to her whereabouts. And unfortunately, it's come up while you're worried about all these other incidents."

"Oh, maybe. I feel jumpy. And confused. Things used to be clear-cut and predictable. Orderly. Now I don't seem to have a hand on the pulse of Winterset."

Rory knew what she meant. "Tell you what; I'll look into it first thing tomorrow. It can be my thank-you gift for your help."

She smiled weakly. "There's more."

"Do we need more wine?"

"Judge for yourself." She got up, brought the bottle over, and filled their glasses. "It's about Axel."

Oh, boy, this was going to be good. He listened without comment. Her story was a little hard to follow, but since Axel was the subject, Rory wasn't surprised.

"Okay, let me see if I've got this straight. Axel helped Ralph Steel, the owner of the Best Western, rummage through a guest's room because he'd already searched the same guest's automobile and found an ammo stash. And this illegal search required Axel to use an illegal set of picklocks to open a suitcase. No, two cases. Am I getting this right?"

"I didn't say it was a pretty picture, just that it was confusing and might shed some light on these other problems."

"All right, tell me the rest."

"According to Axel, the cases contained one"—she held up her pointer finger—"a lot of items one would use for disguising oneself. And two"—her middle finger unfolded—"newspaper clippings taken from murder cases going back ten or twelve years."

Rory sat up straight. "What kind of murder cases?"

Esther balled her fist and tucked it into her lap. "I don't know. Axel didn't know. Sheila Steel caught them in the act of rummaging through the luggage and put a stop to it. She did, however, take pictures of the newspaper articles with her cell phone. Axel is convinced that Jerry Ames is a hitman. Or a serial killer."

"Or a private eye?"

"I tried to convince Axel to come over and tell you about it himself. He mumbled something about getting into trouble when he was just trying to warn me to watch out for the guy. And then said he knew he shoulda known better and now was going off to mind his own business. You know how he is. When I left the house and headed this way, he was camped at the edge of my yard with a six-pack of beer and a police Maglite. I figure he's set up to watch my house for the night."

"You think he's downstairs now?"

"Yes."

Rory grinned. "Better invite him up."

Chapter Twenty-Eight

Axel came up, carrying a six pack by the handle. Three cans still dangled from their plastic neckties. "I'm going to need to work on my stealth," he said, placing the beer on the floor beside the chair in which he sank. "Miss Esther isn't nearly as hard to follow as you'd think or want." A scowl pushed his unibrow down between his steel-gray eyes, and he looked intently at Rory.

"So, you are following her," Rory said. "Anyone out and about?"

"Nah, the sidewalks are bare. But that's no reason for her—"

"I'm a big girl, Axel," said Esther. "I'll manage on my own, but right now, I think we need to make some plans."

Axel's face softened. "Aw, Miss Esther."

"It has to do with your discovery at the Best Western."

He looked around wildly. "You didn't confide in the constable, did ya?"

"Yes."

"But..." Axel's gaze bounced back and forth between them.

"I know about the lockpicks, Axel," Rory said.

The younger man slumped in the chair. "It's not that. It's...well...it's just that I don't want to get Ralph into more trouble with his wife."

Rory tried to keep a straight face. "From what I hear, he doesn't need any help irritating Sheila."

"Geez, you know what I mean."

"I do. What's more, I understand Mrs. Steel is opinionated and apt to react if confronted." Axel nodded, and Rory added, "And that's why I'll need your help tomorrow."

Axel leaned forward and swapped an empty beer can for a full one. After he'd popped the top, he said, "Lay it out for me, Constable."

Rory obliged.

****

Thursday, Rory woke to a Chamber of Commerce Day complete with a cloudless sky, modest breezes, and temperatures in the mid-seventies. As robins chirped and squirrels chased each other around the courthouse lawns, he felt the energy dancing through the air. His roomie Thacker was more than willing to take him over to Steel's Boat & RV Storage to talk with Ralph Steel. The walking cast was still a challenge, but Rory was determined to master it, and he wondered if he should get one of those fancy Bat Masterson canes.

When they pulled into the storage lot, Ralph Steel was outside, moving in a new RV. Thacker let Rory out at the steps to the mobile office and parked out of the way of the drive. Together they leisurely walked the short distance to the boat storage area and verified that Jerry Ames' trailer and car were still parked among the other stored units. They were. Thacker skirted the rig, wrote down the plate number from the trailer, and found the vehicle under the tarp. The trailer had North Dakota tags and a rental sticker. The car had neither.

By the time they finished, Ralph, wearing overalls and a salesman's smile, joined them. "What can I do you for, gentlemen?"

"We're interested in this vehicle," Rory said. He flashed his ID and then tucked it back in his pocket. "You've had it on the lot for what…three days?"

Ralph stuck his hands in his pockets and lost his smile. "Is something wrong?"

"Nope, just interested in this one vehicle."

"If it's stolen, I don't know anything about it. Guy just asked me to store it for a couple of days. He's taking it down to Ashland on Friday for the car show. I didn't ask to see his registration."

Rory pulled out his notebook. "What can you tell me about the man?"

Ralph paled. He pulled a handkerchief from his pocket and used it to mop his face. "Name's Jerry Ames. That's all I know. He paid with a credit card. I'll show you the receipt."

"Officer Thacker would like to see the car without the tarp. That a problem for you?"

"No, sir. But I don't have the keys. I don't require clients to leave a set with me, just a phone number."

"That'll be fine, Mr. Steel." Rory walked around the car with as much dignity as a one-legged man could muster. "Store any other cars, Mr. Steel?"

"No, sir. This here's a boat and RV storage."

"How'd you happen to make an arrangement with Mr. Ames?"

Ralph fidgeted nervously. Rory could almost see the gears moving behind the man's bloodshot eyes. He figured Ralph was weighing the pros and cons of sharing his suspicions about Ames and wondered if he'd confess to rifling through the belongings back at the motel.

Bungee cords held the tarp in place. Thacker worked them free. Rory tipped his fedora back, locked his knee for better support, and waited.

It was a red beauty without the tarp—an All-American sports car with wraparound chrome bumpers and white ragtop. Thacker climbed onto the trailer, placed the palm of his hand on the roof, and bent to look through the driver's window. "Clean as a whistle, boss." He tried the door and found it locked.

"You don't have a key?" Rory asked.

Ralph shook his head. "I told ya, I don't require them to leave one. Boaters don't care. They can carry everything on and off when they take their craft out. RV owners got stuff inside their units and don't want me going through it. I don't want anybody claiming I did."

Thacker went around to the passenger side of the vehicle. "Hey, boss, this side's unlocked." He opened it and popped his head in. "Nothing out in plain sight. But it smells. Wait, there's a funny mark here on the inside of the door. It looks like someone jimmied it open. Looks recent. Whew-eee! Something's off." He extracted his head and made a face. "And the smell…"

"See if you can get into the trunk, Thacker."

"Wait a minute," Ralph said, hustling to the rear of the rig. "You oughtta get Ames' permission for that. Doncha need a search warrant?"

"There's a cable latch." Thacker reached inside the car, and the trunk popped. He sidestepped to the rear, lifted the lid, and then abruptly reared back. "We got a problem here."

"I don't know nothing about files and cross-dressing," Ralph blurted then wrinkled his nose as he peeked around Thacker to look into the trunk. "Hey, that wasn't there yesterday!"

"Looks like Ames is hiding a body, boss."

A pungent smell mixed with overpowering lilac toilet water emanated from the trunk. Rory was all too familiar with the scent. It took a second to hobble over and get a look. The thing that caught his eye was the leather strap binding her wrists together. She lay in a fetal position, her neck hidden by her hair, a gentle gray that spread back from her temples like angel wings.

"Smells like she's been here a couple of days. Better call it in."

Mopping his brow, Ralph pleaded, "I swear it wasn't in there yesterday."

****

"We got to stop meeting like this." Petey Moss tossed his medical bag onto the trailer and then strained to climb on board after it. He took one look in the trunk and said, "I've seen prettier sights. Did you confirm ID?"

"Nothing confirmed," Rory said. "Thacker says it looks like Abigale Sue Bellman. Unless there's a purse hidden under the body, there's nothing to substantiate her identity."

Thacker cleared his throat, preparing to comment. Petey beat him to it. "I can tell you you're right. Abby Sue Bellman, without a doubt. She chaired a committee Viola worked on, and I sit on the board of the children's home with her. You can get next of kin to make it official, but it's Abby Sue."

Rory noted Petey's connections and tried to recall

what Esther had told him the night before. The best he could remember was that she had been concerned because no one had seen Abby Sue for a while. He didn't recall how long.

"Let the boys document the scene," Petey said, jumping down from the trailer. "Confirmed dead from undetermined causes for now. I need a better look when they get her out of the trunk."

The crime scene technicians took over. Petey stood next to Rory while the boys photographed and then lifted the body out. "Damn, Abby Sue Bellman," Petey said. "It's a '62 Corvette, isn't it? Used to be the car of my dreams. Nice piece of machinery."

Rory agreed. "Too bad an odor like that will never come out."

Thacker took Ralph Steel into the portable office. Rory watched as they zipped Abby Sue into the body bag. Then he went to check on the younger man, leaving Petey supervising the loading and transport.

The hobble to the trailer went as anticipated: slow and pitiful. The hop up the steps—excruciating. Rory paused on the landing to let the pain subside after conquering the three cement steps. Then he opened the door and stepped into the tepid air-conditioning.

"Is Mr. Steel interested in confessing?"

"I don't know anythin' about it," Ralph blabbered. "It's that guy, Ames. It's his car. He's the one who wanted it in the lot. I don't know nothin' about the body."

"Mr. Steel is sticking to his story," Thacker said. "Although he now admits he looked in the trunk yesterday and says it was empty."

Rory sat on the edge of the desk, stretched his

booted foot out in front, and said, "Tell me about Mr. Ames."

"I don't…" Ralph started but after Rory gave him a stern look said, "Okay. I thought something was off about him. To tell you the truth, I thought he was the kind of guy that'd bring a porterhouse to a weenie roast. I was sure he had something hidden in the car, and I was interested in finding out what it was. That's all. Honest to gosh. Just plain old curiosity." From his folding chair, Ralph looked up at Thacker. "You can't charge a man for being curious." He switched his focus to Rory. "Can ya?"

"No, you have a point there," Rory said. "But I'd be willing to bet that when the boys are finished collecting all the evidence, they'll find your fingerprints on the car and in the trunk."

"I don't deny it. But mine won't be the only ones. I didn't know she was in there, and I didn't kill her and leave her body in the trunk."

"All right, then tell me about Mr. Ames."

"I just did." Sweat spread in half-moons under Ralph's arms, turning the white T-shirt gray. He wiped his hands on a soiled handkerchief.

"I want to know what else you know about him."

Ralph looked at Rory as if he'd spoken in a foreign language. "I don't know what you want."

"Let's start with the cross-dressing and the files."

Ralph gasped. But in the end, told them everything, right down to Axel's lockpicks and Sheila's tirade.

Jerry Ames definitely topped Rory's list. Only, he didn't want to go into Ames' motel room. Getting a search warrant was a possibility, but he didn't want to tip Ames to the fact they had the body yet. If it was true that he came by the lot every day, there was every chance Ames had already seen them working the scene and knew. If he ran, they would hunt him down. What Rory wanted was the get his hands on the newspaper clippings. Were they trophies? Was Jerry Ames a serial killer?

While Petey worked up the autopsy, he could work up a profile.

Thacker agreed to take Ralph down to the station for a formal statement. Rory took out his phone and set the plans in motion for a visit with Sheila Steel.

Thirty minutes later, Axel picked him up behind the station, where Thacker transferred the scooter from the cruiser trunk to the pickup bed.

Once Rory buckled in, he said to Axel, "I'll do all the talking. Sheila Steel has the pictures. She can't deny they exist if you're there to rebut her denial. You are my leverage. Got it."

"Sure, Constable."

"Remember what we talked about last night? You're just along to stabilize the situation."

"Gotcha, Constable."

"Thacker will keep Ralph down at the station until we've transferred the photographs. That way, Sheila can't go south and accuse him of indiscretion. Nothing wastes more time than an old married couple arguing. You sure you got all that?"

"Are you going to deputize me?"

"Not this time."

Sheila was in the motel office when they arrived. Broad shouldered and thickly built, her stern features screamed no nonsense. Not happy at the interruption, she invited them in. "Detective Naysmith, I heard you had an accident. I didn't realize it put you in a cast." She pushed back from her desk but didn't rise. "There hasn't been a complaint, has there?"

"I believe you know Axel Barrow, Mrs. Steel."

"I do." She gave Axel a slit-eyed glare. "I have a lot of paperwork to do; I hope this won't take too long."

"I don't know why it would," Rory said. He took out his notebook, flipped a page, pretended to read. "I have it from a reliable source that you are in possession of photographs that could shed light on a case I'm working."

For a moment, she looked startled. Then she relaxed and gave Rory a self-righteous smile. "Are you talking about evidence in a homicide?" She didn't take her eyes off Axel.

"No, I don't believe so. This would be background information. Photographs of newspaper clippings."

She closed one eye to sight in on Axel. True to his word, he didn't react.

"Let's see…" Rory flipped another page. "Eight sets of newspaper clippings. Photographed from the collection of a motel guest staying in room number…" He let the sentence wander off, waiting to see what she would do.

She stared at him. Finally, she broke eye contact and shifted her gaze to the door. "Is Ralph with you?"

"No, it's just Mr. Barrow here and myself."

Axel puffed out his chest. Sheila craned to see around him, gave up with a huff, and pulled herself back into position at the desk. She began straightening papers. "Oh, hell. There's no law against a proprietor entering a room in her own establishment. Furthermore, there's nothing wrong with documenting a peculiar item found in that room."

"Is that what you did, found something peculiar?"

Sheila's cheeks flushed. Rory didn't know if it was anger, embarrassment, or plain old frustration at getting caught.

"What I would like, Mrs. Steel, is a copy of those pictures."

"Wait until I get my hands on that little weasel." Sheila reached for the cell phone lying on the desk, tapped the photos icon, and scrolled through the pictures. "Where do you want them sent, phone or email?"

"Both would be nice." Rory wrote the addresses down in his notebook, tore the page out, and handed it to her. "I'd appreciate it if the room was left untouched."

She wrinkled her nose, flared her nostrils, and then snatched the paper from his outstretched hand.

Once Rory heard the whoosh of the send signal, he rose. "Thank you for your co-operation, Mrs. Steel. I hope we didn't take up too much of your day."

As Axel drove back to the apartment, Rory opened the first message from Sheila. It was too small to read. Enlarging the image made it readable, but it was frustrating because he had to constantly slide the image to get the next line on the screen. He'd wait until he could pull them up on the computer monitor.

He scrolled to Esther's number. When she answered, he said, "I need your help. We've located Abby Sue."

Chapter Twenty-Nine

When Esther arrived, Rory brought her up to speed, sharing the briefest number of details. She seemed to trust he'd fill in the blanks later. After he explained what was needed, he manned one computer while she worked the other. The printed photographs taken by Sheila documenting the newspaper clippings found in Ames' Best Western room lay in a pile between them. Even enlarged to fit a standard sheet of paper, most of the print was still too small to read but the headlines were clear: *Woman's Dead Body Found*.

From there, they accessed the originals at their source, the appropriate newspaper websites, bookmarking them, and printing the originals on the laser printer.

The temperature in the war room was ten degrees warmer than the apartment, so Esther insisted they prop the door open. Commander wandered in and out, finally stretching out in a spot between Esther's keyboard and monitor. "Commander, you really aren't much help." She scratched him behind the ear, and he purred his appreciation.

She hit the print button. "I've got the one from the *Amarillo Globe-News* coming out on the printer. Which do you want next?"

"Print two copies. Grab the next one on the pile. Don't worry about the dates. Let's get them where we can read them. Then we'll look for similarities and worry about putting them in chronological order."

Rory noticed Esther was printing two for every one he found. He didn't claim to be a computer expert. And contrary to his own instructions, he had a hard time not skimming through the article before sending it to the printer.

Petey called to say he had Abby Sue on the morgue table and would have something for him in an hour. Then Thacker interrupted to report that Ralph Steel was back at the motel.

"I took him back to the storage lot," said Thacker. "He made a beeline for his car, and I followed him back to the Best Western. He's in there now. Do you want me to set up surveillance?"

"It wouldn't hurt to keep tabs on him. See if he heads out again. The WPD boys still working the crime scene?"

"It looked like they were wrapping up. Lloyd didn't want to share any details. But I did find out that Jerry Ames hadn't shown up. The boys are out looking for him with a warrant."

"Great. Everyone is hopping. Hang out there for another hour. If Ralph doesn't leave or Ames doesn't make an appearance, come on back to the apartment. Esther and I are working on the newspaper clippings."

"What about Sheila Steel?"

"Call me if anybody moves. Oh, and if Lloyd puts a man on Jerry Ames' room, stay out there as well. I want to know if anybody goes in or out."

"I'll call Axel. He can take over when I leave."

"No, he'll want to be deputized. I'd hate to disappoint him."

Esther snickered and printed the last newspaper article. "That does it. We're ready for the next step. How do you want to go through the printouts?"

"Grab a couple of highlighters, and we'll read through them in the living room."

Esther separated the papers into two piles, found the highlighters, and turned off the monitors.

Rory had a sudden thought. "See what you can find on Emily Weir in the *Omaha Sun* and the *Omaha World-Herald*." He opened the drawer containing the Emily Weir documents and took out her autopsy.

Esther's fingers flew across the keyboard. The printer buzzed. "There's quite a few here."

"Print them all."

He had the notebooks containing his notes on Emily Weir in his bedroom, where he'd been studying them the night before. He left Esther and limped down the hall, crossing the living room to his private quarters. The notebooks lay on the bedside table, dog-eared where he'd marked particular passages he wanted to find again. When he made his way back to the living room, Esther was seated on the sofa, booting up her laptop.

"I thought I'd start a spreadsheet," she said.

He rolled his eyes.

"What? I thought it would keep us organized."

"You're right. It's a good idea."

She set the computer on the coffee table and picked up a pile of printouts. "Okay. How do we do this?"

"First, we sort them into chronological order. Then you start with the oldest. I'll start with the newest. We each do four. We highlight the vital statistics: name, age, race, occupation, and marital status if it's listed.

We're looking for similarities. Ames had these clippings because they have something in common. We'll look for as many as we can find. Don't get distracted by anything more specific. That comes next."

"You don't think Ames is…" she let the question drift.

From the glassy look in her eyes, he could see she was uncomfortable, her thoughts circling to tag Ames as a serial killer—the clippings, trophies, and Abby Sue Bellman.

"For now, we'll just log the information. Concentrate on the task. Don't worry about the story, reason, or doer."

"Got it." She started to sort the printouts by date. "You want the articles about Emily Weir in this run-through?"

"Let's keep them separate for now."

They concentrated on their work. The only noise in the apartment was the squeak of highlighter marking paper. When Esther finished her first article, she put it down and started a pot of coffee. While it dripped, she picked up the second.

Despite his instructions, Rory read the *Grand Island Independent* account of Adriana Holmes in its entirety before picking up the highlighter.

Esther brought him a steaming mug before he finished. She hesitated, pausing beside his chair. He looked up. "Thanks. Can we mark the rest before we discuss them?"

"Of course," she said and picked up her third, *Amarillo Globe-News*, December 31, 2002, and started to read.

After working through her pile, Esther took time to

feed Commander, clean up the dishes in the sink, and make a pitcher of iced tea before Rory laid down his final printout.

"Okay. I'm finished," he said. "Fire up your spreadsheet."

"Do you want a sandwich before we start? I can throw a slab of baloney between two slices of bread."

"I'd rather see this come together." She made a stern, not-before-you-eat face, and he added, "But yeah, let me stretch my legs first."

While Rory hobbled around to get his blood flowing, Esther threw some cookies on a plate and brought them to the coffee table, along with tall glasses of iced tea. She put the laptop on the coffee table, where she could type without holding it on her lap.

He used the scooter to get next to the coffee table so he could see the laptop's screen. Sitting sidesaddle on the knee pad, he said, "Let's start with the oldest first." He picked up Esther's printouts, verified he had all eight articles, and they were in the right order, and then started to call out the information.

"January 2, 2000, Madelena Camino, Hispanic, twenty-eight, San Angelo, Texas, occupation unknown, marital status unknown."

"Hold up. Your detective brain is working faster than my bookkeeper fingers. Let me set up the categories. Then I'll ask you for the information bite and populate the cell. We should make a pivot table."

It was all gobbledygook computer-speak to him but he waited while she set up the page.

"Ready," she said a moment later. "That's date, name, race, age, location, occupation, marital status. Go. First date."

"The newspaper article is dated January 2, but it says the body was found the day before. We're going with the date of death. Put this down, January 1, 2000." He watched her type it.

"Name?"

It was painfully slow, but finally, they had the oldest article entered. It took another thirty minutes to fill in the remaining seven.

"I need to look at it on paper," Rory said. I've got this thing about holding it in my hand."

"Can do." Esther made a few swift movements on the keyboard, and the printer came to life in the other room. She went into the war room to retrieve the printed spreadsheet, handing it to Rory when she returned.

After scrutinizing the page, he said, "No particular race, age, or season." He rubbed his head. "No two in the same city. Let's move on to round two."

Taking the articles back and removing the oldest four, Esther handed the others to him. She looked ready.

"Now we log where they were discovered," he said, "by whom, and cause of death."

Esther started through the write-up on Madelena Camino. Rory studied the spreadsheet printout. Sighed. "We need to know more, like if the cases are still open and the backgrounds on these victims. There are a lotta blank squares under occupation and marital status."

"I can do a Google search for information and check social media."

"These cases go back a dozen years."

"Nothing ever leaves cyberspace."

"All right, you try to fill in the blanks. I'll mark for

210

round two."

Commander stretched out across the top of the sofa and went to sleep.

It took Esther twenty minutes to verify they had eight unsolved murder cases. Then they worked for another hour, mostly in silence. Twice she got a text and stopped to read and answer it. Rory didn't ask. He was deep into tabulating a single profile from the victims. He was certain the murders were connected.

Finally, he had as much information as he could glean from the newspaper accounts. "Can you take a break and fill in the little boxes?" He flexed both index fingers to indicate his typing prowess, or lack thereof.

"They're called cells, Rory. And two fingers can type just as easily as ten."

"There's the problem. I have eight fingers and two thumbs." She gave him a get-real look, and he said, "Whatever. I want to see them all side by side, and I don't want to wait to see what pops."

Esther called up the spreadsheet. "What are the new column headings."

"Found, By, and How. Will that work?"

"You're the one who needs to understand what the entry means. We'll start with those." She typed in the headings and then signaled she was ready.

Rory cleared his throat, picked up the oldest account, and said, "Madelena Camino, trash bin, neighbor, homicide undetermined."

Esther filled in the cells as Rory dictated. When he finished, she populated the cells with the information she'd found using the search engines. She saved the file and printed a copy for Rory. Then she went back to hunting for more details.

The oldest case was from 2000; the newest from 2013. Four murders took place in Texas, one in Oklahoma, one in Kansas, two in Nebraska. That is, if you didn't count Emily Weir, the River Girl, or Abby Sue Bellman.

"I have an atlas somewhere," Rory said. "I think it's in the book pile by the bookcase over there." He pointed at the wall beside the large window, where a six-foot bookcase stood. The shelves were overflowing, and the excess books lay in a tall stack along the side. "Would you mind grabbing it? Try the stack first."

Esther complied. After going through the stack, she found what she was after on the top shelf of the bookcase, between a dictionary and a thesaurus.

Rory turned to the front where the atlas contained a two-page map of the contiguous United States. It was titled "Interstate Drive Time & Distance." Lines connected the cities, with the miles between them printed in red and the average travel time in bold black. None of the cities he needed were shown.

He found all eight cities on the "Time Zones" page. He used a thick marker to circle each, studied the page a minute, and then tore it from the book. "Take a look at this. I guess you can tell the same thing from your spreadsheet, but this draws a picture for me."

Esther studied the locations of the circles. In each, Rory had entered a number. The number one was written in the circle farthest south, and then the sequence of numbered circles snaked their way northward, up the middle of the Central Time Zone, and headed toward Manitoba, Canada. She verified that the spreadsheet contained the same information, four states in the central region of the US. On its own, the map looked more sinister than the spreadsheet. Rory's marks laid out a path of death. It made the cases look premeditated and their route northward suggested escalation, where nothing else really suggested that.

"I'm still collecting occupations," said Esther, but I've noticed all the dates coincide with holidays."

Rory hadn't noticed. "US, religious…"

"New Year's Day, Fourth of July, Halloween. Oh, wait. Here's one that's not a holiday of any sort. False assumption."

"Can you find out what day of the week?"

"Sure. Two seconds." She typed, transferred the information to the spreadsheet, typed again. "A variety of days. No Wednesdays, Thursdays, or Saturdays. Do you think it means something?"

"Not yet. Patterns are important parts of discovery. I just thought…" But he didn't finish the thought. The red bulb above the tapestry began to flash, and the rumble of the lift came from the floor below.

He checked his watch: six fifteen. It had to be Thacker returning. "Good. An update and another pair of hands."

The young officer stepped into the living room. "Salutations."

"Hello, Thacker." Esther shooed Commander off the coffee table where he was trying to climb onto her laptop.

Rory used the arms of the recliner to push to his feet. He stood lopsided, his right foot two inches higher than his left, thanks to the walking cast. "Has Jerry Ames turned up?"

"I am getting ten-minute updates from Axel who is currently parked in the Beaver's Best Western parking lot, keeping an eye peeled. Ames hasn't returned to his room. The APB hasn't netted any results, and Lloyd sent Jim Zielinski out there with a warrant in case Ames does show up."

"I thought I asked you not to call Axel."

"He has a mind of his own. Showed up with night goggles, two dozen donuts, and a thermos."

Esther tittered. "He'll be vigilant."

Rory handed his copy of the spreadsheet to the young officer. "Take a look at this."

After a quick glance, Thacker's jaw went slack. He jerked his head up. "You got all this from the clippings?"

"Some, but Esther has been working her magic with the Internet. The sooner we can see what we're looking at, the sooner we'll know if it's important." Esther rolled her eyes. Well, she knew what he meant. "Change into something comfortable and give us a hand?"

As Thacker disappeared down the hall, Rory went back to speculating. "We need a murder board."

"A what?" she asked.

"A murder board. It's a board where you can place scraps of information pertaining to the case yet seemingly unrelated. It helps to see the whole picture. Sort of like the map does."

"Okay. I'm game. Where do we get one?"

"We had a whiteboard in the recovery center when we were looking for your mother. I suppose the church would let us borrow it. But truthfully, any office supply store." He checked the time again. "Too late to pick one up tonight."

"I'll call Pastor Mark. Thacker can run over and

pick it up with his truck. The church will never miss it. They don't even run Sunday school classes during the summer."

"We'll need sticky notes, too," Rory said.

Together they thought of a dozen supplies they needed, and the arrangements were made.

When Thacker returned with the board, Esther had to help him carry it upstairs. It wasn't heavy, but it was awkwardly large. They set it down in the kitchen end of the great room. Esther printed out photographs of the victims, and Rory stuck them up on the murder board, along with the "Time Zone" page from the atlas.

Thacker took over the computer search for missing bits of information. Esther wrote the sticky notes. By ten o'clock, they had all the facts they knew up on the board. Sitting side by side on the sofa, the three stared at it.

"Should it speak to us, boss?" asked Thacker.

Rory rubbed his head. "It stimulates the gray cells."

"I'm really sorry, guys, but it's past my bedtime." Esther stretched. "Maybe my gray cells can be stimulated tomorrow."

"You're right. We should look at it with fresh eyes. Do you want Thacker to see you home?"

"This is Winterset. I'll be fine. But if you're worried, I'll let you know when I get there."

He grinned. "I'll call Axel and tell him there's a change in surveillance targets."

"Don't you dare." She smiled good-heartedly. "I'll call to let you know I'm home."

Rory saw her to the kitchen door and watched her descend to the street. When her car turned down First

Street, he pulled the door closed and threw the deadbolt.

"I'm going to call it a night, Thacker. Will you call Axel and relieve him of duty?"

Thacker laughed. "Will do. Mind if I study the murder board for a while?"

"Suit yourself."

Rory straightened up the mess they'd made assembling the board. After Esther called, he turned in.

His mind was running full tilt. He was sure Emily Weir and the River Girl belonged on the board. The one thing he had noticed was the dates. Six murder dumps, one a year until the apprehension of Tobias Snearl. Then a five-year gap before the next. And three years until the last. Snearl was behind bars, with no chance of parole. If he was a serial killer, it had taken him five years to set up girl number seven? Or was Emily Weir number seven, shifting victims seven and eight up a digit? Nine victims plus the River Girl for a grand total of ten.

Well after he pulled the sheet up, he could see a light shining under the bedroom door; Thacker was still up. And why shouldn't he keep late hours? He was a good thirty years younger than Rory. He didn't need beauty sleep. Rory figured he'd let his subconscious connect the dots. He'd get up early and make sense of the notes.

Sometime later, he heard a scratch at the bedroom door. A quick look at the clock confirmed he'd nodded off and it was after one in the morning. The lights in the living room were out. Before Thacker moved in, Rory had kept the bedroom door open. He liked having the cat snuggle up at his feet.

He slipped out of bed, cracked the door open, and limped back. He didn't hear Commander come in, but he felt the bounce when the cat leaped onto the bed. His brain went through another cycle of connecting the murder dots. That "like" murders had started in 2000 and ended in 2013 complicated things. He'd put Snearl in prison in 2009.

Why wasn't the 2006 killing of Emily Weir part of the collection?

Chapter Thirty

Rory felt his ankle clench then unclench inside its plaster encasement. It was late, and he needed sleep. But how did one get comfortable with an anchor strapped to one's leg? His mind whirled through the details on the murder board, filled with possibilities thanks to Thacker's energy, Esther's skills, and Axel's daft dedication. There was great comfort in being part of their unorthodox team. He snorted in satisfaction, took a pain med, and relaxed into oblivion.

He opened his eyes and found the webbed creature next to his head. A cape covered its head and shoulders, and its eyes flashed like exploding coals. From beneath the fabric folds, a feathered arm raised a twelve-inch hypodermic needle. The vial glistened in the moonlight.

Rory raised his arms to swat it away, but they didn't respond. He tried to rise. Fear and the weight of a hundred sandbags held him in place. Rancid breath brushed his cheek, and a tremble ran down the length of his body. He double-blinked, opened his mouth to scream.

Nothing came out. Where were his feet? He couldn't feel his feet! Gawd, what would he do without his feet! He couldn't work without them. Didn't want to live without them.

Rory woke, drenched in sweat and shame.

His ankle throbbed. He drew a calming breath in

the quiet room. The moon shone through a break in the curtain, and he felt the weight of Commander at his feet—he still had both. Only a dream. The murders, the surgery, the damn pain medicine. He needed to clear his mind. He lay listening to the night, his blood still rushing, and concentrated on slowing his heart down.

Commander growled, a low, throaty, primitive sound. The cat didn't move. Neither did Rory. Then Commander shot off the bed and out of the room.

He was now on full alert. Something had woken him, and he didn't think it was the dream. He waited for the cat to return. It didn't. He couldn't hesitate longer, not if there was something—or someone—in the outer room.

Silently he slipped out of bed and stepped down, cursing his ankle when it hit the floor. He felt the pain up to his hip—mind over matter. Drawing a deep breath, he soundlessly inched his way into the living room end of the great room, taking care to place his cast gently, avoiding the knock it made when planted solidly on the wooden floor. The moon went behind a cloud, and the room grew murky. The message light on the answering machine pulsed. He heard the tick of the clock above the stove and the hum of the refrigerator. He saw shapes and shadows, and they were all too familiar. The murder board blocked his view of the sofa and the tapestry behind.

He felt his way along the wall until the space beyond the whiteboard was visible. He stood for a long time by the sofa, waiting for the tapestry to move. When he was satisfied nothing was behind the rug, he crept to the new hallway and stopped to listen in the doorway. There was something: a muffled noise down the passage, a faint rattle. Commander's claws frantically scratched on wood.

The hallway was windowless. Rory looked into the pitch-black void and felt his knees shake. He was in no shape for this, a one-legged man in a bullfight. He assessed the situation. Three doors off the passage. The doors to Thacker's room and, directly across from it, the war room should be closed. At the end of the hall, the third door led to the two sealed-off offices, the steel-curtained staircase, and the condemned fire escape.

He'd never counted off the steps to reach the third door. He tried to visualize it in his mind. An image of the distance wasn't there. It was too new. He longed for a weapon. Why hadn't he picked up something along the way? He wished he'd brought his gun and radio; both were locked in the safe, along with his competition tomahawk. The cell phone lay on the dresser in the bedroom, next to his keys. He couldn't open the war room or the steel curtain blocking the staircase without them. He remained in the doorway, undecided on the best course of action, feeling old and defeated.

Commander screeched. There was a loud thud. Rory rushed down the hall, stomping his walking cast on the hardwood floor as hard as he could with every other step. He grabbed where he thought the knob would be, grasped it, twisted it, and threw the door open. Commander shot out. Rory stomped in as adrenaline pumped through his veins. The door slammed behind him.

Now it was truly dark—and dank. He froze. If he stepped away from the door, he would lose his sense of direction. There shouldn't be anything in this area; the offices were empty, the staircase closed off, and the fire escape sealed. He sensed someone's presence. Contemplating what he would do if he felt a feathered hand reach for him, he locked the knee above his good ankle, shifted his weight, and waited in the silence.

He prayed for night vision. None came.

He felt the movement before he heard it; the stale air stirred, a whoosh. He raised a forearm and connected with the blow. It knocked him against the door. He balanced on his left foot and swung his right foot up and out with as much force as he could muster, pushing against the door for leverage. The cast found its mark. Rory crashed to the floor, landing on his tailbone. The assailant let out a cry of anguish, scrambled up, and took off. Rory heard him running with a lopsided gait. A door slammed, then silence.

Rory sat in the dark, inventorying his injuries. He wasn't hurt, not more than he'd been before, but he didn't understand what had just happened. The silence was deafening. Finally, he struggled up and went back into the apartment.

Throwing on the lights, he hustled to the bedroom and got the phone and his gun. Then he checked for missing items. He unlocked the war room and confirmed it was just as they'd left it. Knocking on Thacker's door, he called out, "Hey, Thacker, wake up." The young officer didn't answer. He opened the door. "Sorry to barge in, but I—"

Thacker lay on the bed, his neck twisted at an odd angle as if he were double-jointed and asleep with his chin pointed at the ceiling. Rory rushed to his side. He shook Thacker's arm, felt for a pulse, found one. It was faint. "Wake up."

He tapped the young man's face. Nothing. Rory grabbed the department-issue phone from the nightstand, jabbed in 911, summoned the calvary, and then called the station.

****

Five minutes later, they loaded Thacker into the ambulance. He hadn't regained consciousness, and Rory didn't want them playing Russian roulette with his friend. "Have the hospital check for chloral hydrate right away," he demanded. "Call me as soon as there's any word."

Commander came out of the bedroom and sat on the arm of Rory's chair. There had been an intruder. He recounted the evening to Jack Morris, a seasoned WPD officer, who was also Thacker's friend. He didn't mention the webbed creature, and he left out the part about fear. A crew dusted for prints, and an officer took pictures. They were pretty sure the intruder had gone down the fire escape. They hadn't determined how he'd entered. Morris asked if anything was missing.

Before they'd arrived and the rookie had been whisked off, Rory had discovered that the eight pictures printed for the murder board were gone. He didn't mention this to Morris. Esther called them coincidence incidents. Tonight's incident wasn't an accident.

It was deliberate.

Rory got the message—loud and clear.

Chapter Thirty-One

It was a long night for Rory. The boys finally left at four in the morning. The hospital called to say Thacker was stabilized, adding it was a good thing Rory had told them about the chloral hydrate, or he wouldn't have been so lucky. They planned to keep him for a day to make sure. Rory thanked them, relieved.

He sat in the recliner and studied the murder board. Crazy how someone would break in to steal pictures that anyone could get off of the Internet. Theft was not the motive. Diversion? Impeding his efforts? Why would anyone break into the home of a police officer? He had weapons. He knew how to use them.

Between Esther and him, they'd made a good start at laying out the eight victims and possibly tying them to a single serial killer. Did the killer feel threatened? Was the intruder the killer? Rory went back to the eight victims. He needed their complete autopsy reports if he hoped to get anywhere close to seeing a pattern. And he wanted to know how Emily Weir fit on their spreadsheet. The thought brought him to Tobias Snearl and the coming meeting Monday. Was it possible he could be responsible for any or all of these murders? Rory knew there were ways for inmates to remain active from behind bars. He had to prepare before he went out to the maximum-security prison.

At six thirty, Jim Zielinski called. Rory grabbed the

phone. "Detective Naysmith."

"I thought you'd want to know. Jerry Ames just showed up at the Best Western."

Rory could hear the highway traffic over the connection. He noted the time. Where had Ames been for eighteen hours? "So, you have him in custody."

"That's the thing. Officer Lloyd says we've voided the warrant."

"What! Not serving the warrant?"

"That's correct. We're not picking Ames up. Some snafu. I go off shift at seven, and WPD isn't sending out a replacement. There'll be no one on surveillance. Thought you should know."

This was ridiculous! "Do I need to talk to Lloyd about the warrant? Or do I have to pick Ames up myself?"

"Lloyd will be at the station at seven, or you can get him on the horn. I heard about Thacker. Any word?"

"He's going to be fine. I'll tell him you asked."

Rory was mad. What did they think they were doing? It might be circumstantial, but Ames had no business walking around free. Maybe if he had been more insistent yesterday when they'd found the body, Thacker wouldn't be in the hospital this morning. He wasn't calling Lloyd; he'd do a face-to-face, see what the department was thinking. Snafu indeed!

Grooming was a challenge. Rory managed to wrap the cast in a plastic garbage bag and drag himself in and out of the shower. Short pants worked, but he wasn't a Bermuda shorts type of guy. Managing to find an old pair of relaxed-fit jeans, he slit the right leg to accommodate the boot-covered cast.

He threw some eggs and bacon together for breakfast, called the hospital to check on Thacker, and then took the elevator down. He crossed to the Winterset Police Department using the knee scooter and the street and let himself in the back door. He arrived before Lloyd, but not before Sunny.

"Detective Rory Naysmith," she cooed, her voice coming through the vestibule window. "I see you there, trying to sneak in through the back door on your tricycle."

The CCTV was his worst enemy. Sunny must have seen him arrive on the stupid camera mounted in the lobby. Hell, for all he knew, she'd watched him pedal across the parking lot.

"Good morning, Sunny. Lloyd here?" He didn't go into the dispatch office. He was in no mood to face the taunts of Sergeant Powell. Even seeing him didn't appeal to him this morning.

"I expect Lloyd shortly. He called in a ten-forty-five, so he's probably chowing down at the Golden Leaf. They'd be having—"

"Thanks."

Rory parked the scooter by his office door and limped over to unlock it. The cast felt like it weighed three hundred pounds. He tried to ignore it. Instead, he hit the door on the way in and stumbled against the trash can while getting to his chair. His tailbone ached where he'd landed on it earlier. All he needed was another broken bone. He forgot to hang his hat over the camera, but he wasn't about to get up to do it now. Let Sunny watch!

What did he have? A nice lady was lying on a slab in the morgue. A linebacker-sized suspect was on the loose. Marilyn Beauregard's cousin-in-law, who may or may not have known her from childhood, was unaccounted for at the moment. There was a lot of agreement that Cousin Henry had left the party with Abby Sue on Saturday. Henry Beauregard seemed harmless, yet Jesse and Esther were wary of the old codger. Where was that cousin now? How long until they processed the fingerprints on the Corvette? For that matter, how long before they processed the prints from his apartment?

He called Sunny on the intercom. "Sunny, tell Lloyd I'd like to see him when he gets in."

"Ten-four, kemosabe. But he might not be in right away. From what I hear, and you know I hear it all, he had a late night chasing down criminals."

"Just give him the message, Sunny."

Rory booted up the computer. The database he was interested in tapping into was only available on the station's secure line. He wished he knew more about the mystery of electronic data flow, but now wasn't the time. All he knew was that he couldn't link to the NCIC files and the Nebraska criminal database and cross-reference them from anyplace other than the terminal in his office. The screen prompted for his password. He entered it and watched as the connection painfully, slowly verified his credentials and let him in. He took the piece of paper out of his pocket, unfolded it, and smoothed it out on the desk. He typed in Adriana Holmes with two fingers and then waited while the computer gods woke up and fetched the information he'd requested.

At seven thirty, Jim Zielinski called again. "Zielinski, I thought you went off duty at seven?"

"I think you ought to know that Ames just pulled out of the Best Western parking lot."

"Was he carrying his bags?"

"An attaché case and a duffel."

"So, you don't think he's running?"

"Doesn't look like it, not unless he's leaving everything else behind. There's one more thing. Axel Barrow cleared the lot right behind him.

Damn Axel. What was he doing? "Thanks, Jim." Rory disconnected.

He scrolled through the contacts on his phone, found the hippie's number, and tapped it. Axel picked up on the fifth ring.

"Constable!" Rory could barely hear Axel over the country music playing in the background.

"What are you doing? I thought Thacker sent you home last night?"

"A private citizen can do what he wants. For the record, I watched Miss Esther's house until she got home. Then I watched until her lights went out. I figured she was good for the night, so I came back on out to the Best Western. This guy, Ames, he's slimy suspicious. Too slippery to leave on his own. And bingo! I won the enchilada. He comes in at the crack of dawn and leaves soon after. I'm on his tail."

"Where are the two of you headed?"

"Funny thing. It looks like we're on our way back into town." Rory could hear the window roll down and the air rush into the cab of the pickup. "I'll keep ya posted." Axel was gone.

Crap! Rory still had the phone in his hand. He called Esther and didn't even hear the phone ring before she answered.

"Are you okay? Jesse just told me about Thacker. Are you all right?"

"I'm at the station, collecting information. Look, the pictures of the victims got filched. How much trouble is it to get them again?"

"I still have them; they just need to be reprinted. Tell me what happened. Were you hurt?" He heard panic in her voice. "What do you want me to do?"

"I'm fine. But I'm in a difficult position since Thacker is at the hospital and Axel is tailing a suspect. I doubt the chief will assign another set of feet to assist the detective department."

"You want my feet?"

"I'd look pretty funny chasing down a criminal on a tricycle knee scooter."

"Oh, Rory, if I weren't so concerned, I'd laugh. How can you joke at a time like this?"

"I'd appreciate it if you'd come by the station. I need to go somewhere, and I can't work a gas pedal." The phone made the noise signaling an incoming call. "Got to go. There's a call coming in."

He pushed the blinking icon. "Naysmith."

At the other end, Willy Nelson sang "On the Road Again". "Constable. Heads up! We're either heading for Hilly's or the police station."

The phone went dead.

****

The man stood in the door frame of Rory's WPD office. "Naysmith?" he said.

Chancing a glance at the camera, Rory stood.

The visitor strutted into the room and took the visitor's chair. "We need to talk. It might take a minute or two, but sooner or later, the boys are going to match

228

me up to your prints."

Rory sat back down, his eyes trained on the man. "Mr. Ames?"

"I thought I'd save you the trouble of heading off in the wrong direction."

Axel appeared in the doorway and stepped into the room. Rory raised his chin to acknowledge his presence. Ames didn't turn to see who had joined them; instead, he reached for his breast pocket.

Wait a minute! Rory jerked upright, started to stand. Was Ames going for a gun right there in the station? Axel jumped to attention, but then he relaxed as the visitor withdrew a wallet.

"Take a look at this." Ames flipped it open and tossed it onto Rory's desk. Then he sat back in the chair, resting his forearms on the arms and crossing his legs, ankle on knee. "I'm on the Job."

Axel shifted, looming toward the big man. Rory fingered the shield, lowered his gaze, and asked, "Undercover?"

"Special assignment. Serial Crimes Division out of Dallas."

Rory took in the man's measure: noncommittal expression, relaxed posture, platter-sized hands. He knew this kind: adrenaline junkie. Undercover guys, he'd learned in Omaha, were extroverts, good liars, and didn't need energy drinks to get their blood pumping. Worse, they were territorial and cocky.

"I can't keep you out of it," Ames said, "but I don't want you fooling around and getting in the way."

Poking at the wallet, Rory frowned. "Jerome Ash. Cute. Jerome—Jerry. Ames—Ash. And what exactly are you investigating?"

Ames-Ash gave Rory a cocky smirk. "You've got the newspaper clippings." Rory raised a brow. "You'll need the eight dossiers I put together. We can save time if we work together."

Collaborate? That was a first. Rory could definitely use help. He'd just drafted Esther, a civilian bookkeeper, to be his chauffeur. His number one aide was out of commission, and Axel, well, Axel was Axel. Rory's gaze fell on the civilian in battered fatigues leaning against the door jamb. With the handgun threaded through his belt, crossed arms, and drooping mustache, he was the spitting image of Yosemite Sam and sang an equally looney tune.

"Together? How would that work?" Rory knew Ash would take the lead and how dangerous his decisions would be. Although they wouldn't be willing to admit it, undercover agents tended to think they were bulletproof. Rory had reached the age where he was comfortable in his skin. He liked life in Winterset. He enjoyed his part in it, stable and predictable. While the detective still wanted a challenge, he didn't feel an urgency to prove anything. And he sure wasn't bulletproof.

"You know I've got this casket plastered on my foot?"

"Your town—your investigation. You work the body found in the rocks and the Bellman woman. I'll concentrate on the others."

"You know about Abby Sue Bellman?"

"Yup."

"Sounds fair. Where are the dossiers?"

"Here in my attaché case." Ash picked up the briefcase and opened it on his lap. Axel stepped forward to stand over his shoulder. "A fresh pair of eyes never hurt anyone," the undercover said. "I'd like to see your murder board." He slid a plump folder across the desk.

Rory wondered where Ash's knowledge of the board came from. Then he decided that any decent undercover agent lost for eighteen hours could have covered a lot of ground. If he'd been lurking outside Hilly's, would he have seen the intruder? He was confident Ash wasn't the assailant; he'd never have run away.

"You're right, and you might have the information I'm after and save me from using my Neanderthal computer skills on these databases. Axel, show this gentleman how to get over to the apartment."

Rory stood, tucking the folder under his arm.

Ash punched the button to close his attaché case, stood, and held out a palm to Axel.

Muttering under his breath, Axel pulled the undercover cop's shield from his jeans pocket and dropped it into the outstretched hand.

The three men left together, with Rory leading the way on the tri-wheeled scooter. He paused long enough to watch Axel and Ash shoulder each other through the doorway.

Geez!

Chapter Thirty-Two

Ash didn't seem surprised by the setup in Hillard's Department Store. Axel performed the show-and-tell of the two lower floors while Rory went up in the lift.

As soon as Rory was alone, he called the station. "Sunny, urgent police business. Patch me over to Powell."

He heard her chair squeak, and he pictured her leaning back to plant an evil eye on the unsuspecting day sergeant. She must have placed the phone against her chest, because her voice was muffled. Moments later, Powell's growl came in loud and clear. "What do ya need?"

"I need a check run on an undercover operative out of the Dallas PD. I don't have the shield number handy. I had a look. Looked legit. I'm with him now."

"Want to hold, or should I have my people get with your people?"

"Cell phone. I need it yesterday." Powell wasn't going to give him grief. Not today. "And Sergeant, it's life or death. Do you understand? Description and status."

The pause was long enough for Rory to lose heart. Then Powell replied, "You got it, buddy."

The line disconnected.

Ash and Axel entered from the second-story staircase and came down the newly opened hallway.

"Nice setup you've got back there," said Ash. "Do the local boys suspect last night's intruder used the stairs?"

"Not that they've told me. No speculation on the method of entry. Definite use of the fire escape leaving. Can you shed any light on it?"

"While it's true I was close by, I didn't see anyone enter the building last night." Ash stepped to the board. "I like the map."

"So, Dallas," said Rory, taking a seat in the recliner, "you worked the investigation on Camino in 2000?"

"New Year's Day. She was found in a trash dumpster behind the Morning Star Motel. Her body had been doused with gasoline and set on fire, and a maid discovered the body when she went to empty the trash bins. She'd been dead for twenty-four hours, but the fire wasn't her cause of death, just the means of disposal. She'd been missing for two weeks. No one noticed. But we worked that out by interviewing witnesses in the apartment complex where she lived, various store clerks, and people who had worked with her. You know the drill."

"Yup, I've worked homicides."

Ash didn't bat an eye. "Camino taught kindergarten at the public school, lived alone. It was Christmas break, and classes were out. The last person to see her was a fellow teacher at the end of class on December fifteenth. We didn't find any prints. Forensics didn't find any DNA trace from anyone other than Camino. Bruises evident on her wrists and throat. Public school teachers in Texas must submit to a background check, and we identified her through a fingerprint match run on the FBI database, IAFIS. We didn't identify the cause of death."

"I have my suspicions," Rory said.

"This first one looked like a crime of passion. Camino had a steady boyfriend and was hoping to get engaged over the holidays. Only, they had a falling out, and the boyfriend left town. I worked that angle for a while until his alibi proved he was a thousand miles away from anywhere we could place her. The fellow teacher was also a dead end; he'd taken his mother to the Bahamas for a ten-day vacation. It didn't take long until all the leads went cold."

Rory's phone rang. He grabbed it, listened, nodded, and then said, "Thanks. I appreciate the information." Ash had checked out.

As soon as Rory put the phone down, it rang again. This time, it was Esther.

"Hey," he said, unable to keep a smile from his voice. "We have a new development. I may not need your feet after all. Axel is with me in the apartment, and there's someone...something I'd like you to see. Can you join us?" He disconnected. To Ash, he said, "Esther Mullins, she's helping with the murder board."

"I'm familiar with the bookkeeper."

There was nothing to read in Ash's expression. Rory pressed his lips together, scratched his forehead, and frowned at the cast. He should have realized Ash's undercover activities would include Esther. Knowing they included investigation, trailing, and surveillance bothered him. Well, that couldn't be altered. He waved Axel toward the door, indicating he should let Esther in when she arrived.

Ash picked up his story. "In 2000, we thought we had a single crime and didn't suspect a serial crime until Anna Vogel, a thirty-three-year-old domestic worker, was found in Lubbock by a man mowing the grass. That was March 2002. This one was wrapped in a blanket and left behind a restroom in the city park—bruises on her wrists and throat and still no apparent cause of death. The MO was different enough for the locals to miss the similarities. It was some time before it filtered back to me."

"How much t—"

A knock at the door made Rory swallow his question. Esther came in like a whirlwind, her arms full of Tupperware containers. She stopped short when she spied them seated in the living area.

Rory made the introduction from the recliner. "Esther, this is Jerome Ash. He's on a special assignment from the Serial Crimes Division out of Dallas. He's working undercover using the name Jerry Ames."

She dumped the containers on the kitchen table, stepped into the room cautiously, and threw a questioning look at Rory. He tipped his head and raised one shoulder in a noncommittal shrug. Her eyes settled on Ash. "Mister Ash. Or should I call you Agent Ash, Officer Ash?"

"Jerry will do." He indicated the murder board. "I'm filling in the blanks."

"Oh." Esther took a seat on the sofa, sitting as far from Ash as possible, visibly struggling for composure, her voice uncertain. "Special assignment? You are on the trail of a serial killer?"

Rory knew what was going on behind her strained expression: her mind was rifling through the victims, adding them up, and arriving at Abby Sue. It was only natural to zero in on the one closest to home. There were going to be emotions. He needed the big picture. He needed emotional separation. He needed to ignore her alarm. Returning his attention to Ash, he asked, "How'd you link them up?"

"I started to put two and two together when I discovered Vogel hadn't been seen in public for over a week."

"And each one, all eight, with bruises, an unaccountable time before death, and an undetermined cause of death?"

Ash puffed out his chest. "Affirmative."

"How'd you miss Emily Weir?"

"Didn't miss her. I identified a path trajectory, and she wasn't on the path. The obvious conclusion was a copycat murder."

"I can add another one or two to your string." Rory crossed his arms. Three, if River Girl, Abby Sue Bellman, and Emily Weir all fit the pattern.

Ash gave him a stern look. "I'm here to prove it one way or the other."

Was that challenge or standard police no nonsense? What happened to 'we can prove this'? There was no time to be territorial.

"Then let's get the board up to date. Esther can reproduce the photos." When he looked at her, she had shrunk into the cushions.

With the four of them working the Internet and Ash's dossiers, the picture drew itself.

The trail of abduction and murder started in West Texas and coiled its way to Winterset, Nebraska.

Chapter Thirty-Three

The next morning, Thacker stood before the murder board and blew out an astonished breath. "Wow, boss. The undercover agent, Jeromy Ash, had all this information?" He moved from one pinned note to the next. "All the way back to December 2000… when I was in the second grade."

Rory was glad to have the young policeman back. "And yet, here we are."

"This sure makes River Girl look like she's part of a pattern. Serial murder, holy cow. I mean—" Thacker squared his shoulders. "—that is extraordinary. Will the FBI be part of the investigation and apprehension? Where is Agent Ash this morning? Is he pursuing new leads?"

The rookie's deep voice was low and urgent. Rory laughed. "You've only been gone twenty-four hours, son. I'll fill you in on all the developments. I don't know that there is new information in our cases. It's more like our one good lead morphed into something bigger. We had two bodies, the girl found at the river and Abby Sue Bellman. Now we know about a passel of killings." He eyed the board. "I'm convinced our situation goes beyond Bellman and the girl."

Thacker rubbed a hand down his unshaven chin and dropped his shoulders. Rory added, "There's work to do. Take a minute, wash the hospital stink off, and we'll draw up a plan to make sense of the situation."

"Affirmative. I could use a shower. Mom wanted me to come by the house, but she understood when I told her I had responsibilities."

He had no doubt Natalie Thacker had a problem dropping her boy off at the apartment. The sedative injection hadn't done any damage; nevertheless, the shock of her son's attack would bring the gravity of his profession to the surface. He hoped it didn't lead to complications.

"You gave me a scare. Your parents' reaction was probably stronger. Clean up. We'll talk."

The color drained from Thacker's face. "B... but..."

"Don't worry. Nothing will change in the next fifteen minutes. And I'm not sending you home."

Glancing around the room, the young officer let out a huge breath. "Five minutes, then," he said, his voice full of relish and anticipation, and then headed to his room.

Rory raised the recliner's footrest and stretched out, and Commander climbed onto his lap. With only the cat for company, Rory's thoughts turned to killers. Were his girls part of Ash's killing string? Several circumstances bothered him.

First, most serial murderers stayed within a defined geographic area, finding their prey within a comfort zone close to home, family, and job. Ash's eight killings were all over the place. If the cases were connected, the predator had moved beyond the original area and outside his comfort zone. It took years to gain that kind of confidence. Very few criminals crossed state borders. According to Ash's map, this one did and had been doing so for more than a dozen years.

Rory scratched his head and studied the path of dead bodies: Texas, Oklahoma, Kansas, Nebraska. The water pipes rattled. The apartment took on an aroma of shampoo and manly soap, mixed with the scent of summer on the breeze coming in through the open windows. Unless the killer was homeless or a fleeing transient, there was no reason to travel so far from home. A man with a job had to stay where his career put him unless he was a trucker.

Commander stretched, breaking into Rory's thoughts. He ran a palm down the tabby's golden length. "You're right; airplane pilots travel. Salespeople cover expanded territories. Even a race car driver moves between racetracks and speedways." Crap, he could think of a dozen professions requiring travel.

Then there was the problem of time and location. Serial killers studied their prey, stalking them over time and meticulously planning while remaining under the radar. This was hard to accomplish unless carried out in large cities where the activity went unnoticed. Winterset wasn't large enough to get lost in. Major cities, Dallas, Amarillo, Topeka, made sense.

Why move up from Texas, across two more states, and enter Nebraska? Once in Omaha, why move west and then double back to Omaha again? These were bizarre actions for a classic serial killer.

If it weren't for Powell's confirmation that Jeromy Ash was who he said he was, Rory would not have believed it. Shoot, he'd suspected Ames was Bellman's killer until he'd learned Officer Ash had better reasons for being in Winterset.

He heard the water go off as he thought about the

murders piling up in his quiet town. Last December, only days after taking the detective job, he'd handled a murder case. It was the first the town had seen in a decade. Now, six short months later, he had two more deaths plus the possibility they qualified as serial crimes. The statistics said less than one percent of all murders committed in the US fit that classification. You couldn't get two women more different than a socialite do-gooder and a runaway girl. If they fit the profile, why was Ash so happy to push them off on him?

Thacker came into the great room, dressed in fresh jeans and a T-shirt, rubbing his head dry with a towel. "Mom had some interesting information for us. She'd already heard about Mrs. Bellman and the stakeout at Beaver's Best Western."

"I'm not surprised. A full forty-eight hours have passed since we found Bellman's body. Nothing takes more than a minute to make its way down the Winterset pipeline."

"This wasn't gossip." Thacker gave Rory a puzzled look. "Well, I don't think it was speculation. Mom doesn't... I've never known her to..."

"It's okay, son. Tell me what she said. I could use some insight from the Miss Marple brigade."

"She was quite firm that I stay the full twenty-four hours in the hospital." His face, fresh from the razor's scrape, turned unnaturally pink. "I suspect she intended to bribe me to stay put by giving me the information. Truthfully my blinding headache was the determining factor. Anyway, she told me Mrs. Bellman was lying low last week."

"Does it have to do with the Beauregards?" Rory rubbed his hands together. According to the Mullins sisters, no one had seen Bellman during the week leading up to her discovery in the Corvette's trunk. Marilyn Beauregard's account of Abby Sue's whereabouts consisted of numerous outings with her cousin Henry. When pushed, she admitted that she hadn't seen the woman, had no reason to doubt her cousin, and made a firm declaration that Cousin Henry would have no reason to lie.

"It had to do with Smyrola, Georgia, where the family had their plantation."

"I'm all ears."

"Abby Sue told Viola Moss, who told Sophia Becker..." His face grew redder. "I see what you mean."

"Just tell me."

"Mrs. Bellman remembered a cousin to the Beauregard family who went by the name of Dewey. Thought it was probably a nickname for something else. She didn't recall him fondly, nor did she remember him being close to Marilyn's husband, Garrison, who she did remember well. She had some disturbing stories which included that this man was known as a bully."

"She thinks Henry might be Dewey, short for something?"

Thacker raised one shoulder and let it drift down. "A bit of a bully, according to Mrs. Bellman. The way she told it, he was a charming liar who felt no qualms about manipulating situations or people. While he clerked at the First National Bank, the bank president's daughter disappeared. Dewey and the daughter had been close. Two days later, they discovered she'd eloped with her college boyfriend. The ordeal threw a spotlight on the bank, exposed missing deposits, and called for a full audit. The bank president, arrested for embezzlement, denied any wrongdoing. Mrs. Bellman remembers widespread relief when Dewey slipped out of town."

"Was she afraid he was the same man and up to no good here in Winterset?"

"She wasn't sure Marilyn's Henry was the deceptive Smyrola Dewey. But yes, she was avoiding Henry while her sister, who still lives in Georgia, did some checking."

"Dewey Beauregard." Rory leaned back to think. Lightly tapping his fingertips together, he murmured, "Dewey... Andrew..." Tap, tap. "Dewitt, Dwight Beauregard." Tap, tap.

"No, boss. He wasn't a Beauregard—absolutely not a Beauregard."

Rory bolted upright. Commander flew across the room. Abby Sue Bellman had been killed by an impostor from Georgia? "Did we process the prints from Ash's car trunk?" Crap! He'd been distracted by the attack on Thacker and then Jeromy Ash's dossiers. Did the town know more about his case than he did?

The car would be in the impound lot, and the trace evidence waiting at the station. He'd neglected to follow up on his one undeniable case of hometown murder. Ignoring Esther's suspicion that Cousin Henry was more than an irritation, he'd dismissed the Southern gentleman as an annoyance. He'd even gotten a kick out of the competition going on among the townspeople hoping to be the first to receive their DNA results.

Was it possible that Henry was the dishonorable

Dewey? What had Esther called him? Huckster, flimflam man, con-artist, along with spicier descriptions. It was Rory's job to root out the truth. His stomach clenched. He hadn't run the background check he'd promised. There was no excuse for his negligence—broken ankle, wrenched knee, dead body, vicious attack, surgery, coincidence incidents—but who was counting? What he saw plainly was the opportunity for deception, kidnapping, and murder.

"Thacker, bring the car around. If it hasn't been done, it's time we collect Henry Beauregard's DNA and fingerprints."

****

By the time Thacker returned with a city car, but before they headed out, Cecil Rudd phoned. "Naysmith," he said, his words clipped with urgency, "your meeting for Monday. There's a problem."

"Okay." Rory mouthed, *Cecil Rudd* at Thacker, who bobbed his head in understanding.

Rudd cleared his throat on the other end of the connection and then said, "Snearl won't add you to his visitor's list."

"I don't need to be on a list. I'm law enforcement."

"Yeah. I pointed that out. He said he'd refuse to speak with you if you showed up. No surprise there."

Crap! Rory wanted to speak to the convicted felon. Ten years ago, there had been no hint of serial murder. Snearl was an arrogant piece of work, yet Emily Weir's abduction and death appeared an isolated incident. Back then, Rory's reaction had been relief coupled with satisfaction that the sadistic jerk was off the streets. And would be for the remainder of his life. Now Rory had questions.

"What about a look at the log of Snearl's visitors?" he asked. Across the room, the rookie's eyes widened.

"That could be arranged," replied Rudd. "Faxed, even. Only, it's practically the weekend, and it could take some time."

Swiftly shifting priorities, Rory asked, "What if I came there? Walked it through. Picked it up."

As Thacker's brows danced the samba, Rory added, "Snearl may have a change of heart by the time we get there."

"It would need to be quick. And for your information, he doesn't have a heart."

"We can be at the prison in an hour." He disconnected and clipped the phone to his hip.

"Let's saddle up."

Thacker snapped to attention. "So, the game is afoot?"

The detective grinned as he donned his fedora with a flick of his wrist. "Yes, Watson."

Rory used the drive time to ask Chief Mansfield for help collecting DNA from Henry Beauregard without getting a warrant from a judge. Mansfield remained firm, stating the intrusion was unnecessary. Finally, they agreed Officer Lloyd would make an impassioned request of the Southern gentleman. If that didn't work, Rory would file the appropriate paperwork when he got back. Thacker and Rory arrived at the prison ninety minutes later.

Cecil Rudd came down to meet them as soon as they signed in at reception. "Seems to be your lucky day, Naysmith. He's agreed to see you."

Warden Rudd stayed with them through the security procedures, pat search, metal detector, and extended discussion on Rory's cast and boot. A K-9 inspector was brought in—they endured his cold-nosed scrutiny. After all the security requirements were met, Rudd led them to an isolated office. It wasn't the general population visitation room. Rory wasn't certain it was soundproof, but he didn't much care.

The room had plain gray walls, four chairs bolted to a concrete floor, and a metal table. The door held the only window. They took seats facing the door. Rory stretched out his legs, trying to find comfort. Thacker folded his hands and placed them on the table.

Cecil Rudd said, "A guard will bring him over in chains. I don't intend to stay for the happy reunion. When you finish, have the guard radio me. Meanwhile, I'll prod the clerk for the visitors' register." He forced a smile. "I'll see that you get out."

Rory grimaced. The warden left, and the prisoner's arrival was announced by a metallic click. Thacker leaned forward as the door swung open.

A guard in gray led Snearl into the room, watched while he sat, and then snapped the prisoner's ankle chain to a restraining ring anchored to the floor. Snearl stared into Rory's eyes. They sat in silence until the guard left, and then the prisoner's glance drifted to Rory's foot, and he said, "I remember you as a bigger man."

The detective snorted. There was a gleam of haughtiness and coldness in Snearl's eyes. After ten years in prison, his skin had become pasty, and his hair, short and thick, was now receding at the temples. His black eyes, however, still danced like flaming coals. There was nothing relaxed about his strong features and hard muscles. No kindness, or ounce of compassion.

"Still five-eight, a hundred seventy pounds without the boat anchor. Big enough to put you in prison."

Snearl scoffed.

"They treating you well?"

The prisoner's eye's narrowed. "Three squares a day and a private room. Could be the Ritz." His gaze returned to the detective's face. "Why are you here?"

"There's evidence we missed before trial."

"Too late. Spend my days in meditation and performing acts of contrition. I've moved on."

"Let's talk about those moves."

Snearl yawned, drumming his fingers on his jump-suited thigh. "I read somewhere that you'd taken up ax throwing."

When Rory had solved the case last December, it had made the newspaper headlines around the state. The reporters had had some fun with his skill at using a cleaver to break the case open. It was conceivable that Snearl had read the copy. Rory didn't think it warranted a response.

He rubbed a hand over his balding head and said in his civil-service voice, the one he reserved for children, "You used drugs to subdue Emily Weir. Date-rape drugs that you administered intravenously."

"I didn't need help to interest a woman."

"But you needed straps to keep her."

Snearl rolled his eyes heavenward and then brought his focus back, glancing at Thacker.

"I'm here to help you," Rory said.

"Help me?" A shocked expression came over Snearl's face. "You can do that by leaving." He leaned forward, his gaze glinting with challenge. "You're here for something more. And I see you brought a pup."

Retorts blasted through Rory's mind, but he knew that if he unleashed them, he'd lose the opportunity to ask his questions. Instead, one side of his mouth lifted in a wry smile. "Bodyguard."

The killer continued, "Everyone needs a bulldog, blindly devoted, zealous, fierce. Best to get one without his own thoughts."

From the corner of his eye, Rory saw the rookie stiffen. Some pandering and name calling was allowed; they were getting somewhere.

Snearl smirked. "And the foot?"

"Earthly reminder."

Snearl sprawled in the chair with his legs spread wide in a statement of defiance.

"You fascinate me," the detective said. "I always wondered why a good-looking guy needed to abduct a woman in Nebraska. Weren't the girls in Texas interested in you?"

"Never been to Texas."

"How about Kansas?"

Snearl looked hard, arrogant, and unrepentant. "What is this, twenty questions?"

"Besides Emily Weir, did you have other pets?" Rory heard the chain slap against the restraining ring as Snearl bounced forward in the chair. "Friend? Confidant?" Rory added, "Bulldog." He didn't waver, keeping his voice under control and neutral. "How many others did you kill?"

Jerking his head, the inmate yelled over his shoulder, "Guard!"

"Did you boast about your exploits in the yard?" The victims' names tumbled from his lips. "Magdelena, Anna, Morgan, Ruth, Emily—"

"We're finished here," Snearl said through clenched teeth. Veins bulged at his temples.

"Or did you need help?" The prisoner flushed with anger and ignored the taunts. Rory pushed harder. "Couldn't do it yourself. Not alone. Not enough of a man."

"Guard!"

The guard wrestled Snearl out of the room. The prisoner's angry shouts drifted back as he was led down the hall.

Thacker stood by the doorway, watching. "You stirred him up, sir."

"That was my intention."

"He's an angry man, and even from behind bars, angry men can be dangerous."

"That would make two of us."

Chapter Thirty-Four

Warden Rudd came through with a copy of the visitors' log. Rory flipped through the document on the ride back to Winterset. The printout included visits taking place over the last dozen years; still, it was only a couple of pages long. Rudd had included Tobias Snearl's official visitation list. Only two names came up with any frequency: Demetrius Jones and Harmon Free. Rory knew Free to be a crime reporter. Demetrius Jones meant nothing to him.

"There's not much here," he said, thumbing the brim of his fedora as he slid the hat back on his head. "Free works the crime beat for the *Lincoln Journal Star*. According to this, he was a regular visitor the first couple of years."

"Writing a book, you think?"

"True crime," Rory scoffed. "Must not have worked out for him. No visits since..." He flipped through the pages again. "A dozen visits the first year, only one every year after that. The dates coincide with the anniversary of Snearl's incarceration. It might be follow-up pieces—citizens beware. He lowered the pages. "We can check it out when we get back to the station. Read a couple. See what he had to say."

"You can Google the *Star* articles and read them while I drive."

Rory gave Thacker a not-in-this-lifetime glare.

Researching with a cell phone might be second nature for a twenty-something kid, but Rory found it impossible to get his fingers to hit the right buttons—impossible to read the itsy-bitsy screen. Talk about the digital divide.

He pulled the newspaper out and found the page with the sudoku. He'd rather spend the ride time clearing his mind. "I'll wait until we can print them out." He folded the sheet, making it easy to work the puzzle within the confines of the car. Thacker set the cruise control.

They were on the last leg of the trip when Petey Moss called. Rory placed the phone in speaker mode and answered. "Keep it clean. I've got the kid with me."

Petey snickered. "Hey, Thacker. I'm glad I have you both. The test results are finished on the blood samples Officer Lloyd dropped off this morning. Therefore, I believe we're caught up in terms of professional favors."

Suppressing a smile, Rory did a cat-like stretch. "Good. We have a match."

"That would be a...no."

"You compared both?"

"Henry Beauregard and Jeromy Ash, according to the labels. Neither came close to matching the blood type collected from the Corvette trunk. Bellman was B-negative. Your two donors are both O-positive. We got *nada*."

Thacker reached up to adjust the rear-view mirror and tapped the brake. Rory bit his lip, thinking as the car began to slow. He shot a glance at the rookie and said, "What about the DNA?"

A warm chuckle preceded Petey's reply. "Even I can't run a DNA profile that quickly. Ash's DNA sequencing will be on file, since he is law enforcement, but Beauregard's would require some time."

"There is that ancestry site, Family Lost-N-Found. They'll have the DNA sequence on Beauregard."

Thacker stamped on the gas, swerved to zip off the freeway, and fishtailed down the exit ramp and onto the feeder road. He glanced at the side mirrors and hunched over the steering wheel.

"I'll call you back." Rory disconnected, braced his hand on the dashboard, and said, "Pit stop?"

"We're being followed."

The detective twisted for a look over his shoulder. Putting his booted foot down firmly, he gave a push to boost himself up for a look out the back window. His back arched against the pain. "Still there?" he croaked as he sucked in a deep breath.

"I think we lost him."

The detective finally managed a position that allowed him a clear view through the rear. "There's no one behind us."

Thacker relaxed. "At first, I thought it was just someone traveling along with us. It's the interstate. Then I noticed it sped up and slowed at the same rate I did. The other day, I almost stepped in front of a truck as I crossed the street going to the station. This one looked similar, black, fairly new, tinted window. Not so clean. I'd forgotten the incident. Seeing this one reminded me, and I started watching, wondering. That's how I noticed it kept a steady distance behind us. I didn't know him at the time, but Ames, I mean Ash, drives that model."

"As do thousands of others."

"I guess you're right. There are two million four hundred thousand registered vehicles in Nebraska."

It amazed Rory when Thacker spouted statistics off the top of his head. "It's still clear." He carefully settled back onto the seat. "Ash gets around, but I doubt he'd tail us to, or from, Lincoln. Or try to run you over. What reason would he have? Besides, this morning, he had a date with Lloyd and a hypodermic needle."

Rory spotted the sign announcing the freeway rest stop. "My stomach is rumbling. How about a bite to wipe the taste of hospital food from your memory?"

"Affirmative."

They drove in silence, turned into the parking lot, and parked near the entrance. Rory frowned when Thacker suggested he pull the scooter from the trunk.

"I'm working on stamina, son." The truth was, he didn't want the attention the scooter would draw. He felt stiff, sore, and about a hundred years old, but so far, he'd managed the day without the assistance of wheels.

The waitress led them to a back booth. Rory kept up with an effort.

After placing menus on the table, she said, "Shall we start with drinks?" They agreed on a coffee and an iced tea.

As soon as the waitress was out of earshot, Rory said, "We need to discuss our next move."

"I'm ready, boss."

Rory gave Thacker a one-eyed squint, and the rookie pinked.

After busying himself with the napkin roll, Rory placed the knife and spoon on the right side of the paper placemat, the fork on the left. "Let's talk about the

252

black truck you think had a tail on us."

"Well, it seemed like—"

"It might have been. Tell me why someone is following us?"

"We're detectives?" Thacker wrinkled his nose and added in a tentative voice, "One of us is a detective."

"Tell me why someone shot you up with sedatives. Attacked me the week before." The senior officer began to count the incidents on his fingers. "Put surveillance in my hospital room. Broke into Henry Beauregard's car. Accosted Jesse Wallace. Waylaid Petey Moss. Killed Abby Sue Bellman. Swiped the photographs off the murder board."

Thacker, wide-eyed, lifted one shoulder. "You think there is only—" he swallowed hard "—one reason?"

"I'm asking what you think."

Before Thacker could respond, their orders arrived.

"Think about it, son. I'm eating my burger while it's hot. I advise you do the same. We'll need all the energy we can gather."

Rory ate with relish. Thacker pushed his fries around until the detective relented. "Here's what I believe. Finding the body behind the 4-H building stirred up a hornet's nest." He squeezed more ketchup onto his plate, picked up a fry, and pointed it at Thacker. "First, because we weren't supposed to find her so quickly. And second, because she's the key." Pausing long enough to drench the potato, he stuffed it into his mouth, chewed, and swallowed. "Everything else has been to slow us down."

"But—"

"Hear me out. We find the girl, and twenty-four

hours later, someone attacks me. Sure, I hurt my ankle being careless, but someone exploited my injury. Maybe they hoped to put me out of commission. Petey does an autopsy. The autopsy discloses similarities to Emily Weir. Then, not satisfied with the findings, Petey heads to the state lab to conduct more detailed testing."

"And he's rerouted on his way home."

"That's right. Not hurt. Delayed."

"Why murder Mrs. Bellman?"

"I'm still working on that one."

Thacker picked up his burger and took a huge bite. Rory said, "Discovering the girl by the river brought Ash to town. I'm convinced his Tahoe raised the alarm at Marilyn's townhouse. Ash was checking out Henry. It wouldn't be hard to discover he was new in town or where he was staying. I'm pretty sure he scouted out the rest of the town, He might be responsible for your close call with that bumper. Directly or in some obscure way, the diversions link to Tobias Snearl."

"So, our visit to the prison wasn't to question Tobias Snearl as much as to prod him into making a move?"

"Yup. Or an unnamed person linked to Snearl. Right now, our best move is identifying a murderer on his visitor's log. We'll figure it out. Go ahead and eat your burger."

After they finished their meal, Rory raised his mug to signal the waitress for a refill.

Thacker gulped from his glass of tea and then wiped his lips with the back of his hand. "Harmon Free or Demetrius Jones."

"We'll know soon enough."

Setting the glass down, the rookie took out his

phone. "I'll call Miss Esther and have her start the internet search."

As the waitress poured the hot liquid into his mug, Rory's mind drifted to fond thoughts of the tall brunette.

"Ready for dessert?" She held the empty pot, her eyes playing over the family climbing into the next booth. "A nice slice of cherry pie?"

"We'll take the check." Lowering his gaze to Thacker, Rory said, "Everyone has met a diversion except Esther Mullins." He flipped his hat onto his head, picked up the ticket, and reached for his wallet.

"She's not answering, sir. What kind of message shall I leave?"

Gripping the edge of the table, Rory struggled to his feet. "Try her landline."

"I guess she's not home."

The meal, so satisfying moments ago, turned over in his stomach. His mouth went dry. Tossing two twenties onto the table, he said, "We need to get to Winterset—*now*."

Chapter Thirty-Five

Esther flipped the fan switch from medium to high. In her opinion, July was always humid, but this year, it seemed hotter than usual. Balancing books is tedious and being sticky only accentuates the misery. The old house she'd inherited from her grandmother didn't have central air, not air conditioning that she was comfortable using anyway, and today there was no breeze.

Four years ago, she'd switched from propane heat to an electric heat pump. It had been a substantial expense and required construction modifications. She had no regrets; it eliminated the need to refill the tank. And although the cost was nearly the same, she didn't have gigantic semi-annual bills but instead made budgeted monthly payments. The true luxury promised before the conversion was cool air to offset the summer heat. Ha!

Unfortunately, when the dehumidifier attached to the heat pump was engaged, it worked overtime. The constant gurgle of water trickling through the pipes after being drawn from the air drove her crazy. She imagined pennies flowing from her wallet, moisture collecting on rafters, and ceilings crumbling beneath undiscovered leaks.

If she wanted to finish her work, cooling the house was the only option. She wasn't sure ductwork and drainpipes were the same as chimneys, requiring a yearly cleaning to keep them functioning without mishap. No one had ventured into the attic since the installation. Before she turned the air conditioner on, the attic needed an inspection. She looked through the window at Axel's house. His truck wasn't in the drive. Thacker was out of the hospital, but he'd taken Rory to Lincoln before noon. Jesse was at work. Esther couldn't think of anyone else she'd feel comfortable asking for help. If there was going to be relief from the heat, she was going into the attic.

Access to the attic was in the bath linen closet and behind a false ceiling that required a ladder to reach. She began the task of removing all the linen and then the wooden shelves. Sweat trickled down between her breasts before she finished. The kitchen table was piled high with towels, bedsheets, and blankets. After checking once more for Axel's truck, she wiped the sweat from her brow. She sighed and then went to the basement for the eight-foot ladder.

Standing on the ladder, she could see the silver ducts snaking from the central unit to each room. The dehumidifier was on the left, attached to the main box by flex pipe, and a small tube led from it to the eaves and a location she couldn't make out. The top rung allowed her to step over the lip and onto the wooden floorboard. She reached for the overhead rafter to steady herself. At six feet tall, she couldn't straighten to her full height, so she had to stoop to make her way to the central unit.

It was understandable that the attic was hotter than the rooms below, but she also found the Whirlybird fan off. After her first complaint of insufficient cooling, the contractor had suggested that the attic fan was pulling the cooled air from her living space up through ceiling cracks and lighting fixtures. It was an old house. She flipped the switch. Whirling blades sucked hot air through the vent and stirred sixty years of dust. Through the electronic hum, she heard the cell phone ring in the office below. Pausing to consider the climb down, she decided the caller would leave a voice message if necessary. A hasty inspection revealed no damage or blockage, not that she knew what she'd expected to find. She called it good and headed down.

She arrived at ground level, gritty, sweaty, and frustrated that there was still bookkeeping to finish. She replaced the false ceiling, folded the ladder, and turned on the air. After closing the opened windows, she picked up the cell phone. One call from Thacker. No voicemail. She suspected the men were on their way back and trusted their visit had been beneficial. With her arms outstretched, she stood in front of the table fan, relieved Rory had finished with Tobias Snearl.

She heard the kitchen screen door close. A glance through the window told her it wasn't Axel. Something was wrong. Brushing damp hair off her face, she went to investigate. Esther stepped into the kitchen and found a man standing at the table. His back was to her as he bent over the linens. Blankets lay on the floor. The wall phone rang.

"What are you—"

As he turned, she recognized him. "Oh, it's you. Is there something wrong?" She stuck out her chin, though it wobbled.

He looked her up and down, then gave her a slow grin.

The phone rang twice more and then stopped. The room was deadly silent. Nothing. Only the faint sound of moving air and then a gurgle in the dehumidifier water line.

She opened her mouth and shut it again. Panic shot through her veins.

"You won't feel much," he said.

Chapter Thirty-Six

Rory estimated it would take thirty minutes to get to Esther's from the rest stop. His call went straight to voicemail, which sent a bad feeling up his spine. He called the station. Sunny picked up. "This better not be something new, Mr. Detective. Only got two hours until my weekend, and you know how much I love a weekend."

"Yeah, sure. A simple request."

"Tell me you're not fool enough to ask for a special favor late on a Friday afternoon."

Keeping his voice under control, he said, "I need a car sent to Esther Mullins' house on East Peach Street."

He heard the huff, followed by the sound of chair wheels rolling over linoleum. "Garth and Nguyen are on that side of town."

"Miss Mullins isn't answering her phone, and I'm a half-hour out. Have them do a drive-by and check for suspicious activity."

"You're not taking advantage of the police department to check up on your girlfriend, are you?"

He winced. "No."

His phone beeped, announcing an incoming call. "Got to take another call, Sunny. We good?"

"Your wish is my command."

He switched to the incoming call. "Naysmith."

Cecil Rudd said, "Thought you'd want to know

Snearl made a call shortly after you left."

"Any idea to whom?"

"No, but the timing is suspicious. He's not much for talking."

"Thanks." Rory lowered the cell.

Thacker said, "What do you think, boss?"

"I think we need to hurry."

When they pulled up to Esther's, a police cruiser stood at the front curb, lights flashing, both front doors open. Thacker pulled in behind. A second cruiser arrived and parked at their rear bumper. Rory was halfway to the front door, his heart thumping in his ears, when Officer Nguyen stepped out through the front porch.

"Is she in there?"

"It's empty, sir. It's untidy, but there is no sign of blood."

Rory brushed past him, hobbling at top speed, the best he could do in the walking cast. He stopped when he hit the kitchen. The table usually against the wall was in the center of the room. One chair lay on its back, and blankets, wadded fabric, and boards littered the floor. Esther kept a spotless home. The disarray clenched his already queasy stomach. How had he been so careless?

"Didn't need to hurry." Garth's voice came from the bath off the kitchen. "Looks like she's been rearranging. I'd say she started with the linen closet. There's no sign of foul play, only one helluva mess in the kitchen, and, well…in here."

Rory stuck his head into the bathroom, noticed the dust, ladder, and empty closet. "What's in there?" He indicated the closet.

"Attic," said Garth. "Looks like she's been up there this morning. What do you want to do? There's no evidence that anyone committed a crime."

Rory wasn't so sure. "Let me talk to Nguyen and make a couple of calls to see if anyone has seen her."

"Right. I'll call it in."

The rookie met Rory on the front porch. "Axel's not home." He lowered his phone. "He's down at the lodge, watching the ballgame with the Kaulburg cousins. He said Miss Esther was working at her computer all morning. And he'll be right over. I can question the other neighbors."

A heavy blanket of depression fell over Rory's thoughts. He lifted his fedora and ran a hand over his balding head once, twice. Nguyen joined the two patrolmen at the second squad car. Reseating his hat, Rory eyed the other two men. Then said to Thacker, "This doesn't feel right, son."

Thacker shook his head. "According to Nguyen, the doors were open. It's messy inside, but that's not a crime."

"We're dealing with a murderer who abducts women."

Rory didn't want to let his mind go there. He'd seen the body dumped by the river and the one unearthed in the rock quarry. If this wasn't the work of Tobias Snearl, it was someone just as dangerous, just as sadistic, and using his recipe. Rory couldn't keep his thoughts from going down that track, even knowing Esther was intelligent, resilient. His heart sank.

As if reading his thoughts, Thacker laid a hand on his arm. "We'll find her."

"We'd better hurry."

****

The day sizzled. With hardly a cloud in the sky, the sun burned down as Rory made calls to Jesse Wallace and Marilyn Beauregard. Neither had seen Esther. Like Axel, they were prepared to drop everything.

"No," Rory said to Marilyn. "Your offer is appreciated, but she's just out of pocket. There's nothing to be concerned about yet. Is your cousin around today?"

"He left about an hour ago for an appointment in Omaha. I don't expect him back until evening. I doubt he saw Esther, but I'll ask."

Rory scribbled on his notepad. "That would be good. Have a nice day."

Jesse was more insistent when he inquired. "No, I've been busy. Is something wrong?"

"I haven't seen her since last night and wondered if she was with you. Nothing to worry about."

"Where have you checked?" she asked, her voice winding into a panic.

"Marilyn Beauregard, you, a few others. No one has seen her, including the neighbors. I'm sure it's nothing."

"We said that about Abby Sue; we were wrong."

Rory agreed he'd wait at the house for her to arrive.

Jeromy Ash said he was at the impound lot, seeing about the release of his car. He, too, would head over.

Thacker sat with Rory on the front step as they waited for their motley crew to assemble. The other policemen had gone; still, they were hesitant to enter. Rory had been inside, as had Nguyen and Garth, and he was concerned the house was a crime scene. It was too early to report a missing person or call for forensic techs. There was no need to contaminate the area. It was the right time to worry.

From the alley, he heard a car door slam. Then a second. Ash's and Jesse's voices came down the sidewalk from the side of the house. Thacker went to meet them. Rory got to his feet. Axel's truck squealed around the corner and flung gravel as it swung into the driveway. Jumping out as soon as he threw it into park, he shouted, "Constable, what news?"

Rory was glad Axel hadn't accused him of anything. He felt guilty anyway and a little off-kilter.

Jesse tossed her head defiantly and called out, "This makes my day. What happened?"

Only a step behind, Agent Ash reached out to restrain her. She wiggled from his grasp. "She wouldn't go anywhere without leaving a note." She glared at Rory. "I'm going in. Don't try to stop me."

He thumbed back his hat. Her nostrils flared as she brushed past him and kept going.

"Thacker, you and Axel check the cellar," he said. "See if it's been disturbed. Ash and I'll search for the note."

Jesse had righted the kitchen chair and was rifling through the towels when he joined her in the kitchen. "Why couldn't you protect her?" she said without looking up at him. He knew she was thinking about her mother, whose disappearance six months earlier had ended badly. She needed more time to put her grief where she could live with the loss. Esther was all the family she had left. And he couldn't blame her for being upset.

She kicked a blanket against the wall before

sinking into a chair. "Why, Rory? Why did you have to involve her?" Her eyes were bright with unshed tears. She buried her face in her hands.

Lowering his voice to a whisper, he said, "I couldn't stop her."

Ash stood in the doorway. He cleared his throat and announced, "Nothing in the living room or the bedroom. How's it going in here?"

Rory shook his head slowly. "We're still looking. If you help Dr. Wallace here, I'll check the office."

His body was stiffening up, but he managed to thump his way into the room Esther used for bookkeeping. It was as neat as a pin and smelled of library books, shredded paper, and the floral scent Esther liked, jasmine, lilac, or something faintly woodsy. He found a manila file folder marked "INVOICES" open on the desk by the computer and an iced tea glass that had left a damp circle on the mouse pad. No note tacked to the bulletin board. No message on the desk or the filing cabinets. Frustrated, he pounded the ham of his fist on the desk. The mouse jumped, bringing the computer screen to life.

At first, he wasn't sure what was on the screen. There were words, but it looked like any other document you'd write on a computer. It wasn't until he sat in the chair and began to read that he realized it was a message meant for him. "Ash, will you step in here?"

The agent read over Rory's shoulder.

Detective Naysmith,

I have Esther Mullins.

She has not been harmed.

Follow my instructions, and she will not be harmed.

If you raise the alarm, she will die.

If you try to find her, she will die.

If you notify anyone, she will die.

Cooperate, and you will see her again.

I do not negotiate.

This is not a game.

You cannot win.

If you want to see her again, follow these instructions.

Remove all the files on the Weir murder from your private collection.

Seal them in cardboard boxes.

Leave them at the foot of the stairs on the store's first floor.

Midnight tonight.

I will retrieve them when I know it is safe.

If the documents are not complete, she dies.

I will know.

I am watching.

If I am satisfied, she will be released in 24 hours.

Agent Ash spoke first. "Son of a bitch."

Rory slammed his open hands on the desk. "Sonofabitch has Esther."

"How do you want to handle this?"

"Midnight." Rory's voice cracked as he shoved away from the desk. "He expects me to do this tonight."

"What are you going to do?"

"How do I print this without messing up fingerprints on the keyboard?"

Ash reached over Rory's shoulder and pushed a button. The printer hummed to life.

The detective rose to his feet, knocked Ash back, and grabbed the page from the tray. He pivoted for the door. Through gritted teeth, he spat, "Comply."

When he looked up, Jesse was in the doorway, blocking his exit. She hugged a folded towel against her chest. Her eyes were wide, her mouth slightly open. "Rory?" She sounded like a frightened child.

"He has your sister. And we're getting her back." He elbowed past her and stomped through the kitchen. He let the screen door flap behind him. He couldn't breathe. He couldn't think. Not Esther. Not sweet, kind, never-hurt-anyone Esther.

The message couldn't be clearer. Rory had what the kidnapper wanted and was willing to take Esther to get it. He couldn't call in the forensic crew with a madman watching. Bruises, leather straps, and images of the decomposing body by the river sent a shiver up his spine. He needed to believe the message and hoped she was alive and unharmed. Tightening his fists, he knew hope couldn't be his strategy. Even if Esther were physically unharmed, she'd suffer trauma from being overpowered and restrained. The cellar door thumped closed behind him.

Thacker called out, "Nothing down there except canning jars and spiders, boss."

Rory slapped him in the chest with the printed message. "Read. She's gone." His voice sounded angry—he didn't care.

"I'll check the basement," Axel said, moving from the cellar door to the back stoop. "If Miss Esther is down there, I'll find her."

"We need to identify the doer. Learn where she is and"—Rory struggled to say it out loud—"if she is compromised."

Thacker glanced at the paper and thrust it at Axel.

"We'll need gloves and evidence bags." The rookie took off at a run, rounded the corner of the house, and disappeared from sight.

"Have you called for backup?" Jesse stood at the door, looking pale and vulnerable. Ash stood behind her.

"No," Rory said. "There are five of us, more manpower than the chief would assign to a crime. I'm not risking her life."

Ash patted his shirt pocket as if searching for a pack of cigarettes. He didn't take his eyes off the detective.

"Thacker talked to the neighbors earlier," said Rory. "No one saw anything suspicious, so no witnesses. We'll make a thorough search, going room by room."

Ash gave up on whatever he wanted from his pocket. "I'll climb into the attic. Might as well eliminate that now."

Rory gave him a curt nod. "Axel, you are downstairs. Jesse, you handle the bedroom."

The search didn't turn up anything. They congregated in the kitchen. "Who has keys to the house?" asked Rory.

Jesse and Axel both started to speak.

"Good," Rory said, holding up a hand to silence them. "I want all the windows and doors locked. Axel, you do that after we leave for the apartment."

"Not without me. No one is taking Miss Esther and getting away with it."

"Fine." Rory glanced at Jesse. "I don't suppose you will go home?"

She folded her arms across her chest. "You may

need a doctor. She's my sister, and I want to find her."

"I plan to confront a might-be and probably-is serial killer. He'll be desperate. You may be hurt."

Her eyes narrowed, and her jaw clenched. He didn't have the heart to refuse. "All right. We need packing boxes. See if you can find six and bring them with you."

She agreed.

"You'll want to dress in dark, comfortable clothing." Looking at each of them, he added, "All of you."

It would be a long night without air conditioning on the first floor. "It will take at least two hours to locate and pack the documents demanded in the message." Rory took out his phone, frowned at the screen, and checked the time. "We'll meet in the apartment at eight tonight. Don't speak to anyone between now and then. Prepare for a long night. Don't park any closer than Front Street. Any questions?"

Blank faces. Ash was the first to move, going into the bath and coming out with the eight-foot ladder.

"Put it back, Ash. We want everything as is if we need the forensic boys tomorrow."

The bigger man paused, studied the detective, and then returned the ladder to the closet.

"That's it, then," Rory said. "Two hours."

Chapter Thirty-Seven

Winterset was never truly dark, not with moonlight, streetlights, windows lit from within, and storefront signage flashing. By nine thirty, the sun had set, and the night was as black as it was going to get. Rory felt they were ready, his small army, Thacker, Axel, Jerry Ash, Jesse, and himself. Each had an assignment. He thought about all the historic battles he'd studied. Attacking before daybreak was good. Under a full moon was always better. He expected the kidnapper to make the pick-up at or just before dawn.

Rory addressed the crew. "There will be no talking once we're in place." They each wore a black shirt, dark pants, and running shoes. Rory had a running boot but planned on doing none. He flopped the fedora onto his head. The others donned WPD ball caps. Axel squared a pair of night goggles on his forehead.

"All the doors are locked. The lights on the first floor are out like any other night. He knows how to enter the building and has done so on at least two occasions. Anyone who has a change of mind, say so now."

They were silent. Rory put a hand on Jesse's shoulder. "You don't have to do this."

She wore a flak vest and had tucked her hair under her ball cap. She inhaled deeply and let the breath out slowly through parted lips. "I want to."

"It may be a long night. It will be sweltering, nerve-racking."

"She would do it for me."

Jesse had him there. Esther's life consisted of one sacrifice after another.

"Son," he said to Thacker, "put Commander in the war room. We can't have him loose on the ground floor."

While the rookie took care of the cat, Rory went into the bedroom for his gun. Axel followed him in—a Bowie knife threaded through his belt, arms bare, Yosemite Sam mustache waxed. Standing back as the detective unlocked the gun safe, he said, "I'm up for the tomahawk."

The detective hesitated. "You have a hunting knife."

"Yep."

Rory said into the open safe, "The plan is to disarm the kidnapper and rescue Esther."

"Look, it's cool, Constable. I won't use it unless, well, you know, I absolutely have to."

When they rejoined the others, Axel's knife handle glistened from a sheath strapped to his arm, and the ax swung from a belt loop.

Ash eyed the weapons, patted his shirt pocket, and dropped his hand. "At times like this, I regret giving up cigarettes." To Axel, he said, "Fancy getup. Did you leave anything at home?"

Rory waved him off. "We'll take the radios and phones down. Set them on silent. I don't want any tipoffs to our presence. Let's load up."

After stacking the boxes on the knee scooter, Ash pushed it into the elevator. The five warriors went down in the lift together. On the second floor, Jesse and Axel stepped out. Rory rode to the ground floor with the other two. They exited, left the lift open, and secured the gate on one side.

The windows were blackened, and the fairy light string Axel and Thacker had strung was out. A faint smell came from the gas generator, as well as a steady hum. The battery-powered motion detector lights came on in the stairway when they stopped to stack the boxes in front of the bottom step. They looked insignificant in the gigantic space. Rory knew the killer's identity was in one of the three cardboard boxes, and he wished he'd found it.

He checked the gun in his shoulder holster. Thacker moved to the far corner by the manikins. Ash cocked his head left, indicating the west wall. Rory nodded, and the undercover cop moved in that direction. Rory walk-limped to the door and rattled the handle, checking the lock. He heard the bar on the outside jump and settle back into place. He limped back and settled sidesaddle on the scooter and in the shadows against the staircase wall.

He knew where Thacker and Ash were. From his position, they were invisible. There was no doubt they were hidden from each other. By this time, Jesse and Axel would be in their positions as well: Axel by the hidden stair to the apartment above, Jesse at the head of the stairs coming down.

Silence settled in as they waited for a predator, a madman without restraint, social filters, or conscience. He would attack with instinctual shrewdness. Rory hoped they were ready, and he prayed the villain never made it to the second floor. He fingered the St. Michael medal hanging around his neck—the patron saint of police, defender in battle and protector. He counted on Thacker's youth, Ash's strength, and his own experience to prove worthy of the task and knew Esther's life depended on it.

For a long time, it was quiet. Traffic passed on the street without stopping. Once, someone walked past on the sidewalk, but they kept on walking. It was a man with a dog, because Rory could hear the man's one-sided conversation. "We can do it, boy. It's our daily constitution. Just one more block. Then you'll be able to enjoy your new chew bone." Then the voice faded from hearing.

Rory had plenty of time to think. The downtown department store was an odd place for the retrieval—particularly this department store, within two hundred feet of a manned police station. It made their man arrogant as well as tricky, overconfident like Agent Ash. What he knew about the Dallas-based agent was minimal. His identity had been verified by Sergeant Powell, he seemed genuine, and he was undoubtedly cooperative. But if their kidnapper turned out to be the serial killer that Ash was hunting, his cooperation could come to an abrupt end. Rory wondered what Ash did with the disguises in his hotel room and how he filled his days.

A pigeon walked along the outside windowsill. Through a crack where the cardboard was missing, Rory could see the bird pacing back and forth. He was almost lulled into letting his guard down. His foot tingled; he needed to walk it out. Standing, he moved in front of the stairs and looked up. Jesse was there somewhere at the top, but he couldn't see her.

Once his sight fully adjusted to the dim lighting, he tried to spot Ash and Thacker again. Even knowing where they hid, he couldn't make them out. That was good. He'd trust Axel with his life, but he hoped the man was behaving. Moving slowly, he crossed to the windows, peeked out at the dark street, and found it empty. He'd served enough stakeout hours over the years, maybe as many as four or five hundred hours altogether, hanging in limbo, waiting while nothing much happened. It was time enough to learn that at dawn, it would be too dark to identify a man on the other side of the street, but within minutes, he'd be able to read his alma mater off the ring he wore. He expected something to happen soon—knew there was plenty dark-of-night left.

Deciding to take a swing around the room to stretch his legs, he limped a circuit along the walls. When he passed Thacker, the young officer was squatting between armless manikins with his back against the wall. He raised a hand in salute. As Rory rounded the other side, Ash offered a thumbs-up from his position at the throwing targets. Rory noticed the agent had blackened his face and draped camouflage netting over his shoulders. When Rory got back to the stairs, Jesse was perched on the second step.

Rory put a finger to his lips, and she nodded. "What's wrong?" he whispered. "Why didn't the lights come on." He looked beyond her and up into the shadows, anxious.

"Axel showed me how to disconnect the motion detector."

"Reconnect it. I want to see when someone uses the stairs."

"It's after midnight. Will it be much longer?"

There was no way to know. "You can wait in the apartment. Have Axel take you up the rear stairs."

"No, I'm fine. I heard you moving and thought you'd want to know the time."

"Where is the air horn?"

She looked over her shoulder. "At the top of the stairs."

"Go back up. Reconnect the lights. If things go wrong, we'll be busy down here. I'm counting on you to hit the horn and call the station."

She stood to comply but stopped after mounting the third step. In a husky whisper, she said, "Do you think Esther is okay?"

He couldn't let himself think differently. He wouldn't voice a lie, either. He turned his back to her and moved into the shadows. After a moment, he heard her climb to the second floor.

He didn't want Jesse to see his pain. The unknown was always ugly, and her fears mirrored his. He didn't have time to dwell on them. He needed to do what he did best, work with the information, figure out its meaning, and identify the enemy. He started with Snearl's phone call and the unnamed person at the other end. Three men made the cut: Demetrius Jones, Harmon Free, and Henry Beauregard.

Marilyn said her cousin had gone to Omaha for the day. He could have just as easily slipped over to Peach Street to abduct Esther. Henry could be the notorious Smyrola Dewey. Henry had murdered Abby Sue Bellman because she could identify him. Henry planned to fleece the town with an ancestor-locating scheme. The problem was Rory had no proof of any of it.

While Thacker packed the Weir files, Rory ran preliminary internet searches for the two men on Snearl's visitation log, Free and Jones. Free still worked for the *Journal*, with nothing iffy on him popping up. He warranted a closer look. Demetrius turned out to be a pathologist. There hadn't been time to discover more. So, what if Demetrius Jones turned out to be the notorious Dewey? Demetrius nicknamed Dewey, sort of worked. But so what? Something that happened twenty years ago in Smyrola didn't explain a string of murders. Or Snearl's phone call.

Rory pushed his hat back, wiped his forehead, and looked at the street, speculating. A movement caught his eye. Something was in the shadows beyond the pigeon window. He froze, holding his breath. The movement stopped, and he could see a man's outline through the dingy pane. Rory's heartbeat quickened, and he flexed his bad leg to get the circulation going. Jitters settled in his stomach. He squared the walking boot on the floor and tightened his muscles.

The man moved on.

Rory exhaled. The enemy had arrived.

Moments later, the bar on the alley door rattled and then fell silent. The silence stretched to minutes. Blood rushed through Rory's veins, and he became aware of his anxiety, fear mixed with eagerness, foul body odor, a dry mouth filled with a metallic taste. Dread had been growing in him since Esther's abduction. He didn't fear death or ordinary pain. Failure, helplessness, and shame fed his angst. He would not lose Esther.

Trying to slow his heart rate, he rubbed a hand along his jaw. He was ready to face the next bit. It was the bit after, and the next, that he put out of his mind.

Instead, he pictured his opponent moving around outside the building, making his way in and coming onto the first level. By now, he'd be inside.

Rory glanced at the cartons and listened. Nothing. Only the faint sound of air stirring, not the whisper of movement. Creepy coward. Where was he? Rory felt for the gun in his shoulder holster. It would be hard to draw under attack, impossible if they grappled. The draw motion would put his arm at his chest, where it could be pinned, rendered useless to match his useless leg. He removed the pistol and held it at his side. Adrenaline pumped. He made an effort to control his breathing, willed himself to remain calm with the knowledge that the rookie was prepared, and Agent Ash had converted to bulletproof mode.

He managed two deep breaths and then felt the presence beside him.

Shifting his eyes, he saw a phantom shape in his peripheral vision. Instantly he understood his disadvantage. The specter stood on the side with his damaged leg, opposite the drawn gun, and well within Rory's personal space. Pungent heat radiated in a wave to assault the detective's senses. Rory swallowed hard and stiffened.

A bark, low and throaty in Rory's ear. "He's here." It was Ash's voice.

Rory jerked his head to confront the agent. "What are you doing over here?" Incredulous. He had a rogue operative. He whispered harshly, "You're supposed to stay hidden."

Ash grinned. There was a maniacal glint in his expression. "He'll never see me."

Indeed, Ash was wearing a sniper's cape and had

approached without detection. Now was not the time. As the detective took in the undercover agent's measure, Ash raised an arm and patted his shirt pocket. The cape spread like a webbed appendage. The hackles rose on the back of Rory's neck.

Ash withdrew a package of chewing gum, unwrapped a stick, and put it in his mouth. Chewing with vigor, he spat, "He's not smart enough." His hot, fragrant breath landed on Rory.

The detective held his expression steady while his mind popped the pieces into place. Webbed arms. Exchange the fennel scent with licorice chewing gum. First, the night he was attacked. Later, the night of the dream and Thacker's trip to the hospital. Ash, the liar. Manipulating situations and people. A madman without restraint or conscience—a predator holding Esther hostage. Bold enough to work within their ranks. Agent Ash *was* the Jones from Smyrola, Georgia.

He locked eyes with Ash and slowly raised the gun to firing position. Through clenched teeth, he said, "Not this time, Dewey Jones."

Jones swatted the gun from Rory's grip and backhanded him in one swift movement. The force threw Rory to the tiles. The pistol clamored to the marble floor and spun in a lazy circle, stopping just short of the scooter.

Jones' voice was a growl from his throat. "You have no idea who I am."

Vivid memories mixed with debilitating stomps leaped into Rory's mind's eye. He shuddered but managed to get to his feet, astonished that the man allowed it. A glimpse of Jones' distorted face convinced him the coward still felt invincible.

"It wasn't hard to figure out."

"Is that right?" There was a swagger in Jones' expression, a bravado he couldn't suppress.

"Let's see if I have this right," Rory said. "Jerry Ames comes to town after the body turns up at the river. And with the sole purpose of keeping abreast of the investigation. Then, when it became apparent the WPD is zeroing in, you conveniently became Jeromy Ash, an undercover agent from Dallas." Rory moved toward the scooter, keeping his voice as even as possible. "Making the connection to Dewey Jones was harder."

Jones smirked and relaxed his stance.

Rory led with his cast. Mother may I. He took one smooth baby step. "But not impossible."

"Too bad about your friends. The bandito, doctor sister, the Boy Scout—and the charming bookkeeper."

Rage and fury kept the pain in Rory's foot at bay. Fearing for his friends, he inched closer to the scooter. Keeping his voice as matter-of-fact as he could, he continued. "Putting the body in your trunk. I have to give you credit there. It looked like a separate doer, but it turns out Bellman was the only person in Winterset able to recognize you weren't Jerry Ames but, instead, a guy from Smyrola, Georgia, named Jones." He offered a wry smile. "Rather than a diversion, it added another name to a list of aliases. Jerry Ames, Jeromy Ash, Dewey Jones. I'm confident you've masqueraded as others."

Jones pulled a pair of gloves from his pocket and started to put them on. "Intriguing. A fascinating theory. So, you got a Jones in Georgia. Big deal."

Rory rubbed his forehead. "Well, yeah, it is a big

deal. You see, I believe you are *that* Jones." He tilted his head at the cardboard cartons. "I believe Dewey Jones is continuing a string of brutal murders for Tobias Snearl. You know Tobias. I believe the proof is in these boxes. And to continue your fun and games, you can't afford to have that proof uncovered."

"Don't be ridiculous." A hypodermic needle materialized in Jones' hand. "You checked my credentials. I'm Jeromy Ash."

"The fingerprints in the car match your prints. Your prints don't match those on the union card for Jeromy Ash, Dallas undercover agent."

Jones feigned a shrug. "The Boy Scout?"

It had only been a guess. But one that confirmed a switch. When this was over, he would backtrack that trail. Rory said, "Thacker is more than a pretty face."

Seeming to tire of the discussion, Jones took a quick step toward Rory with the raised needle.

The detective summoned the strength to lash out with his plaster-encased foot—a swift kick straight to Jones' knee. But the scooter got in the way, and Rory found himself on the floor, jerking in agony, and the coward still advancing. He kicked the scooter, and the handlebars slammed into Jones, blocking him and twisting into the cape. The big man went down in a tangle of camouflage webbing and metal.

Rory reached for the gun. Where was the bull horn? He expected Thacker to rush forward and glanced fleetingly toward the manikins and his friend's hiding place.

But unbelievably, a shape detached itself from the opposite wall. Traveling low and swift, it charged straight for Rory. Damn! If Jones lay in front of him, there was a second man as well, an adversary that rattled the door and circled the building.

The sinister silhouette outside the window had made it in aided by the distraction from Jones.

Rory's heartbeat quickened. When the advancing figure reached the center of the vast marble floor, Rory fell, rolled, grabbed the gun, and got to his feet, surprised he could get up at all.

He locked his knees and raised the barrel.

Chapter Thirty-Eight

Rory kept the barrel pointed at the advancing enemy. As it approached, its momentum slowed. Arms shot into the air, waved a pistol, and then leveled. "Stand down, Special Agent."

When he was close enough, Rory could see his face. *Brown. The hospital roommate!* Another pump of adrenaline. Gawd, this was one revelation after another. Was anyone who they were supposed to be? He didn't have time to digest it, instead the detective swung back to Jones, pinning him in place on the floor.

"Police! Don't move!"

Muscling past, Brown kicked the hypodermic out of reach, cuffed Jones where he lay, and looked up at Rory. "Special Agent Jeromy Ash, Dallas PD."

Phantom Special Undercover Agent Jeromy Ash had a scar running through one eyebrow. It made an artificial lift in his brow, which lent an attentive look to his expression, as if he anticipated every question and appreciated all answers.

Agent Ash added, "Better known to you as Mister Brown."

Rory took a deep breath. "Thanks for the assist. Where is my crew?"

"The doctor is unharmed and locked in the room with the cat."

"Axel?"

"Ah, the guy with the mustache that matches his brow. I sent him across the street for the cavalry." A commotion sounded from the alley. Voices grew louder, and leather boots slapped the ground as people entered the building.

"Thacker?" Rory didn't wait for the answer. As the police made their way in, he speed-thumped to the manikins. Thacker lay in a heap, unmoving. A whiff of ether lingered, and a discarded rag lay by his head.

"Clarence?" Rory bent over, checked for a pulse, found one. "Thank God." He whipped his hat off and drew a deep breath. "Son, I need your legs."

Thacker moaned and slowly opened his eyes. "I… I…didn't hear him coming, boss."

"It's all right. We got him."

Camouflaged and blackened, Jones could have easily snuck up on the young officer and render him helpless. Even if Thacker had seen him coming, he wouldn't have expected such evil—not from within their ranks. It was a miracle the coward hadn't done more damage. Rory prayed he'd been as considerate to Esther.

The rookie's eyes found Rory's. "Did he release Miss Esther?"

"No. But I know where she is. We're going to save her just as soon as your legs start working."

Groggy, Thacker struggled to his feet, leaning heavily on Rory. "I'm really—"

"It's all right." The rookie was upright but unsteady on his feet. He draped an arm across the detective's shoulders. The extra weight made Rory feel like he had a piano on his back.

He couldn't describe the throb in his ankle. Or the

ache in his heart. "Son," he said, "I'm going to need you to walk out of here on your own."

As if drawing on a superpower, Thacker straightened and squared his shoulders.

****

Leaving the scene to Agent Ash, they used both lights and siren to speed down Main Street, swing onto Maple, and race to Peach Street.

"You think she's there, sir?" Thacker's deep voice sounded hopeful.

"I know so." Rory refused to consider her condition. "If I know Esther, she's wondering what's taking so long."

"We searched the house."

"Yes, but we weren't all on the same team—sleight of hand, misdirection." He clutched the dashboard and willed Thacker to hurry.

The cruiser fishtailed into the drive between Esther and Axel's houses. Rory threw off his seatbelt and bolted from the car.

Thacker beat him to the back door. "It's locked."

"Kick it in."

The door frame was no challenge for the young officer, and it gave way and splintered at the first try. They entered the kitchen, flipped the light switch, and stepped over the linen still on the floor. The wall clock read ten to four, and fear rose in Rory, choking and thick. Esther had been captive for over twelve hours.

"In there," he croaked, jutting his chin at the bath. "She'll be in the attic." His pulse was pounding so loudly in his ears that he could barely think. God, let her be alive. Let her be all right.

Thacker balked at first, but then he stepped past

Rory, unfolded the ladder, and set it in place. When his foot hit the bottom rung, Rory threw his hat to the floor and grabbed the rookie's shirttail.

"She's my girl, son. I'll go up first."

Thacker stepped down, allowing him access. "Right behind you, sir."

Adrenalin is a fantastic drug. Climbing one step at a time and leading with his non-booted foot, Rory managed the cast's dead weight without effort. The rookie pressed behind him, so close his breath lifted the hair at Rory's neck. Once the false ceiling was out of the way, Rory popped his head through the opening.

The attic was black save for the thin beams of light filtering in at the eaves and down through the vent. The heat pump loomed straight ahead. The duct byways looked smashed and loose. "It looks like a war zone up here. I need—" The rookie tapped Rory on the shoulder with a flashlight. "—a flashlight."

Playing the beam around the attic, Rory spotted her lying by the dehumidifier, a small mound tucked in a fetal position. "Quick."

He boosted himself through the opening and made his way to her. She was unconscious, and leather thongs bound her hands and feet, but she was alive. He dropped to his knees and took her in his arms. He couldn't find his voice.

Through a fog of shame and guilt, he heard Thacker call for the ambulance, and he cradled her against his chest and buried his face in her hair. His throat ached with emotion. He was sorry. So very, very sorry.

Rory had no sense of time passing. When the EMTs arrived, he lifted his chain from around his neck, pulled it over his head, and placed the St. Michael medal around her neck. Then, gently kissing her forehead, he released her into their custody. Unable to stand, he scooted to the opening, clumsily made his way down the ladder, picked up his hat, and stood aside. The medical technicians lowered her limp body and carried her to the ambulance.

Darkness stood with him on the driveway. It was not yet dawn when he removed his fedora and gripped the rim mercilessly, watching as they pulled away. He wondered how even a madman could look at her lovely face and do her harm.

Esther had always made him feel special. Now, he only felt hollow.

His heart ached.

He had let her down.

Chapter Thirty-Nine

Rory phoned Jesse while Thacker secured the house. After giving a brief explanation of where he was and what he'd found, he said, "Esther is going to be okay. The EMTs just pulled out. Her vital signs are good. She'll want you at the hospital."

"Did he hurt—"

"No. But she was drugged."

He didn't mention the bindings. Sitting on the step of Esther's front porch, he extended his leg. It had begun to ache now that he was coming down from the adrenaline rush. The streetlight at the corner threw a circle of light on the street, and the windows glowed behind him. Someone hammered a piece of plywood over the splintered kitchen door. In the early dawn, the blows echoed.

"I imagine she'll have a story to tell when she's rested.

"Where'd he put her?" Jesse asked. "What did she say?"

"Why don't I answer those questions when we're face to face. I'll join you at Winterset Memorial when I finish up here."

"Agent Ash, the true Agent Jeromy Ash, has your killer at the station."

"Good." Jones would go into the holding cell tonight, transfer to county jail tomorrow, and then move on from there, depending on agency and jurisdiction. Rory couldn't summon the energy to care where the murderer was, as long as it was behind bars. The whole case was far from over.

"They are calling in the state police, Rory. Maybe the FBI. Ash says the important thing is a serial killer is off the streets." She talked fast and loudly, both unlike her. Jesse would stabilize when she saw her sister if relief didn't turn her giddy. He needed Jesse's connections to see that Esther had everything possible to ensure her recovery.

"He's right. Go on to the hospital, and I'll join you as soon as I can."

It took more reassuring to get her calmed down and headed out. Then he called the station and asked for Agent Ash.

"I understand Jones is in the lock-up. Miss Mullins is on her way to the hospital, and as soon as I'm able, I'll head that way. When she is stable, I will come to the station. We good?"

"Take whatever time you need," Ash said. "The paperwork alone will tie us up for a couple of hours. Your Officer Lloyd is most accommodating. Axel Barrow is standing guard at the department store and the apartment. A crew is over there, and I'll be here until it all gets handed off."

"About my files, the three boxes containing the Weir documents…" Rory let the request trail off. He wasn't sure how to get his hands on his files so he could search the contents again. He also knew the ransom note, and the files would be part of the evidence collected from the department store.

"I thought that might be the case," Ash said. "They

are still at the scene. Call when you're ready, and we'll get Lloyd to witness the inspection."

They exchanged cell numbers and disconnected.

After finishing at the house, Rory asked Thacker to drive him to the hospital. It was a sad ride full of fear and regret. Without a doubt, the FBI or Nebraska State Bureau of Criminal Identification would take over his case. He and Thacker would do clean-up and discovery. However, his disappointment took second place against his concern for Esther.

When they walked through the ER doors, Jesse rushed over and grabbed him in a bear hug. "She's going to be okay." Jesse still wore dark pants and running shoes; the WPD cap was gone. A white lab coat covered her T-shirt. "Esther is stable but not aware of happenings around her."

"All good news," Rory said, swiping the fedora from his head. "Let's hope it's chloral hydrate. And nothing more."

Thacker said, "She'll have a dandy headache."

"Oh, Thacker." She grabbed him for a hug, too.

"It's all over in twenty-four hours." The young officer's face turned bright red, the radio on his belt crackled, and Jesse let go.

They listened to a conversation between Jim Zielinski at the department store and Lloyd at the station. The officers' exchange was peppered with police 10-codes to cover the content. Jesse looked bewildered; Rory understood. They had wrapped up the scene and were ready for the detective. They mentioned his name.

Jesse's eyes went wide. "Esther is resting and expected to recover. Go. Do what you do. I'll stay with her and tell her you were here. Nail the bad guy."

He wanted to stay. But he wanted to see Dewey Jones put away for a long time, even more.

****

"Ash tells me the documents are still at Hilly's," Rory said as the two policemen headed back. "I'd like you to drop me off and then run an errand."

"Sure, boss."

"Better hear what it is first."

"Nah, it won't matter. I'm upset with this guy. First, he's a tourist named Ames. Then he's an undercover agent named Ash. But all the time, he's a serial killer who stole an identity, messed with our evidence, our friends, our lives, and then hurts Miss Esther."

The young officer was staring out the windshield, clutched the steering wheel with white-knuckled hands. Rory said, "I think that sums up my feelings exactly."

Thacker's ears were pink when he glanced at Rory.

"After you drop me off, go into the station and get what you need to legally search the room Jones had under the name Ames at the Best Western. You might take a warrant, but I think you'll only need to ask Sheila Steel to open the door. It will be best if you had a witness with you, so, maybe take one of the guys."

"What am I looking for?"

"Ames had all eight dossiers when he showed up at the station. Half were possible kills by Tobias Snearl. We can attribute the other four plus River Girl and Bellman to Jones, a man of disguise and deception. I want something connecting him to Snearl. The bonus would be an explanation for the killings or the theft of the photos from our murder board."

A low whistle escaped Thacker's lips.

"Heck, son, I don't know. Just see what you find."

****

The sun was up when the detective entered the department store and crossed to the cardboard cartons sitting by the staircase on the first floor. He'd been through every document. First, leisurely in his search after suspecting similarities between Weir and River Girl. And then, diligently as he packed the paperwork into cartons to satisfy the ransom demand. Both times he hoped to find a link—a name. Yet, both times he didn't honestly know there was a connection between Snearl and the killer using the same device. But now he knew for sure. And he knew it was in the boxes.

Rory moved the cartons to the desk area that held the ax targets and began unloading the documents and separating them into piles of like items. Scanning each page before setting it down, he searched for "Jones," "chloral hydrate," and the word "unknown."

The first run-through resulted in a dozen documents containing "unknown." No paper had the word chloral hydrate. Nothing mentioned Jones. He wasn't discouraged.

The connection was in the piles.

He dragged a weight bench over and sat before starting the second examination. Axel came down in the lift with Commander and joined him.

After filling the younger man in on Esther's condition, he explained his task. "Sometimes, I don't see a word because my mind skips right over it. I know what should be there and see what I expect to see."

Axel raised his brow.

"You can help by reviewing this pile." He pointed

at the pile containing his notebooks. "Don't try to read them. I use a form of shorthand, and it will make that hard to accomplish. When I have a question, suspect a falsehood, or want to follow up, I end the passage with double question marks. It would help if you run through the notes taken during the Snearl investigation and find the places that tweaked my spidey-sense."

"Roger that."

Commander wandered the floor. Axel found the knee scooter and, using it for a chair, began his hunt. "You want me to show you the page when I find your double-doubt mark?"

"Nah, dog-ear it, and I'll look when you're finished with that notebook."

"Ten-four." Axel picked up the top book and began to hunt and fold.

Rory started the second swing. Hunting for a needle in a haystack wasn't any more manageable when you knew what the needle looked like. He wondered how Thacker was faring. And if Esther was in a room resting.

He picked up Emily Weir's final autopsy report, sighed. He'd read it countless times and began one more read. Finished, he shook his head. There was nothing there, just the ugly, scrawling signature of the attending medical examiner—the very distinguished Dr. J. B. Barnes. The physician's signature was illegibly messy. The more Rory stared at the scribble, the more he didn't see the doctor's name but something entirely different. A "J." And "nes" following, but it didn't spell out J. Barnes, it was—

"Axel, are you in the notebook containing the Weir autopsy?"

"Un-huh."

Rory snatched the notebook from Axel's hands and frantically flipped the pages. Finally, he found the double question mark on a dog-eared page containing notes he'd written while questioning Barnes on the autopsy.

Intern D. I. Jones?? Barnes assist??

D. I. Jones was his connection. Demetrius Jones, the pathologist. Jones, the constant visitor to Tobias Snearl. It would only be a matter of legwork to identify him as Dewey Jones, a younger man who moved from Georgia to Nebraska, then from a pathology lab in Lincoln to the prison and connecting the doctor to the inmate.

Gotcha!

Rory's cell rang. "Naysmith."

It was Thacker. "Boss, checking in. I'm in Ames' room. It's taped off and Jim Zielinski is with me. There's a lot of stuff, incriminating stuff."

"Can you be more specific, son?" Rory set the phone on speaker and laid it on the desk where Axel could also hear the conversation.

"To begin with there's a case with costumes, a case with weapons, and a case containing fraudulent identification documents. It doesn't look like he tried to conceal much."

"He thought he was above the law."

"Jim says, the FBI will collect the goods. They will be interested in the burner phone and the laptop computer. But one thing may interest you. The printouts, the ones that Miss Esther did for our murder board. I found them tucked in the front pages of a scrapbook."

"That doesn't surprise me." Nothing would surprise him—not ever again.

Rory filled Thacker in by telling him about the signature on Weir's autopsy. "I'm going to have Axel run me back to the hospital. It's been a long night. You should try to get some rest, and we'll sort things out later."

He disconnected, picked up the autopsy report and the notebook. There would be hours—no days of legwork.

And no matter who ran the operation, Detective Rory Naysmith, WPD, would do his part.

Chapter Forty

The problem with an injured foot isn't the foot itself but the swath of time and space needed to move from one point to the next. Rory dressed, arranged for a ride from Axel, and arrived at Winterset Memorial Hospital's Wingding thirty minutes before it kicked off and half an hour behind the rest of the county. Or so it seemed. The Wingding was well underway.

Purple and gold streamers hung in the community room. Music played softly through overhead speakers. Cafeteria tables lined one side of the room, with decorated baskets sitting at one-foot intervals down their length. A small crowd moved along in front of the tables, inspecting each silent auction item. Conversations created a happy buzz. Occasionally someone leaned down and scribbled on the bid sheet lying in front. The sound of happy voices spilled through open doors leading to the additional tables on the patio.

Rory limped into the room. His gaze landed on Esther, in a summery, scoop-necked blouse and seated with her sister and Marilyn Beauregard, both in lavender outfits. Esther looked what he would call lovely-serene. Beyond them sat the local dignitaries, including Mayor Becker, Chief Mansfield, and the hospital administrator. Petey Moss waved a hand.

Esther materialized at his elbow. "Hello." Her eyes

were bright. "I saved you a seat."

"Great." He felt awkward. And undecided on whether to be embarrassed or excited to see her. Their last conversation had been what he'd call uncomfortable.

After being drugged and bound, she'd come to in the hospital and discovered she was wearing his medal. She insisted he take it back. He thought she needed the protection. Things had gone sideways. Women were not weak, his job was dangerous, she wasn't Catholic, she didn't need a good-luck charm. Jesse had arrived in time to avert a war. He'd slipped off, claiming a need to wrap up the case. That had been three days ago.

Since then, he'd decided her reaction had resulted from feeling powerless and had not been an objection to his gift.

"Nice turnout," he said, noticing the chain still hung around her neck.

She laced her hand through his arm. "Sit with me. Marilyn and Jesse will abandon me to run around and see that things go smoothly. I have no intention of getting in their way."

As they passed the auction tables, he asked, "Did you donate a basket?"

A blush rose on her cheeks. "Not so much donated as indulged in blatant self-promotion. Bookkeeping service for a year. I'm looking for new clients. Preferably someone with simple expenditures."

"So, your basket contains a solar-powered calculator and a flex folder."

"It's the one with red, white, and blue ribbons. And also stuffed with homemade cookies, chocolate candies, and a coin purse."

"Nice touch."

She giggled and squeezed his arm. It was nice to see her smile.

"I hope I get at least one bid. But if not, I know the three cakes I donated for the cakewalk were appreciated."

"I'm sure there'll be takers."

"Then you haven't heard that the ancestry letters started arriving yesterday. People are only here to compare results."

"And delivery times." She looked at him askance, and he added, "I heard a contest was underway. We're talking first results. Best pedigree. Most notorious, outrageous, famous…" He let his voice drift off. She wasn't listening. He followed her gaze to the local dignitaries' table.

"Who is that man, Rory? The one talking to Chief Mansfield."

The only person she wouldn't know was the man with the artificial lift in his brow. The man avoiding his calls. Rory had been busy after the arrest of Demetrius Jones, but Ash had been busier, and not so willing to share.

"That is the real Jeromy Ash. Come, I'll introduce you."

Ash and Mansfield both stood as the couple approached. Mansfield clasped Ash on the shoulder and offered his hand to Rory. "Getting all the details from our man here. Ingenious and harrowing, the real cloak-and-dagger stuff. Great police work. Glad to see you're walking."

Rory shook the outstretched hand and then lifted the walking boot. "Walking slower, I'm afraid." To

Ash, he said, "I'd like you to meet Esther Mullins." Placing his hand over hers where it still lingered on his arm, he rattled off the agent's long title in one breath.

She smiled appreciatively. "Our good luck you weren't a gardener."

Ash tugged an earlobe. "About that. I hope you don't think I was harassing you."

"I thought you'd picked the wrong gardener-ette and were a poor student of horticulture."

"Touché."

After exchanging greetings with the other dignitaries, Rory said, "Chief, do you mind if we borrow your undercover agent?"

Ash followed Rory and Esther back to a side table. He held the chair while she sat, and Rory maneuvered to face the larger community room. "I thought you might have some additional questions," Ash said after they were seated.

"Winterset Memorial," Rory said, "Moving into my hospital room couldn't be a standard operating procedure. A little extreme, even for undercover."

Ash laughed. "Truly undercover. I knew Ames. You don't mind if we call him Ames, do you? It's complicated enough with all the aliases but depressing when your identity has been stolen."

"Sure, you are Ash. He can be Ames, a.k.a. Demetrius Jones, a.k.a. D.I. Jones, the intern attending to the body of Emily Weir, a.k.a. Dewey Jones." Rory had only discovered the name of the young intern assisting with the autopsy in 2006, and he'd traced the connection to the pathologist named Demetrius Jones.

Ash relaxed his posture. "As I was saying, Ames had been on my radar for a while. When the MO for the body in the river hit the databases, I was confident he'd be involved. I came to town looking for the evidence. Knowing and proving are quite different. Miss Mullins, you may not be aware, but being a police officer requires some cunning. I found Ames after he hurt Detective Naysmith."

Esther gasped. He gave her a hundred-watt smile.

Rory wasn't buying it. If Ash knew or even suspected Ames was the killer and was in town, he had a responsibility to report in at the department to identify himself and tell what he knew. He was starting to fit Rory's idea of the typical undercover agent, extrovert, liar, and cocky. Well, Ash wasn't cocky. But if he'd been shadowing Ames and was outside the department store the night of Rory's attack and not prevented or helped—that wasn't going to cut it. Rory could feel the heat in his face.

"So, you were in the second bed to protect me? Why not just notify the department?"

"Like I said, knowing and proving are quite different. You have to understand. I've been tracking these cases for a long time, and Ames was here. I'm afraid he knew I was getting close."

The detective thought about that for a moment. Why hadn't Ames left town after the body was discovered? For that matter, why had he stuck around until it was found?

Esther leaned forward. "Did you hurt Jesse?"

"No, ma'am. Those incidents, the car, the detour, and the mugging, those were all on Ames. I'm afraid they started once he discovered Abby Sue Bellman lived in Winterset. He couldn't afford for her to recognize him."

"And you knew?" Rory slapped his palm on the table. "Needless deaths."

"I didn't expect another killing."

"No, that wouldn't fit your MO. Keep your head down and your behind lower."

Esther blinked rapidly. Ash shrugged.

Axel chose that moment to hustle into the room, and he made a beeline for their table. He had on a purple Wolfman Jack T-shirt, a pair of cut-off jeans that exposed skinny knees, and a gold scarf tied around his head, sweatband style. "Miss Esther, Constable, I thought you'd want to know. The Kaulburgs aren't descendants of the kaiser. It turns out they come from a long line of master brewers. They're down at the lodge, buying drinks for anyone who wants to hear about it."

Rory inhaled deeply, counted to ten, and exhaled. "Go on, son, I'll find my way home."

"That's not all." Axel squinted at Ash, pulled a chair out, turned it so he could sit with his arms draped over the back, and sat. "Turns out that only half the DNA results people were expecting came back." He twisted one end of his mustache between his fingers. "Yup. If you bothered to mail it in, you got the enchilada. But if you ordered the deluxe handling with the quick turnaround, Cousin Henry pinched your moola, and your swabby sample ended up in la-la land. There's a lotta—"

Rory turned to Esther. "Where is Cousin Henry?"

Axel answered first. "He's done the boot-scooting boogie."

Esther said, "Marilyn told me he went to Omaha on Friday and isn't back yet."

"FBI," Rory and Ash said together, rising. Rory's

glance darted to the chief. Ash pulled out his phone.

"Oh, poor Marilyn." Esther ran a hand through her hair, stood, and craned to locate her friend.

"And one other thing," Axel said. They turned to him. "There are about fifteen hundred bids for your basket. The last one puts it up to two hundred and fifty dollars. 'Course, now that the Kaulburg cousins are downtown—"

Esther touched the chain at her neck and said to Rory, "You donated a basket?"

"It's only a take-out container from the Golden Leaf with handlebar streamers inside."

"You're donating your scooter?"

"Don't need it anymore." He cleared his throat, hoping she approved, especially after all the effort Jesse had made finding it. But dang it, it was in the way unless he was using it for a weapon. "It's a worthy cause."

A grin spread across her face. "Are you sure?"

Ash said, "He hasn't missed a trick, including those I threw at him. Bowling ball anchor and all. Naysmith is what we seasoned officers consider a true asset to the law enforcement community."

Rory decided the agent's scar gave him an eager, honest face—he was a man whose judgment should be trusted. Well, as far as you could throw him.

"If you'll excuse us, Esther, we need a quick word with the chief. Ash, you with me?"

It didn't take long to bring the chief up to date. Rory called Thacker, relayed the information a second time, and arranged for a ride back to the apartment. The undercover agent slipped off to do whatever covert things needed doing, and Rory rejoined Esther.

"Jesse is getting ready to close the silent auction bids," she said. "Do you want to make a final swing past the baskets?"

The piped music was interrupted, and Jesse's voice came over the public address system. "If I could have everyone's attention for a moment. The bidding for the silent auction will close in five minutes. If you have your heart set on a particular basket, now is the time to place that final bid. The lawn dart tournament starts at four sharp, and no one wants to see the fire department take the trophy for the fifth consecutive year. Be sure your team is signed up by checking in at the judge's station in the senior park. Now, have fun. And get those bids placed."

The announcement appeared to make an impact. A small crowd swarmed in front of the basket tables. Rory steered Esther to where his basket sat. "Good grief," he said, reading down the list. "The highest bid is for over three hundred dollars. Axel bid six times, and #133 seems determined."

"How do you know it's Axel's bid? They are confidential numbers, not names. "

"Not so secret if you know Axel insisted on using #666."

She laughed.

He thought perhaps the ugly experience hadn't left her traumatized. Images of her desperate and helpless gripped him. Emotion welled at the back of his throat. He swallowed. When he glanced at her, she was smiling. Her dark eyes communicated tenderness and admiration. He felt overwhelmed.

"I'm going to find Marilyn," he said. "While you check the baskets, I better find out about Henry. I'll be back in a moment."

There were enough people placing bids that he figured he wouldn't be seen by Esther when he approached her basket at the other end of the tables. There was one entry on her bid sheet, twelve dollars for a full year of bookkeeping services. He drew a line through it, added his secret number, and filled in a bid for two hundred and thirty-three dollars. It was the amount he'd paid last year to have his federal income tax filed. If she needed more, he'd find it.

The Wingding crowd spilled out onto the patio and the lawns beyond. He walked to the park between the hospital and senior center without spotting Marilyn. It probably wasn't the right time to question her about Henry with the charity event going on. The truth was, he just needed a moment to center himself.

He stopped at the cakewalk, placed a quarter on square twenty-four, and won a chocolate cake. If he couldn't eat it, Thacker would.

When he reentered the community room, Jesse was talking to Esther. He fell in line with the others reviewing the baskets and slowly worked his way toward them. When he was close enough to hear their conversation, they giggled, not realizing he was there.

"I think your neighbor has designs on Rory's scooter."

"Knowing Axel, he'll challenge someone to a one-legged race in the back alley."

"Under the full moon."

"Blindfolded," Esther said. They giggled louder. Esther snorted. It made Jesse double over and grab her sides in glee. Rory felt the smile tug at his lips. Silly girls.

When they sobered, Jesse said, "So, you and Rory, you're okay?"

"Sure."

"I didn't want to ask what the spat was about."

"It wasn't a spat. He was feeling kind of manly, and I was feeling kind of womanly, and…" She let the thought drift off.

"He's a good guy, Es."

Esther pulled the medal from under her blouse and swung it by the chain. "I think we're going steady."

There was pride in her voice. She looked around expectantly and caught Rory's eye. Her face brightened, and her lips twitched into a sweet smile.

His heart pounded. Jesse would see that Esther got counseling. Therapy if it was needed.

She was a survivor—a warrior.

Without a doubt, she was the best of women.

Epilogue

It took days to sift through the evidence against Demetrius Jones. His arrest for the murder of Abby Sue Bellman was a slam dunk, as was the tie-in for the murder of the girl found at the riverbank. River Girl's identity had finally been established, a college student living alone, abducted from a gym parking lot in Omaha after a late-night workout. The FBI worked the details, including where Jones held her before the dump behind the 4-H building. All agencies admitted Abby Sue didn't fit the serial killer's pattern and was a defensive maneuver rather than a planned murder. It didn't help. She was dead, and Winterset mourned.

Rory and Thacker were hard after Jones' movements, culminating with his involvement to carry out Snearl's murdering ways when Cousin Henry knocked at the detective's WPD office door. He let himself in, looking every bit the dapper Southern gentleman in a Panama hat and seersucker suit. He still had a scar and mustache but no longer spoke with an accent.

"I come to exonerate myself and beg for leniency," he said, tipping his hat.

"Pull up a chair." Rory took his walking-boot off the wastebasket lip and straightened. "Thacker wondered why you vanished."

The rookie dipped his head, then asked, "FBI?"

"Federal Bureau of Investigation, yes. Special Agent Henry Beauregard." He held up a hand, palm facing them. "Before you ask, no relation to Marilyn Beauregard. And I wasn't permitted to notify anyone I was with the FBI, or in Winterset. Such information is protected from public disclosure, by current law and Department of Justice and FBI policy."

Thacker did the low whistle thing. "Marilyn knows?"

"I did take her into my confidence. I needed a place to stay, and she is an excellent sport. Not to mention a patriot. I can say, my goals included increasing the local enthusiasm for an ancestral search."

"Promoting Family Lost-N-Found, specifically," Rory said.

The agent took a seat next to Thacker. "Operations are often misunderstood by civilians."

"Why set up an operation in Winterset?"

"Chance. Fate. Happenstance." He glanced between Rory and the rookie, then added, "I have no obligation to explain my actions."

Rory did a slow-growing smile. When it reached capacity, he asked, "So, why are you here?"

"Abby Sue Bellman."

The detective gave a nod.

"And this phase of the investigation wrapped up. I should say, fieldwork wrapped up, paperwork is underway, and more charges are pending. These things take years."

"What can you tell us?"

"My only concern was Family Lost-N-Found. Most details, I can't divulge. I'll say there is fraud and extortion, financial gains elicited through Federal mail, and tax evasion. In short, nothing sexy, but all criminal acts."

Rory drummed his fingers on the desktop. "I think I've seen this movie."

"And the public, deceived," added Henry. "Abby Sue Bellman was an unfortunate complication. First because my cover story was compromised. Then later, because her hometown of Smyrola, Georgia played in the history of your serial killer." Henry cleared his throat. "Thanks to Marilyn and the citizens of Winterset, I've been able to expose numerous infractions and close down Family Lost-N-Found."

"Wow," said Thacker softly. His face conveyed his concern for his parents' loss of lineage distinction. The Thackers of Winterset would never know if they were related to the Earl of Sandwich or Robert the Bruce.

"I wanted to fill a gap, so it doesn't get in the way of other investigations you have underway."

Rory stood and offered his hand. "As they say, 'no news is good news.' I, that is, we appreciate your consideration."

Henry rose, returned the handshake, and headed for the door. Stopping with one hand on the knob, he turned back. "You can't say you heard it from me, but the FBI's working theory is that Demetrius Jones became enamored of Tobias Snearl while assisting Dr. Barnes at the state pathology lab. And after witnessing Snearl's handiwork firsthand.

"If you're looking into Jones, you'll find he's a bad customer. I never understood the workings of the mind or what draws one person to another, but those working the connection say Jones found a kindred spirit in Snearl. They are both addicted to evil.

"Besotted, charmed, who knows how, or why? The theory is Jones sought approval and needed encouragement. It's a known fact Snearl gets off on control. They say there is no doubt it took both men to continue the serial killings. Plus, cell phone records eliminate the uncertainty."

Then he added, "I'll deny you heard it from me."

Cousin Henry touched the brim of his hat and was gone.

When the door closed, Thacker leaned forward. "Do you think he's really Henry Beauregard?"

"Not for a minute."

"Spooks," said Thacker. "It was just a coincidence that Agent Beauregard was in town while our killer was here."

"First rule in detecting: there is no such thing as coincidence, son."

"Just our bad luck."

"Stroke of luck. But it takes hard work to earn a break." The rooky made a face like he'd opened a pop and found the carbonation gone. Rory added, "Good fortune, godsend, windfall—*la compétence*—all necessary in a detective's toolbox."

Rory glanced at the clock. "Let's call it a day. Miss Mullins is preparing a special dinner in my honor. And if I'm not mistaken, it's meatloaf night at the Thacker house."

Thacker brightened. "Some things you can always count on."

Rory grinned as he donned his fedora with a flick of the wrist.

"Second rule in detecting: little things are big."

A word about the author…

Terry Korth Fischer writes mystery and memoir. Her memoir, Omaha to Ogallala, was released in 2019. Her short stories have appeared in The Write Place at the Write Time, Spies & Heroes, and numerous anthologies. Transplanted from the Midwest, Terry lives in Houston with her husband and their two guard cats. She enjoys a good mystery, the heat and humidity, and long summer days. Visit her website at https://terrykorthfischer.com